"Tell me what you want," Daniel whispered

He took Lara's hand. "I think you want it all."

"You're so wrong. *All* is exactly what I don't want. Unless you mean—" she nodded toward the house "—in the bedroom."

"Okay," he said. "What's your idea of a hot sexual fantasy affair?"

Lara dropped her gaze. "I already told you. I'm a...gameswoman."

"And your favorite game?"

Her body brushed against his. He could feel the tight beads of her nipples through her dress and it was making him wild. Soon he was going to turn into a ravening beast and take her for pure, raw, animal sex.

"That would be tag, Daniel. Winner takes all." She quickly tapped him on the arm. "You're it!" She flew into the house, shutting off lights as she ran.

He rubbed his hands in anticipation. Winner take all? Suited him. He'd never been bested yet.

Blaze™

Dear Reader,

Picture this: A desperately excited woman runs through the forest. A dark, savage man chases her. Is the danger real? Or is it just a game?

There are some books an author can't give up on. *Playing with Fire* was mine. Several years have passed since the opening chase-through-the-forest scene came vividly to life for me. I still remember holding my breath while I wrote it—very quickly. Unfortunately those pages seemed destined to languish in my filing cabinet, labeled "too hot for category."

Until *Blaze.*

Brava *Blaze!* I'm thrilled to join its roster of daring authors. And to the readers who demanded more of our provocative stories—thank you!

All my best,

Carrie Alexander

P.S. Please look for my other books, as well, wherever they might pop up—Temptation, Duets, Superromance,. And I love to hear from you. You can write to me in care of Harlequin or by e-mail at CarrieAlexander2@aol.com.

P.P.S. Don't forget to check out the special Blaze Web site at www.tryblaze.com.

PLAYING WITH FIRE

Carrie Alexander

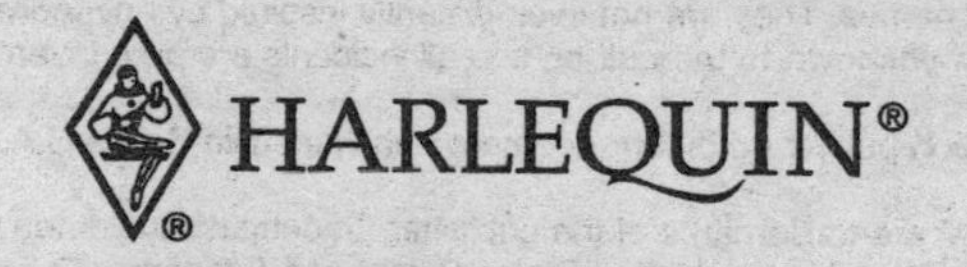

TORONTO • NEW YORK • LONDON
AMSTERDAM • PARIS • SYDNEY • HAMBURG
STOCKHOLM • ATHENS • TOKYO • MILAN • MADRID
PRAGUE • WARSAW • BUDAPEST • AUCKLAND

ISBN 0-373-79024-4

PLAYING WITH FIRE

This edition published by arrangement with Harlequin Books S.A.

Visit us at www.eHarlequin.com

Printed in U.S.A.

Prologue

SAVAGE WAS hunting her.

Lara sensed his presence in every cell of her body—from the prickling hairs at her nape to the heat zinging through her bloodstream to the nervousness of her dancing feet. She panted shallowly, trying to calm herself. To quell the urge to flee. If she lost her head and ran without reason, it would be as easy as child's play for him to swoop down and snap her up.

This was anything but *child's* play.

Holding her breath, she crouched in the parchment leaves to listen for him. Was he near?

She heard only the normal sounds of the forest—minute raspings and tickings and scattershot scurries of tiny claws. The wind sighed, passing overhead with a scraping of bare branches and the whispered brush of evergreen boughs.

Several orangy-gold leaves drifted to the ground. Her alert gaze followed their meandering path. A woodpecker's rat-a-tat-tat sounded in the distance, echoing the beat of her racing heart.

She bowed her head, allowing herself to slowly exhale like a leaking balloon even as she remained on edge, every sense deliciously heightened. Her instincts had never been sharper; her reactions were hair-trigger.

A pheasant flapped through the undergrowth right beside her and she reflexively jerked forward into a ready position as if under the starter's pistol. Her pulse escalated. A frisson of fear rippled across her skin.

Savage *must* be near! And yet there was no sign of him....

Waiting for him to pounce was unbearable. At a sudden loud cracking sound in the forest behind her, Lara sprang forward. Knowing her flight was both precipitous and foolhardy, she raced through the stand of mixed hardwoods, dodging broad trunks and saplings alike, leaping fallen logs, her loose hair streaming behind her like a lick of golden sun-fire.

"Aye-yi-yi-yi-eee!"

The barbaric howl was bloodcurdling. Lara skidded to a stop, moccasins kicking up a flurry of dry autumn leaves. Slowly she turned toward the hunter's call.

Savage was there, silhouetted on the crest. His legs were set firmly apart, his arms hanging relaxed at his sides even though he had to be as wired as she, consumed by the thrill of the hunt as he searched the forest floor for the sight of her.

Lara licked her lips, eyes feverishly skimming the woods to plot an escape route before being drawn relentlessly back to the man who was determined to claim her as his own. Even knowing that he would soon spot her, would descend upon her—conquering, powerful male to the core—she could not move. Her skin crawled with a tingling heat.

Savage's chin lifted. His nostrils flared.

She swallowed thickly. *He could smell her.*

Ohhh. Her knees weakened, as if a swoon was imminent. It was only a matter of time before—

Stop. She gritted her teeth. Slammed shut her eyes, fighting the yearning to succumb to his strong pull, his treacherous and insidious spell. From the start, something in the man had spoken to her. And she to him. Even now, hunter and hunted, they were...they were...

They were one.

She knew the instant he saw her. Her lids flew open. Her heart gave a leap. Of apprehension...and excitement.

He did not move. Instead, he watched her, his fingers slowly curling inward, the muscles of his thighs clenched in preparation.

He cocked his head. Through the slanting rays of the low sun she could see the predatory glint in his eyes. "Lara," he called, voice low and smooth as he dragged her name out until it merged with the sighing wind. "La-a-a-raaah..."

For a moment she was frozen. Mesmerized.

Only when he started down the hill to complete her capture did she shudder back to life with a shrill yelp. She shot off through the woods again.

The forest blurred into a tapestry of golds and grays and greens. She was as fleet as a doe, her legs flying, the hem of her red print skirt bunched in either hand, bare thighs and knee-high moccasins flashing with each scissored stride. She had little trouble placing Savage now. He was crashing through the woods behind her, no longer tracking her in silent stealth. And he was gaining—rapidly.

She had the advantage of knowing the terrain better than he. Disappearing over the top of a ridge, she slid on her heels down the steep slope opposite. Taking a few precious seconds, she camouflaged her obvious trail with leaves, scooping up crisp handfuls and scattering them over the gouges she'd made in the dark, soft earth.

Temporarily out of sight on the other side, Savage whooped again. The primal sound of it sent icy fingertips tapping up and down Lara's spine, but this time she didn't stop.

Finding the worn path that wound around the base of the ridge, she followed it north toward home, leaving no footprints on the hard-packed dirt. Back on the hillside, Savage scuffled through the leaves over her skid marks. She knew that at any moment he'd skirt the thicket of balsam and pine and catch a glimpse of her brightly colored dress.

She left the trail, slipping silently beneath the fragrant drooping boughs of an ancient evergreen. A pinecone crunched underfoot and she froze, not even daring to breathe as she listened for her hunter.

The electric silence was a bad sign. Very bad. Lara knew she'd run out of options. The house was less than a half mile away, but she'd never outrun him. Instead she caught a vertical limb of the nearest big elm and swung, kicking her legs up in a froth of white petticoat to hook around a branch. A few moments later she was halfway up, pressed to the trunk and trying not to pant as Savage appeared on the path, only seconds behind her.

He moved as soundlessly and swiftly as an Indian scout, ducking in and out of her line of vision as he continued past her hiding place. She let out a silent breath and relaxed just the slightest bit. Perhaps for once she'd bested him.

In her head she counted out sixty seconds, then sixty more. When she was fairly certain he'd continued on, she forced herself to move away from the relative safety of the tree trunk. Cool golden leaves, gentle as a lover's palm, caressed her face and shoulders as she inched along the sturdy branch. Holding tight to the tree's limbs, she ducked to peer past its foliage, scanning the empty trail and surrounding wood. Savage was nowhere to be seen.

She breathed a sigh of relief, head dropping forward in a prayerful bow, eyes closed. He was gone. Another deep breath.

She'd avoided capture.

She'd won the game. Sort of.

After a minute, an uneasy foreboding began to nibble at Lara's triumph. Slowly she lifted her face.

And found herself staring directly into Savage's molten pewter eyes.

He smiled.

Like a wolf, like the natural predator that he was.

1

Three weeks before

THE MAN WAS a hunter.

Lara Gladstone felt it in the unwavering focus of his dark, hungry gaze. His was not a piercing stare. It was a steady, mesmerizing one, so visceral she shuddered beneath it as if he'd taken her nape in his strong hand and held her just so, close against his body. Trembling, but still.

Captured.

"Captured," Lara mouthed to herself, pausing in her restless tour of the dining room. She touched her prickling nape, feeling his eyes upon her. *I will not look.*

Deliberately she tilted her head back and lifted her gaze to the yellow, red and golden-brown flecks of glass glowing overhead. A different kind of self-knowledge came over her. A sense of calm. In the midst of the noise and confusion of the cuttingly hip restaurant opening, she gazed at the kaleidoscope of colored glass and let herself slowly drift away. To a dream of home—a restless, yearning sort of dream, underlaid with her awareness of the man who'd been watching her for the past fifteen minutes.

She was in the woods near her house. The autumn leaves shimmered around her, glorious colors, yellow and red and golden brown. It was quiet, but she was not alone. There was a man. A dark, hungry man. He was stalking her. She must flee. Yet even as she ran until her heart was bursting in her chest, deep inside she knew...she knew...

She wanted to be captured.

THE WOMAN WAS a tease.

Daniel liked that about her.

Absently he raised a glass of red wine to his mouth, wetting his lips as he tracked her circuitous route through the crowded restaurant. When she stepped momentarily out of view, he craned his neck for another glimpse of her. Such impatience, however limited, was unlike him.

Ah. There she was, looking up at a large piece of stained-glass artwork suspended from the ceiling on chains. She swayed ever so slightly, her shoulders moving sensuously, her hand going to her nape and lingering there for an instant before slowly slipping around to stroke her long arched throat. An answering caress sensitized Daniel's palms, as if already they knew the feel of her moving beneath them. The warm silken glide of her skin under his fingertips.

A pretty young man approached her. He was garbed in downtown artiste de rigueur—clingy shirt and trousers, both made of thin black wool, a pair of glasses with blue lenses and heavy black frames and, for that Bohemian touch, one indiscreet piercing. In this case, a small silver hoop through the septum. Useful, Daniel decided, if the boy needed to be convinced of his impending departure.

The young man put a hand on the woman's shoulder and whispered in her ear.

Several heads turned when she laughed. Despite Daniel's sudden inclination to make judicious use of the nose ring, the exuberant laugh prompted an answering smile to tug at one corner of his lips. He might have known. No lockjawed, nasal *hunh-hunh-hunh* for this woman. Her laugh was full-bodied, natural. It revealed her zest for life.

So, he thought with a measure of self-congratulatory swagger. She had brio. She would be his match.

The lazy interest that had stirred inside him at the sight of her expanded into pervasive desire. A feeling to relish. One he'd been missing for too long. Already the thrill of the hunt was thrumming in his veins—a low, slow, steady drumbeat keeping pace with the first hot flush of stimulation.

The woman stood out in the crowd like a tawny lioness, regal and reserved among a pack of craven hyenas begging for scraps of attention. She was all in gold, from a cloud of amber hair to the sharp tips of her narrow suede sling-backs. Her dress was an alchemist's dream—a fluid piece of fabric that skimmed her lithe curves, softening the angular edges of a trim, athletic figure.

Her head seemed a tad too small, set on a long neck above broad swimmer's shoulders, counterbalanced by the riotous mass of her pinned-up hair. A private thought made Daniel's smirk slip sideways, lifting the other side of his mouth into a generous smile: She had the kind of wild, thick hair that was meant to be spread across a pillow.

He saw her prone on his own bed, stretched out upon cool Egyptian cotton sheets, long, tanned limbs spread in flagrant invitation, her eyes bold...provocative...teasing.

Yes. It would happen. No question.

After another laugh and an indulgent pat on the cheek, the woman turned away from the pretty young man. Toward Daniel.

He drew a quick breath through his teeth, his chest expanding. As much as he desired the body, it was the face that was truly captivating, that continually drew him in. Her face was small and round, unexpectedly full in the cheek when compared to the lean length of her. Cherubic, he might have said, except that her mouth was wide, her nose narrow and her eyes…

Ah, her eyes were feline—aloof but curious, distant yet riveting. Sparkling with life.

They looked full of naughty thoughts.

Mentally Daniel gathered himself in preparation. Attuned to his wavelength, she responded with a flick of her lashes. Her head cocked in his direction. For the fourth or fifth time, he intercepted a surreptitious glance. Not by default. She wanted him to know that she was as aware of him as he was of her.

Without a doubt, the woman was a tease.

Her elusive gaze slid away again. With the lift of a bare shoulder, she swiveled on her heel, presenting him with her backside.

The dress, so demure from the front, was cut in a deep slash that bared her back to the very dimple at the top of a tight little bottom. A second slit traveled upward from the hem, exposing the entire length of her right leg. Daniel took his time examining the effect. He'd never devoted himself quite so fully to the erotic qualities of the curve of a muscular calf, the hollow of a knee, the tender flesh at the back of a woman's thigh.

When he took a step in her direction, she moved swiftly away, maneuvering past a knot of hors d'oeuvres munchers. Her long, sure stride split the slashed skirt beyond daring. His heart gave an unwieldy thump. The woman was one dropped stitch away from public indecency.

Intent on following her, he set his wineglass on the thick polished slab of marble that made up the bar. The interior of the new restaurant was a marvel of look-at-me architecture—all stuccoed curves juxtaposed against sharply angled half walls of brushed steel. Exposed steel I-beams were crusted with the perfect degree of rust, in contrast to the slick black terazzo floor. At least fifty guests occupied the toothpick chairs clustered around stainless-steel bistro tables. Others jammed the padded banquettes that encircled the space. The overflow stood in clusters, nibbling at the free food, attacking the champagne and assorted wines with gusto. Taken together, it was all too pretentious for Daniel's taste. He preferred history and age to cutting edge design.

Tamar Brand, his companion for the evening, aimed a wordless question at him as he passed. He volleyed with a shake of his head. She raised just one of her elegant black brows—a neat trick she used sparingly—her amused smile both forgiving his curtness and informing him that she knew exactly what he was up to. As always.

Daniel didn't pause. No words were needed; after eleven years together, Tamar knew him far too well. If left to her own devices, she would, with no reproach, take a cab home and charge it to his expense account. Along with a pricey bottle of wine and take-out dinner from one of the city's ritzy delis.

Bribery, he thought, but Tamar's silence and skill were worth it.

He turned the corner. Only quick reflexes prevented him from walking straight into his prey. The lioness stood directly on the other side of one of the angled silver walls scattered around the main room like sculptures. No chase, then, he thought, slightly disappointed. She was waiting. For him?

Of course.

He saw it first in the rounded innocence of her eyes, then in the smile ready to burst from her lips as laughter. Yet there was also a certain tension in her squared shoulders and elongated swan's neck. He presumed that although she was confident in herself, she was not *entirely* sure of him.

Good.

He said the first thing that sprang to mind. "Where's your piercing?"

Her lashes widened. "Are you certain I have one?"

The voice was lovely—a contralto as rich as her laugh. He gestured at the crowd with spread hands, then dropped his arms to his sides at once, far too aware that his palms still itched to stroke her long, bare arms. To sink into her untamed hair.

He said, "Everyone under the age of thirty does."

"But I'm thirty. Exactly. On the very cusp of your anthropological hypothesis."

"Then your piercing must be hidden." He let his gaze drift across the golden dress before rising again to her quirkily beautiful face. She hadn't used cosmetics to alter her complexion. Her childishly plump cheeks were unshadowed, the pale sun freckles dotting her nose unconcealed. Only her eyes were elaborately enhanced with a muted palette of copper, bronze and green.

The painted lids lowered. "And yours?"

"I'm too old," he said evenly.

"How old?" Without pretense, she inspected his suit, an impeccably tailored designer deal for which he'd paid a shocking amount, enough to have funded his entire school wardrobe of jeans and tees and the single off-the-rack suit he'd worn to every college function right up to graduation.

The woman's gaze had lingered long enough to make him wonder if she was studying the suit...or the body beneath it.

He stayed perfectly still, even though his blood thundered with primal urges. "Thirty-six."

"Married?"

"You haven't answered *my* question."

"The woman," she said, ignoring his diversion tactic, "she's not your wife?"

He was fairly certain that the lioness had arrived after he and Tamar. She couldn't have seen them together—they'd separated almost at once. "What woman?" he asked carefully.

Her eyes, green as a tropical sea, met his. She smiled, patient and knowing.

He conceded the point. "She's not my wife."

"Longtime companion?"

"No."

"You hesitated." A mildly playful taunt.

"Does it matter?"

"Yes." Her voice became serious; her eyes were less so. "I don't play fun and games with married men."

He tried not to betray his surprise. Or his conclusion, even though the odds-on possibility that she'd already made up her mind about him—about *playing* with him—had sent shock waves crashing through his system.

"I see." He kept his voice gentle but suggestive, asking without actually asking if she meant what he hoped she did.

Her small nod granted the unspoken petition. She was a queenly cat. "Yes, I believe that you do." Her head tilted. "Convenient for both of us."

A pocket of silence enveloped them. Daniel, for once, was uncertain. Had they agreed to a sexual affair? A dalliance?

If so, it wasn't enough. He wanted more. Suddenly he wanted more.

"A guess," he said. "Your tongue."

Her brows were brown, several shades darker than her hair. They drew together. He saw as her mind clicked into his place in the conversation. "Wrong," she said, teasing again. She stuck out her tongue so he could see that it was not punctured by a metal stud. Her tongue was pink and moist, as long and narrow as the rest of her. The gesture was oddly intimate. Perhaps because he instantly pictured her licking a path down the center of his chest.

The air between them shifted, thickened.

His heated gaze zeroed in on the tight peaks of her breasts, clearly outlined against thin gold fabric. Unpierced. "Then where...?"

She folded her arms, stroked the hollow in her throat. "Not so fast, sir." Her voice was light.

His felt dense and needy. "I had the impression you liked it that way."

"Mmm." She regarded him frankly. "Yes, I do. And I've made up my mind about you."

His smile was all confidence, his demeanor assured.

She turned and walked away.

"IS THAT YOUR TAIL I see," Tamar said when he returned, "tucked between your legs?"

Daniel thrust his fists into his trouser pockets and scowled. "Hardly."

Clearly Tamar was enjoying his failure, but she knew not to take the teasing too far. She set an empty champagne flute rimmed with berry-red lipstick on a passing waiter's tray. "Shall we call it a night? Bairstow's already gone, so we've done our duty."

"You're free to leave."

She shook her head at Daniel's scowl, making the blunt ends of her hair brush bony white shoulders bared by a skimpy black sleeveless top. A matching pair of loose silk pants were secured by a drawstring knotted half an inch below her pierced navel; wide etched metal cuffs encircled her toned biceps. Tamar Brand was the type of woman who was not pretty, but whose impeccable style and confidence made other females stare through narrowed eyes as they tried to discern her secret.

"Like a dog with a bone," she commented dryly, taking an engraved compact out of her tiny evening purse. She flicked it open and frowned at her lips.

Daniel snatched away the compact and snapped it shut. He held it out of Tamar's reach, though she wasn't one to reach. His thumb rubbed the engraved initials. It was familiar; after a beat, he remembered giving it to her two birthdays ago. She'd gone to Tiffany's to select it, then had it wrapped and delivered to his office. He'd meant to pick out something personal, but as usual she'd beaten him to the punch. She was *too* efficient that way.

Tamar waited in silence. She could be as inscrutable as the Dalai Lama when she chose.

He dropped the compact into her open purse. "Go now."

She sucked in her already-hollow cheeks, making a face at him. "Thanks, boss."

"Take the car."

They'd arrived in a hired car, a perk from his employers, Bairstow & Boone, the Wall Street brokerage house. Frank Bairstow's dilettante daughter Ophelia was one of the partners in the restaurant's ownership, thanks to daddy's money. As Daniel was fresh off a promotion to junior partner, his attendance at the grand opening fete had been mandatory. He'd persuaded Tamar to be his "date."

"You don't need the car?" Tamar abandoned the goldfish lips. "My, my, Daniel. So the woman really did shoot you down." She pretended to examine him for wounds. "Are you bleeding? Was it fatal, this blow to the ego?"

"My ego is fine." His teeth gritted. Never in his life had he given up so easily, and Tamar surely knew that. She was merely trying to get a rise out of him.

"Perhaps you're losing your skill?"

He didn't consider himself a ladies' man. If he'd had success in the field, it was because women couldn't seem to resist a man who could resist them. His sights had always been set on other goals.

"I'm skilled enough for both of us," was what he told Tamar. "There's a guy at the bar. A trader with a hair weave and a platinum Rolex. He's been eyeing you all evening—"

"Say no more," she interrupted, withering with disdain. "I'm gone." With a saucy flick of a smile, she tucked her purse under her arm and wended her way toward the industrial steel doors at the front of the restaurant. Daniel watched, curious if she'd leave alone—several men had approached her—but she appeared on the street unescorted, signaling for the car.

Daniel moved closer to the wide front window, keeping a protective eye on Tamar until the sleek midnight-blue town car glided up to the curb. The woman was an enigma, even to him. Although in some ways she was his closest friend, he knew her a fraction as well as she knew him. She was adamant about keeping her personal life out of the office. Tamar Brand's vision was clear but narrowly focused. From the start, she'd made it clear that she did not care for questions or complications.

Perhaps that was why they got along so well—Daniel had been accused of the very same thing.

But not tonight, he thought. Tonight, he'd been struck

blind. Tonight, he wanted to plunge headlong into a messy, unplanned, completely indulgent affair.

He thought of the lioness who'd refused to be his prize for the evening. And he smiled, a renewed anticipation spiraling through his bloodstream. He *would* have her.

A hand touched his shoulder. "You were supposed to come after me," she said huskily into his ear, the action causing her breasts to brush lightly across his back. As if he needed the invitation.

"In another minute, I planned to."

She made a small sound in her throat. Sexy—it shot tiny splinters of sensation under his skin. "I was always too forward for my own good."

He didn't turn. "There's something to be said for cutting *to* the chase rather than cutting *out* the chase."

"Yes, I could tell you were that type." She leaned a little closer, resting her chin on his shoulder. He felt her breasts solidly this time, round and firm, pressed just below his shoulder blades. "All right, I'll let you chase me," she purred, her lips so close to his ear that his lobe vibrated. "And perhaps I'll even let you catch me."

Perhaps she'd *let* him? He managed a dry chuckle.

Her hands closed around his upper arms. Long fingers, a strong grip. "Should we make it a dare?"

He was incited to a profligate degree, in mind as well as body. The latter was potentially embarrassing in such a public venue. "By all means," he said, turning fractionally away from the banquettes beneath the front windows. The large stained glass piece she'd been looking at earlier hung directly over their heads, its myriad colors illuminated by several carefully placed spotlights. Their warmth was getting to him. A sheen of perspiration had risen on his forehead.

"I wouldn't want to be just another of your popsies."

He still hadn't looked at her, but the black window reflected a pale image of her face, tilted beside his. "Popsies?" he asked, watching the dark shadows formed by the hollows of her eyes. Frustrating—he couldn't gauge her reactions except in her voice. But she was holding on to him, forestalling his pivot.

"Lollipops." The husky contralto hummed in his ear. "Sweet little suckers that last an hour, tops."

"What makes you think I have a sweet tooth?"

Her grip tightened in concert with her voice. "Men like you…" She didn't finish.

He let that one go. For now. Even though she was dead wrong. "And what is it *you* want?"

"Is this a negotiation instead of a dare?" She smoothed her right hand along his shoulder, switched her head over and said silkily in his other ear, "Shall we set up a list of rules, then? Would that suit your nature?"

His Adam's apple bobbed when she reached past his shoulder and tugged playfully at his tie. Her fingertip followed the motion, flicking the bump above his collar as if chiding him for his hesitation. If only she knew. He was getting hard—so hard he had to shove a hand into his pocket and make a little room so his arousal wasn't readily apparent. He swallowed again.

She said, drawing away, "I suppose you always follow the rules."

"Not always." He couldn't turn.

"No?" She became playful. "By day, a by-the-books businessman. By night—" in the window, her head cocked "—a lawless scalawag."

His lips compressed, withholding a laugh. "Scalawag?"

"Scoundrel, then."

He chuckled.

"Libertine?" she suggested, stepping to his side, her eyes searching for his. "Lady-killer?"

"You're way off base."

She pretended to pout. "How disappointing. I was counting on your lawless streak to show me a good time."

He turned quickly and took her by the elbows. A fleeting look of alarm passed over her face before her expression settled into an unblinking, wide-eyed stare. "You have no idea," he said, startled by his own ferocity. His desire for her was quickly becoming rapacious. "What do you know about me? Not even my name."

"It's Daniel." She rolled her bottom lip between her teeth, another small signal of uncertainty. "I heard your wife say it."

"Tamar is my executive assistant."

"Your assistant?" A spark lit the feline eyes. "Aha. A substitute wife. Of course. I get it now." She placed her palms on his chest and pressed lightly as her upper body swayed toward his. "You're one of those driven Wall Street types. No time for a family, but you've been with your secretary for ages. She knows your likes and dislikes better than you do. She manages both your professional and personal life with an efficiency that's frightening. She fusses over you like a wife."

"Tamar doesn't fuss." He moved his thumbs against the soft skin of her inner elbows. "Otherwise, your assessment is accurate enough to be unsettling. I wasn't aware that I'd become such a cliché."

She studied his face, her lips puckering ever so slightly. A half smile. "There's more to you?"

He said "Yes" with some intensity.

Her eyes were wide, bright; they reached into his, asking a question he couldn't decipher. Suddenly she turned away, disengaging their linked arms with a shudder so small he might have missed it if they weren't so attuned.

''What do you think of the restaurant's decor?'' she asked in a social make-nice voice. Pressing her knuckles to the hollow of her throat, she tilted her head to study the panel of stained glass that hung above them like a misplaced church window.

Distracted by the loose tendrils that coiled against her neck, he barely glanced at the piece. He wanted to blow aside her hair and run his fingertips over the bumps of her vertebrae until he reached the hollow of her back. Her dress was so open, so provocative, he might reach inside and cup—

''Daniel?''

''Belongs in a church, not a restaurant,'' he said without thought.

Her chin lowered. ''Really.''

Damn. He'd said the wrong thing. Aside from a casual interest in photography, understanding Art-with-a-capital-A was a challenge he hadn't yet set his sights on. Probably he was supposed to have used words like *stunning agony* or *fascinating dichotomy*.

But it was only a piece of stained glass.

He looked up at it. Yeah, sure, it was a nice piece of stained glass. The wood-framed panel was large, roughly five feet by three. It contained thousands of tiny pieces of glass—green, gold, orangy-brown and red predominately, with flecks of white, silvery blue and a stark, clear lapis lazuli. No rhyme or reason to the placement, that he could tell. Thinking *modern art* with a certain derision, he stepped back to better view the piece. The shards of colored glass coalesced into a whole.

''A forest,'' he said, surprisingly moved by its beauty. ''Sunlight shining through the leaves. Autumn leaves.''

It wasn't Art Speak, but the lioness seemed pleased. "You like?"

She'd been testing him, he thought, not sure why. Although, he remembered belatedly, she *had* been at the center of a group of people who'd studied the piece like connoisseurs, all of them narrowing their eyes and nodding sagely. Except her. She'd looked highly skeptical.

"Yes, I do like it," he said, his curiosity renewed.

She spoke directly in his ear once more, the sultry resonance of her voice overriding his newfound appreciation of art. "Let's go."

He stared into her face. "By all means."

She threw back her head, her eyes slitted. "Perhaps not *all* means. Can we start with the usual one?"

Missionary? he wondered, then tried to banish the mental picture he'd conjured when it made heat surge lavishly toward his lower body.

"Walking," she said, smiling just enough to further tease his senses.

He nodded and gestured for her to proceed. They'd negotiated the crowd and were nearly out the door when a tall man of indeterminate age broke away from a cluster of guests and hurried over to stop them. "A moment, my dear," he called, and Daniel's companion winced as if she'd touched a fingertip to a red-hot stove burner. By the time she turned, a pleasant expression had been plastered across her features. But he saw the grit of her teeth.

"You mustn't leave so soon." The other man was several inches taller than Daniel's six feet, suited in double-breasted charcoal-black with a glossy onyx tie. His face was patrician and immobile, except for the eyes, which were avid. Freshly clipped platinum hair lay close to his skull.

"The Peytons have arrived," he continued, with the

faintest trace of exasperation. He reached for her elbow. "They are *important.*"

She brushed away his hand. "Another time."

Daniel opened the door, drawing the other man's assessment. And puzzled dismissal. He tried for her elbow again, eager to tow her back inside. "I know this sort of thing isn't your cup of tea. However—" he drew out the word, laying it on thick as a dollop of too-sweet jam "—you did agree—"

The lioness kissed the man soundly on both cheeks, effectively shutting him up long enough for her and Daniel to slip out the door. "Hurry, hurry," she said, taking his hand and moving swiftly along the sidewalk in a race-walk step that had to be doing interesting things to her slitted dress. Sure enough, from somewhere behind them a wolf whistle pierced the brisk night air.

"He's not after us." Daniel slowed, using their clasped hands to draw her in closer.

She glanced back. "I guess we're safely away."

"Who was he?"

"Kensington Webb." She gave no other explanation.

"And you are?" Daniel asked.

She did not hesitate. "Camille."

"Camille…?"

Her profile was unwavering; her eyes stared straight ahead, avoiding his. "Let's keep it to first names for now."

"Fine." *For now.*

He was strangely enthralled by her reluctance. Nothing like a good chase, he thought as he slid his arm around her waist. Except, of course, the capture and the sweet surrender that would follow.

2

SOHO ON A FRIDAY NIGHT was familiar, but as far from home as Lara Gladstone could imagine. There had been rain earlier in the evening, enough to freshen the air and make the elaborate facades of the cast-iron warehouses gleam. An abundance of lights, pedestrians and traffic blurred together into a melange of city life, an animated stream that flowed continually along the narrow street. Its cobbled Belgian bricks glistened like fish scales, reflecting and refracting the carnival of color.

Lara looked up, forgetting that the stars weren't visible the way they were at home; the glow of city lights hung like gauze across a patch of charcoal sky. Remembering the deep night skies and woody wet cedar smells of her home in the Adirondack Mountains made her shiver.

"You're cold." Daniel took his hot palm off the small of her back—he'd placed it where the open vee narrowed—and shrugged out of his suit jacket. Standing close behind her, he dropped the jacket over her shoulders. She shuddered into its warmth. His fingers brushed across her nape to gather up the loose strands of her hair. A small tug at her scalp, and he'd pulled her straggling hair free of the collar. Her head rolled to one side, like the blossom of a tulip grown too heavy for its stem. She was touched by his chivalry.

"Better?" he asked huskily, shooting sparks along her spine.

She straightened, nodding. "I had a wrap. I left it inside."

"Should I go back?"

"No!" She gripped the jacket's lapels, thrilled to have avoided a second round of meet-and-greet with her dealer Kensington Webb and his well-curried art collector clients. Kensington would be disappointed in her, no doubt, but she couldn't take another minute of explaining her "vision" to the uptown elite.

There had been a time when she'd sworn to conquer that scene. No longer. If she'd had her choice, she'd have skipped tonight's event altogether and stayed at Bianca's to laugh and gab and eat with her real friends. But Kensington, in his subtle slinky octopus way, had worked hard to convince her to attend. And he *was* trying to push her work beyond craft, into the realm of museum-quality collectible art. Too many people believed stained glass belonged only in craft fairs and church windows.

In no hurry to move along, Daniel put his hands on her waist. She leaned even closer, remembering the expression in his eyes when he'd stepped back and really looked at her stained-glass panel. He'd gotten it, without her having to explain in complicated, pretentious jargon. His reaction was the kind of simple reward she cherished, more precious than the prestige of having her work selected for display at SoHo's newest chichi eatery.

She slid her palms along his shoulders, down his arms. Her fingertips fluttered toward his. His eyes were locked on her face as he took her hands. A heated awareness of every magnificent inch of him flushed across her cheeks. He threaded their fingers, giving her a small half smile. Enchanted by the moment—*the man*—she looked her fill, staring like a greedy child until it felt as if her skin had grown plump and glossy with satisfaction. He was uniquely her match. She knew it instinctively.

Pedestrians continued to flow around them. Finally someone muttered, ''Get a room,'' and they widened their eyes and laughed, breaking apart, then coming together again. They walked to the corner with their hands linked. ''We'll go for a drink first,'' he said, and she thought, *Daniel,* so chock-full of pleasure at the sound of his name in her head that she only belatedly wondered what came ''second.'' They crossed the intersection among a flurry of traffic and turned toward Mercer Street, their footsteps ringing on the metal vault covers of the loading bays.

Lara's head was catching up to her impulses. She was astonished at her daring, but intrigued by the direction it had taken her. How far would she let it go?

Earlier, Daniel had drawn her attention as soon as she'd shed Kensington's fawning attentions and taken a good look around the restaurant. There were other business types mixed in with the artsy uptown crowd, but only Daniel had exuded such a distinctive aura. Already feeling unlike herself in the costumey dress and out-of-use social mask, she'd decided right then to play a little game with him. At first the relationship she'd sensed between him and the pale woman with a casque of ebony hair had been disconcerting, but that had turned out all right.

She and Daniel were free, young and single—there was no reason not to follow her impulses. True, the strength of the attraction was alarming. She wasn't sure how to curb it.

Or even if she wanted to.

He held her hand tightly as they plunged through a milling crowd of revelers who'd just emerged from one of the upscale loft buildings. She shot him an oblique glance. Chemistry like this was rare. Why not play it out?

They entered a trendy bar—was there any other kind in SoHo?—through vast glass doors, a place known for its funky pseudo-Adirondack style. It was packed with club crawlers, the black-and-white cowhide couch lined with preening fashionistas. Lara lifted her face toward the heavy log beams that spanned the ceiling, seeking a gulp of untainted oxygen. The air was thick with smoke and a constant buzz of gossip.

It was strange to think that she'd once belonged to a similar crowd, though hers had put less emphasis on designer labels and more on individuality. After a few years of struggle by day—she'd tried everything from waitressing to window dressing before her art had become self-supporting—and partying by night, she'd burned out on both and had taken herself to the country. It was there she'd found her best inspiration.

Daniel tugged on her hand. "Follow me."

They'd been granted a tiny table for two, where they shared a brocade padded bench tucked away in a dark corner beneath a set of antlers. Two icy cold green-apple martinis arrived at the table and she downed a third of hers in one big gulp, hoping the liquor would cut through her otherworldliness. The animated stream of Manhattan nightlife was now wavering like a dream sequence; she blinked and watched the colors weave in and out.

I am light-headed. A bubble of hysterical laughter rose in her chest and she swallowed it down again.

It was because she'd been alone so much, she decided. But she hadn't felt out of place at Bianca's with all her old friends, even though she'd lost touch with many of their current references. What was truly odd was returning, older and wiser, to play dress-up among the glitterati of SoHo. The liquor wasn't helping in that regard.

No, that's not all, Lara amended in the next instant. The blame was mostly Daniel's.

Each time he turned his sharp gray eyes upon her face, she lost touch with the principles that guided her hard-won sense of self. Her intentions—to say nothing of her caution—tumbled into the chasm his eyes blasted into her concentration and when, after several minutes, she came back to herself, she was...unrestrained. Loose all over, like butter in the sun. Oiled like a hinge. The harsh lights and vivid colors burned her eyes. She found herself saying the most provocative things.

Helpless to resist, she leaned toward Daniel, drawn by his compelling masculinity. He was as magnetic as the great Broadway actor she'd met years ago at her father's stone farmhouse in Umbria. In a swoony Welsh accent, the notorious old goat had told Lara that he wanted to take her to his homeland, that she must see Aberystwyth and the Vale of Glamorgan. His spell was so potent she'd been all but ready to hop a boat...until he'd stuck his hand up her skirt.

Daniel was less inclined.

Thus far.

Lara laughed freely at nothing in particular, except perhaps the heady whirlwind of an attraction that was so deeply sexual it had to be more than sexual. She sensed a possibility of long-term desire...if she played her cards right, remembered her limitations and kept her cool. The latter didn't seem likely. She crossed her legs, widening the gap in her skirt.

Daniel put his hand on her kneecap. Her nerve endings hummed with pleasure.

She buried her nose in the mahogany-brown hair that curled behind his ear. He had the ears of a satyr; she wanted to nibble on the tip, suckle at the lobe.

"Mmm, Camille," he murmured when she licked at his ear.

The name was part of her game. It provided the mask that was her safety net. Having grown up as the daughter of a legendary Man of Arts, watching the sycophants, dealers and scholars that revolved around him, hungrily snatching at his soul, she understood the value of simple anonymity.

"Tell me about yourself." Daniel caught her chin in his big hot hand. She wanted to feel those hands all over her, blasting their heat into every hidden crevice like a relentless Mediterranean sun. "Let me guess. You're...an artist?"

To avoid his intense gaze, she ducked under the tumbledown mess of her hair. "Some might say so."

"What does that mean?"

"Well. You know." She shrugged. "It's a man's world. Women's work isn't taken as seriously."

"It's the twenty-first century," he said.

She laughingly overrode him, insisting, "No, no, in the art world it's still 1900."

"What do you do?"

She swallowed a private smile. "I sculpt."

"Were you one of the artists with a piece on display at the restaurant?"

"Yes."

When he frowned, two lines intersected in a vee an inch above the bridge of his nose. His brows were luxuriously thick, but as well-groomed as the rest of him. His nose was a strong beak, matched by a granite jaw. "I'm sorry. There was a lot of art there, but I don't remember seeing any sculpture. Did I overlook it?"

"Probably. But that's to be expected. Auguste gets all

the credit.'' She puffed wisps of hair out of her eyes, amused at Daniel's confusion.

''I'm lost,'' he said, absently stroking her collarbone, sending the tempo of her pulse sky-high.

''As am I.''

''You're being deliberately obtuse.''

She ducked under his arm and snuggled against him. ''That's the fun of it.''

''All right. I'll play along.'' He said this with such a weightiness she laughed again.

''It's the weekend, Daniel. Forget about Nasdaq and Alan Greenspan and all the bulls and bears and other nasty beasties. Take a few hours off. Have some fun.'' She crinkled her nose at him. ''Do you know how to do that?''

''Oh, yes.'' His baritone went right through her. ''I know how.''

''I'll just bet you do.'' She gave her response equal weight, teasing him.

They skipped briefly over his career at a stuffy old brokerage house and how the world would spin off its axis if ever the market were to crash. She said that he could prop it up on his shoulders. He chuckled and nudged his untouched glass toward her empty one. She liked it that he could laugh at himself, though it was clear that he took his position as a Bairstow & Boone financial analyst—and newly minted partner—very, very seriously. There was an ambition in him that matched her own. Not a naked, greedy, soulless ambition, but the driven, meaningful, solid-as-bedrock sort.

''Harvard Business School,'' she guessed, even though he didn't seem Ivy League.

He nodded and narrowed his eyes, looking her over. ''Cooper Union?''

She'd gone to Rhode Island School of Design. ''I apprenticed to a sculptor in Paris,'' she said, spinning her tale. ''He was older, famous, domineering. He'd seduced me by the time I was twenty-one. Abandoned me some years thereafter.''

Daniel scowled, carving out another vee. ''This Auguste guy?''

''That would be the one.''

''Never heard of him.''

She waved a hand. ''He's dead. But you can see his stuff in museums across all continents.''

''This is a joke?''

''It's a universal truth.''

He looked lost again, but he was catching on. ''Poor little artist,'' he said. ''You need a patron.''

''Oh, no. I prefer my Bohemian existence. Living day by day, scrounging in flea markets, peddling drawings for pennies, having fabulous affairs with rich, important men who grovel after every twitch of my skirt...'' His opening.

The man was not slow on the uptake. ''In this particular skirt,'' he said, running his fingertips along her bare right leg, making her glad she'd skipped the hose, ''a twitch is a mind-bending experience.''

Little did he know. Her recent garb was anything loose and sloppy—oversize shirts and elastic-waist shorts, long knit tunics paired with pajama bottoms. A by-product of having no one around to impress. Being fashionable was rather nice, for a change.

''What,'' said Daniel, leaning closer so his lips were a millimeter away from touching her cheek, ''are you wearing under this dress?''

''Besides a piercing?''

''Mmm.''

Her lashes dropped. ''Don't you want to find out on your own?''

"Now?"

She lifted a shoulder, challenging him with her silent acquiescence.

He reached, pressing against her. His hand curved around her bare thigh. Her breath caught short. With a placement that was devastating in its precision, he inserted his fingertips into the seam of her crossed legs from behind. Suddenly she was hot as a coal furnace, the muscles in her belly and inner thighs quivering as she squeezed her legs together. The noise of the bar receded to a distant hum; all she heard was the heavy sound of their combined breathing. Her pulse beating hard and fast. *Pom, pom, pom.*

"Up another inch," she said. A dare.

His fingertips slid a tickling half inch. *Pom-pom-pom.*

She was molten. "Nearly there."

His thumb brushed across the critical juncture. *Pom-pompompompompom.*

"I can't," he said with a gust of an exhale, briefly squeezing her buttock in his hand. "Not here." His breath was hot and lusty. "Let's go. I'd rather grope you—" he grinned "—in private."

She was giddy, feverish. "No one here cares."

His voice seethed in her ear. "You little exhibitionist."

Apparently so. Another surprise. It was this man and this man alone, she thought again, downing his drink in several long gulps, not even caring if he was trying to get her drunk. She was becoming determined to see how far they were willing to go. Probably not the wisest move she'd ever made, but she'd been cooped up alone too long, working in blissful solitude. This weekend was her chance to break free.

What she needed was an adventure.

A...game.

With no rules.

But one.

THEY SAT AND CHATTED like normal people for another fifteen minutes. Daniel's fingertips tingled. The tragedy of the near miss. Although he had trouble concentrating, nothing Camille said seemed to make a lot of sense anyway. Airy remarks about Montmarte, the art academy and Auguste's betrayal. Daniel believed she was toying with him. In most circumstances, he wouldn't tolerate it. Tonight, however, her frank desire had trumped his need for control.

She'd knocked him off balance. And here he sat, nodding and happy, all because he had to know what, if anything, she wore under her dress.

Blast. She'd reduced him to pliancy, and he was never pliant. Not since his youth in the backwater of West Virginia, when he'd looked at his unenterprising parents and his good-for-nothing older brother and set his mind upon the goals that would save him: education, career, success.

No distraction had been attractive enough to stay him from his course...until Camille.

What a woman.

What a tease.

He focused on her face. The small round face with laughing green eyes. He memorized the shapes her lips made as she prattled on about Paris. He stroked her hand. Suddenly her words were tumbling over each other like upended building blocks. She stopped and caught her lower lip between her teeth, then excused herself to find the ladies' room.

He stood to watch her legs as she walked away, only to be punched in the solar plexus by a desire so strong it took his breath away.

Where were they going with this? Unmoving amongst the push and pull of the enthusiastic weekend crowd, Daniel took a silent inventory. He was on top of his game—thirty-six, single, gainfully employed in the toughest market in the world. All his goals had been achieved. From here on out, maintenance was the key. He didn't intend to slack off—ever—but he could finally afford a bit of...recreation.

He wanted Camille for more than a one-night stand. It was only supposition at this point, but he imagined that she might be the kind of woman who'd change his life.

"*Good,*" he said to himself rather fiercely, and there was such emotion in his voice that the exotic eyes of a young woman with hair like a black satin waterfall lit up with interest. She smiled an invitation, but he had already turned away and seated himself at the small round table, thinking only of Camille. He excelled at narrowing his focus to what mattered most. Tonight the lioness was in his sights.

Feeling less pliant, he removed his cuff links and rolled up his sleeves, then sat back to wait for her return. She didn't take long. He couldn't keep the smile off his face as she slid in beside him. Beneath his draped jacket, her body was long and lean in the matte gold dress. A sylph.

"I have a humble flat on East Tenth," he said. "Between First and Second Avenue. It's not far."

"Really." She looked stunned. "The East Village."

"We can go there," he explained patiently.

"Ah, hmm."

He took her hand. "Come with me."

She resisted. Out of sheer feminine contrariness, he supposed, as up to now her signals had been blatant. "Not so fast," she said, tugging free. "You wanted terms."

"I don't remember asking for terms."

She traced a blunt unpolished fingernail through the hair on his arm above the wide band of his steel wristwatch. "Let's strike a deal."

He froze. Was she a professional? Surely not.

Then again, how many men got so lucky without there being qualifications?

He assumed his fiercest analyst's expression, good for facing down squirrely traders and instilling confidence in wishy-washy clients. "Money," he suggested, heavy on the dubious connotation. Money was a commodity he valued. Money was both straightforward and negotiable. He valued it less for the lifestyle it bought—although he could appreciate that—than for its clear-cut measure of his success.

He didn't want this to be a matter of money.

"Money?" Camille's eyes rolled. "You have got to be kidding. This isn't a *business* deal."

"Then what is it?"

She slid her palm over his forearm, her strong fingers massaging into muscle. He felt the touch deep inside, as if she'd been granted unlimited access to the very heart of him. "It's pleasure."

His head inclined. "A pleasure deal?"

"A pleasure game."

"With terms?"

She nodded. "Let's keep this straightforward right from the start. Makes for fewer complications later."

The feeling inside him spread fiery tentacles. As long as there would be a "later," he'd go along with whatever rules she set. "I'm game," he said, reaching under the jacket, still thinking about what did or did not lie beneath her dress.

She shifted, momentarily bringing her breast into contact with his hand. It was a perfect handful, firm and round, unbound by a brassiere. Every thought in his head stuttered to a halt until he realized with a jolt that she was only leaning forward to shrug out of his jacket. He removed his hand. As slowly as possible.

She stood and tossed the jacket over his shoulder, pressing down when he started to rise. "Stay here."

Part of the game? He was ready to toss her on the nearest flat surface, audience be damned.

"But—" he said.

"Not tonight." She leaned over him. "Tomorrow. Let's both think this over, decide on terms, and then make a clear-headed decision about continuing." Her peacock lids blinked. "Tomorrow is soon enough." He opened his mouth and she plucked at his lips, giving him a soft, supple kiss that set off a few alarm bells in his head. The loose tendrils of her hair brushed his face like cobwebs. "Tomorrow," she promised.

"But," he said again, feeling thick and stupid with desire, "I don't know your name. I don't know where you—"

"Camille." Her eyes danced. "Camille Claudel."

She might have caught him in her web, but that didn't make him gullible. He grunted. "Camille. Right."

She flicked the tip of her tongue against his lip, said in a throaty whisper, "Your move, Daniel," then turned and walked swiftly out of the bar. He stared, the subtle jiggle of her derriere smiting him between the eyes. As the crowd closed around her, he decided with a dead-on certainty that she'd worn not so much as a stitch beneath her dress the whole time. And as badly as he wanted to go after her, he found he could not move. He was stone. Dank, dense stone. His face was hot; sweat beaded on his upper lip.

Eventually his brain began to clear. The jacket slid off

his shoulder. He caught it, reaching absently for the fancy silk square that Tamar had folded into the pocket right before they left the office.

The swatch of fabric was pressed beneath his nose before he realized that it wasn't a pocket square at all.

The scent…

Pure enticement.

He lowered his hand, watching in stupefaction as Camille's tiny silk panties blossomed like a golden lotus across his leaden fingers.

"CAMILLE CLAUDEL," Tamar said with her usual crisp efficiency the next morning. Daniel always worked on Saturdays, but Tamar did not. She'd met him at the office by personal request. "Lived 1864 to 1943. She was an artist—a sculptor. The apprentice, collaborator and mistress of Rodin."

"Auguste Rodin," he said, wishing he'd taken that college course in art history.

"Best known for The Thinker and The Kiss." Tamar handed him printouts of the famed statues, still warm from the printer. "Rodin, that is. Claudel's work sank into obscurity until revived by a fairly recent interest. There was a movie, *Camille Claudel,* starring Isabelle Adjani. Shall I get you the DVD? And the screenplay?"

He was usually thorough to the smallest detail in his research. This once, as the project pertained only to his personal life, such lengths weren't necessary. He wasn't evaluating a multinational conglomerate—just outfoxing one naughty little seductress.

"Yes," he blurted anyway. The stakes were high. He'd barely slept.

And the lioness *had* dared him to make the next move.

"Tamar?" he asked, stopping her in the doorway. "I

hope you enjoyed the party at the restaurant. Did you get home okay?''

Tamar blinked. Since she was so circumspect about her personal life, he'd learned not to ask. ''It was fine,'' she said, her dark red lips moving in a deliberate manner. ''Enjoyable.''

''No hardship to come in this morning?'' He studied the photos of Rodin's sculpture, keeping one eye on his assistant, who was taking too long to answer. ''I didn't disrupt any of your plans for the weekend?''

Her head tilted. ''Certainly not.'' She waited a beat. ''Daniel?''

He looked up. ''Yes?''

Tamar didn't answer, but her right eyebrow rose to Alpine heights. Two times in two days, he'd provoked her into impatience.

''See if you can track down a man called Kensington Webb,'' he said, reverting to form. ''I believe he's an art shark. Last night there was a piece of stained glass on display at the restaurant. Get the artist's name from Webb. And, uh, situation. Any information he'll provide, in fact. I want—''

''To buy it?''

''No. Maybe.'' Not like him to be equivocal. He turned away from Tamar's frank stare. ''Say whatever it takes to get the goods. I want the artist's address. A phone number, at the least.'' He thumbed through the sheets of Camille Claudel's biography. Her father had been an esteemed figure in French literature. ''A bio might be helpful.''

''Yessir.'' Tamar's voice was arch.

He waved the papers at her. ''Go on. And shut the door.''

''But of course.'' She exited silently, followed by a soft thunk.

Daniel went to the window and its view of the bleak gray canyon of Wall Street. The memory of the lively color and sound of SoHo on a Friday night made him admit that a degree of sameness, even stodginess, had begun to infect his personal life. By concentrating on his climb up the financial ladder, he had neglected other concerns.

Not to say that he was ready for the monastery. He had a social life outside the office. Still, his career dedication seemed to annoy the women Tamar wrote into and then crossed out of his date book. They started out praising his success. After a month or two, they were peeved by his neglect. They wanted weekends in the Hamptons; he wanted to work. They eventually wanted to discuss commitment; he wanted to work.

Success was a fine thing. A regimen of all work and no play was something else. Had he been so determined to avoid ending up like his parents that he'd become a drone instead?

Maybe that was why his reaction to "Camille" had been so volcanic. Or maybe it was only that she'd aroused his primal instincts, then disappeared, setting him off in hot pursuit.

Who was she? He closed his eyes and inhaled, remembering every detail with perfect clarity. The fake name had been only a part of her game, not an escape plan. Surely she knew he'd run her to ground.

Daniel smiled. The lioness had left a small but crucial piece of her lingerie in his possession. If he needed an excuse—and he doubted it—he could always say that he wanted to return the panties.

She would laugh, he knew. Already he relished the thought of it. Her boisterous laugh would be his congratulations for a deed well-done.

Yes, he decided as he swung around to his teakwood desk, *I need this.*

I need her.

It was nearly a minute before the statement rebounded inside his head.

He needed her? That was new.

He'd learned not to need his parents by the time he was eight. They were well-meaning but essentially useless. Lovable layabouts, going from one menial job to another, doing only enough to pay the rent and put tuna casserole and hot dogs on the table. They had no ambition beyond that which provided a steady stream of cigarettes, Mountain Dew, cable wrestling matches and bingo cards. Purchasing lottery tickets was their lame attempt at bettering themselves. Their sons were treated with benign neglect.

Jesse, the older brother, had gone one route—fast living and easy money, scams and petty crime, occasional jail time. Daniel had gone the other—hard work, long study, strict discipline. All on his own. While his parents had proclaimed their pride in him, they'd also arrived late to his high school valedictory speech because of a flat tire, and had missed his college commencement altogether. Now he visited them once a year, at Christmas. They were always happy to see him, but no more and no less than the check he sent monthly.

Daniel dismissed family connections.

Then…did he need his job? Yes and no. It was completely intertwined with his self-image. Yet he was certain that he could always get another. Probably a better one. He had offers all the time.

So, no, he did not need *this* job.

He caressed the fine leather that banded his desk blotter, readily admitting to himself that he needed Tamar. They'd been a team since he'd landed at Bairstow & Boone fresh out of Harvard, M.B.A. in hand. She was one or two years his senior—perhaps—of mysterious origins, rarely emotionally forthcoming. But she was an executive assistant extraordinaire—smart, efficient, dependable. Although Daniel's career could survive without her, he wasn't eager to test the theory.

Counting Tamar as a friend was trickier. Despite his best attempts, their relationship was mainly a one-way street—certainly not his idea of a proper give-and-take friendship.

None of the guys from the office could be counted as close friends, either. They were co-workers, occasional off-hour buddies. Likewise the tenants in his building: a middle-aged woman who holed up in the third-floor attic apartment, claiming to be a writer; the gay couple on the second floor who used his garden in return for their decorating expertise. Educating Daniel's eye was their ongoing project.

Daniel liked them all; he did not, even remotely, need them.

But, suddenly, he *needed* the lioness?

That was definitely new. And a mighty strange sensation.

Particularly as he still didn't know her name.

With a certain triumph, he thought of the silk panties he'd tucked away in his own underwear drawer for safekeeping. The commingling of their intimate apparel gave him a kick.

And a kick start.

Names were not always necessary.

3

"IT WAS LIKE a fever dream," Lara said, closing her eyes as the previous evening spun through her thoughts, a series of colorful, blurred images anchored by the dark, solid presence that was Daniel. "Psychedelic. Unreal. I couldn't grasp it."

"Bah! You weaseled out." Bianca Spinelli soaped her hands at the sink in her grand charivari of a kitchen. The walls were chili-pepper-red, the cabinets guacamole-green, the clay tiles on the floor and countertops all the wonderful variegated umber shades of a sunbaked Mother Earth. Folk painting in primary colors formed a border around the room. Numerous pieces of stained glass glittered in the only window. For Lara the gaudiness was both welcoming and inspiring.

"I didn't weasel out," she said. "It was—well, it was happening too fast." She sat on a tipsy stool beside the breakfast bar, on the opposite side of the cheerfully crowded living area that had been fashioned out of the back half of Bianca's art-glass studio. Double swinging doors divided the front from the back, though not so anyone would notice. The entire space was an unofficial Grand Central Station for every glass artist and creative type on Avenue B.

Lara put a black olive between her front teeth, bit it neatly in half and swallowed the salty pieces whole. *Daniel lives in the East Village. Only a few streets away.* The coincidence was disturbing, especially after she'd pegged him for the stuffy five-thou-per-month Central Park condominium type. Aware that he was taking shape for her, becoming more than just the prize in a sexual game, she wondered what else there was to discover about him.

"Too fast? Eh. You never were the slow-lane type—" Bianca shot her a sour look "—until recently."

Lara grimaced. "All right, it's true. I got scared." *By my own daring...and his.*

Wiping her fingers with a napkin, she paused to admire the way she'd arranged an immense platter of antipasto. There were plump mushrooms, eggplant and tomato slices, zucchini flowers and sticks, roasted bell peppers, several varieties of sausage and thick creamy chunks of mozzarella, mortadella and provolone cheese. In addition, she'd sliced up a sweet, juicy melon and started a pan of leftover risotto warming on the stove.

Friends and customers—one and the same, in Bianca's book—would soon begin dropping in for a nosh, a cup of wine, good conversation or a rousing debate. Mornings were reserved for Bianca's solo studio time; afternoons, she opened up the shop, taught classes and ran what Lara referred to as either the salon or, for those times when the music was loud and the wine was truly flowing, the *cantina.*

Bianca had returned to scrubbing her hands free of traces of the chemical solvents used in glasswork. "You see?" she said, shaking her black wavy hair over the sink. "Moving to the upstate wilds has done you no good, Lara. Remember the days when you kept a string of men on call as need demanded? You had no qualms about... um...*managing* them."

"Daniel's different."

"Oh? How so?"

"He's a grown-up." Lara unhooked her feet from the rungs and drew them up so she sat cross-legged, perched atop the stool like a stork. "Me, too. In those good old days you mention, I was newly graduated, ready to take the Manhattan art world by storm, or so I believed. I was young and crazy and rebellious. I thought independence equaled indiscriminate adventure." In fact, she'd been trying to imitate Bianca, her mentor. "Now that I'm thirty, I've outgrown casual sex." Despite their accelerated attraction, she knew that sex with Daniel would not be casual. It would be cataclysmic.

"A shame." Bianca grinned. "Casual grown-up sex is even better." She flung her expressive hands in the air, sending droplets flying. "*Dio mio!* Until a man is forty, he knows nothing about how to please a woman in bed. You don't know what you're missing."

"I'm not celibate," Lara argued, laughing. "I just didn't want to rush. And Daniel's thirty-six."

"Bosh. You're a fool to pass up such chemistry."

"I have not passed it up. Merely postponed it."

"Chemistry, chemistry," Bianca sang, doing vigorous battle with a hand towel. "Good chemistry is like catching lightning in a bottle. Don't miss out because of this silly game of yours."

Lara smiled. "Daniel found the game provocative, I'm certain. I did tell you about the surprise I left in his pocket."

Bianca enjoyed her own laughter so much it was contagious. "Yes, that was good." She chortled. "And so naughty of you. I'm proud, *chica.* My Jennifer Lopez dress works every time, even when you insist on wearing it backwards."

A huge smile broke across Lara's face. "After that stunt, he's sure to find me."

Bianca sobered. "But how?"

"Oh, I'm sure he has resources. He met Kensington, so he might think of asking at the gallery."

"Would they send him here? Ai-yee, I hope so. This man, I must see."

"I don't know. It depends how persistent he is." *Very,* she thought. If she knew anything about Daniel, that was it. The intense ray-gun heat of his eyes was not characteristic of a laid-back man. "The gallery doesn't hand out information to every guy off the street. And I go home tomorrow. Daniel may have to continue the hunt there."

"The hunt?"

Lara wiggled her hips; the stool rocked. She grabbed the tiled edge of the counter. "Yes. He's a hunter."

"And you...?"

"Blame it on the chemistry," she said with a lick of her lips. "I am dying to be caught."

"But not encaged, hmm?"

"Nor engaged," Lara said drolly.

Bianca scowled.

Lara squared her shoulders. "You know how I feel about that." She'd decided early on that she was the go-it-alone type. She couldn't see subordinating her independent desires for the security of a marriage ring, as her mother and sister had done.

"Lovers, yes. Love, no. Marriage, never." Bianca leaned her elbows on the breakfast bar, put her chin on her hands and stared broodingly into the spirals of food Lara had arranged in the pattern of a nautilus shell.

Despite the glum expression, Bianca looked as beautiful and exotic as a bird of paradise. Bright clothing, plenty of makeup, gold hoop earrings large enough to touch her shoulders. Lara had been strongly influenced by her mentor's style and attitude, and was grateful for that. She might have turned out like her sister otherwise.

"Bianca?" she coaxed. "You've always agreed that I am smart to guard my freedom."

"In your experimental twenties, yes." Bianca pulled on her lower lip. "But one grows up and begins to appreciate the advantages of settling for stability."

"You're forty and you haven't settled."

"Forty-one. And I have become an old woman." With a groan, she banged the heel of her palm against her forehead.

"Ha!" Lara had done her best to acquire a portion of Bianca Spinelli's zest for life. It was a matter of attitude, not age. Of finding your bliss, to be Oprah-ish about it.

"There's nothing like an energetic eighteen-month-old to make a woman feel ancient," Bianca said, hoisting her daughter off the floor. She plopped little Rosa into a high chair, buckled her in and scooped a handful of crayons off the floor. "Try the yellow one, *cara mia.* In this house, we don't need the dingy old grays and browns."

Rosa gurgled happily, reaching for the stubby crayons.

"You adore being a mother," said Lara.

"Of course." Bianca took a dozen bright blue and pink and green ceramic plates of various sizes from an open cabinet. Nearly every item in her house and studio was colorful and handmade; she bartered with an extensive circle of artsy-craftsy friends. Lara had followed the cue in her own home, though she preferred earthen shades.

Bianca petted her daughter's curly crop of flame-red hair. "Listen, don't tell the *bambina,* but there are nights I miss my club-hopping escapades. My soul still yearns to dance even when my feet are dragging." Suddenly she picked up Rosa, chair and all, and swung her around the kitchen. Crayons flew. "Once I was Queen of the Discotheque. Now, I dance barefoot in the kitchen with my little bay-bee-yeee!'' Rosa giggled in delight.

Lara played along as Bianca danced, laughing and clapping to encourage the frivolity that was so dear to her heart.

Fourteen years ago, she'd wandered into Bianca's little shop as an aimless teenager, having been harshly disabused of a childish notion that she could become as great a painter as her father. The flamboyant older woman had welcomed Lara with open arms, soothed her wounded pride and started her on a beginner's pattern of stained glass that very day. The resulting piece was uneven and bumpy and amateurish, yet it still hung in Bianca's kitchen window. Whereas the crayon drawings Lara had executed at her father's feet were dissected for line, perspective and color sense, then discarded.

Staggering, Bianca set the high chair beside Lara's stool. ''You see? I'm out of breath.'' She put her hands on her hips and bent slightly, panting. ''I've become an old woman.''

''You need a lover, is all. A new romance would perk you right up again. And soon restore your stamina.''

''A man is easy enough to find.'' Bianca waved a hand in casual dismissal. ''It's the reliable baby-sitter that's a tough get.''

''Ooh-lo-lo,'' Rosa burbled. She waved a chubby hand, looking so like her mother despite the Titian hair, that Lara had to plant a kiss on the child's forehead.

''Ah, the mother's eternal lament,'' she said. ''Listen, Bianca, why don't I stay home tonight with Rosa?'' She snapped her fingers for the little girl's amusement. ''You go out and have a good time. The *bambina's* stuffy nose seems to have cleared.'' Rosa had been congested the evening before, putting the kibosh on their plans to attend the restaurant opening together. For all her casual ways, Bianca was a devoted mother.

"Oh. I don't know." Peripherally, Lara glimpsed her friend's covert calculations. "What about your hunter?" Bianca asked ultracasually.

"He probably won't show. You may have the entire evening to go out and find yourself a dashing young lover. I doubt it'll take even that long." Men of all ages were attracted to Bianca. She oozed a warm sensuality that was like honey to bees.

For a woman who'd just complained about slowing down, Bianca was strangely hesitant to take Lara up on the offer. Lara, guessing why, aimed her knowing smile at the toddler. There had been a time when her mentor was indeed the Queen of the Discotheque. In fact, they'd both taken Manhattan nightlife by storm. Bianca's single motherhood and Lara's rededication to her art and the resulting move out of the city had altered them both.

"Unless you've already made plans?" Lara cooed at Rosa, abandoning finger snaps for patty-cake.

"No plans." Bianca spun away. "You know how I feel about being pinned down by schedules. I go where the wind takes me. Rosa was born with a kite string instead of an umbilical cord."

Lara didn't let herself be distracted. "What about all that talk of settling and stability?"

"Achh. Did I say that?"

"You did."

"Then I didn't mean it."

"We are both getting older."

"Mature," said Bianca, reaching for a bottle of red wine.

"Perhaps you should..." Lara hesitated. How could she convince Bianca it was okay to fall in love and marry when she herself had no intention of doing either? The assurances would be hypocritical, and Bianca would know it. She'd seen Lara through too many gripe sessions about the constriction of women's role in marriage and the perfidy of husbands to be fooled now.

Bianca pulled a corkscrew out of an earthenware pot. Her glance was sharp. "Perhaps, what?"

Lara swallowed. "You could admit you're already in—"

The shop doorbell chimed. *"Buon giorno!"* a male voice with a bad Italian accent called from the storefront, and Bianca's face lit up like the Rockefeller Plaza Christmas tree. Total admission, Lara thought, if only Bianca had been looking in a mirror to see it.

Eddie Frutt came through the swinging doors, holding a bunch of sunflowers in one hand and a square envelope in the other. A large, shambling, redheaded man, he possessed a rapidly enlarging bald spot that he'd been passing off as a receding hairline for one too many years. Bianca called him Old Baldy, but kissed the top of his head every time she passed his chair on her way to the kitchen.

Eddie, who owned a shoe store across the street, greeted Bianca with a smooch. He did a sloppy Fred Astaire twirl and handed the flowers to Rosa, then waved the envelope at Lara. "I ran into a courier out front. This is for you. I want a hug in return."

"Of course." Lara went to him and was enveloped by his big, cushy body and strong arms. He smelled of leather and the peppermints he kept in a brandy snifter by his register. "It's been too long."

"Enough, Eduardo," Bianca complained. "You're smothering the girl."

Eddie whispered, "She's jealous," to Lara, then stretched out an arm and snared Bianca into the embrace, snuggling them to his chest until Rosa yelled, "Frower!" and smacked her tray with the bouquet. Exclaiming in spicy Italian, Bianca ran to rescue the flowers while Eddie turned aside, muttering over the corkscrew. Amidst the chaos, Lara ended up with the envelope. It was inscribed across the front with her name.

Unsuspecting, she tore it across the flap and took out a plain card with an embossed border. It read, "Tonight."

And that was all.

Daniel's face flashed before her. He was smiling in invitation, and his eyes were the color of pussywillows, velvety with seduction. The man was pure temptation. Sex incarnate.

All the blood drained from Lara's face.

Tonight, she thought, strung taut with anticipation.

One word was enough.

"THERE'S A LIMO," Eddie Frutt bellowed from the storefront. "A limo for Lara!"

"A limo, a limo for Lara," echoed the group gathered around the long farmhouse table. The elegant white-haired woman stationed by the bedroom door passed on the word. "Your limo has arrived, Miss Gladstone." Genevieve peered through her half-moon glasses and gave a small shake of her head, looking appalled. "No. Not the red leather. Try the plain black shoes with the chains. You'll look like an S and M Holly Golightly."

"Did Daniel come to the door?" Lara said, hopping on one foot as she changed shoes. Bianca's bed was occupied with onlookers. Getting Lara ready for her big date had turned into a neighborhood event.

The question was relayed to Eddie, who guarded the front door like a concerned father. The answer made its way back via Genevieve, who had once been an editor at

Vogue and now ran a vintage clothing store in Little Italy. With an unerring fashion instinct, she'd supplied Lara's dress.

"No Daniel. Just the chauffeur."

"Ooh, a chauffeur," said one of the gang on the bed. "How bourgeois," chimed another voice. "But fun," said a third.

Bianca handed over a silver beaded purse, another loaner since Lara hadn't come to New York expecting to be swept off her feet. They embraced. Lara said, "You're sure it's okay for me to leave after I offered to babysit—"

Bianca grabbed her face and smacked a kiss upon both cheeks. "Go. Have a good time." She pushed Lara toward the door, clearing discarded shoes and trampled scarves with a sweep of her foot. "Gah, I feel just like a mother sending her daughter to the prom!"

A smattering of applause broke out when Lara was paraded through the living space. Eddie enveloped her in another of his big hugs when she reached the studio. "But something's missing," he said worriedly, holding her out to look her over. "Little black dress. Gloves. Pearls. Bow in the hair. I know. The sunglasses. I might be balding and middle aged, but I saw *Breakfast at Tiffany's* too, ya know."

"Sunglasses at night? That's overkill," Bianca said. "You have no subtlety, Eddie."

He made a comical face. "Isn't that the point?"

"I knew it." Lara tore the silly black silk bow out of her hair, leaving in the rhinestone pins. "We've gone over the top."

"No, no, leave the gloves," Bianca urged as Lara went out the door, tugging at them.

The chauffeur waited at the curb, holding the door open

on a long black limo. Lara stopped. Her stomach did a flip. She turned back to Bianca and Eddie, who were watching arm in arm from the lighted doorway, along with the crowd pressing behind them and up against the studio windows.

I can't back out with everyone watching, Lara thought, bolstering herself. The front of the glass studio was painted with bright, boisterous graffiti that distracted from the chipped cement and gritty windows. The place was on the shabby side of humble, but it was her safe home in the city, far more comforting than her parent's expensive town house in Gramercy Park.

"I don't know this guy from Adam," she blurted. "I don't even know his last name. What am I doing, getting into his limo? This is crazy." She offered up a smile, recognizing the drama. "Crazy, I tell you!"

Eddie's brows knitted. "Maybe she's right...."

"Savage, ma'am," said the driver. "Daniel Savage. I have his address for you. He said you might be concerned."

"Oh. That was thoughtful of him." She took the card and stepped over to press it into Bianca's hand with a hollow laugh. "In case I disappear, you'll know where to start looking."

"This is *romantic,*" Bianca reassured her. "Don't look so worried." She pinched one of Eddie's love handles so he'd stop frowning. "You're going off with a chauffeur, not a white slaver."

Lara muttered, "Uh, yeah, thanks for bringing *that* up," but she allowed the driver to escort her into the car. It was luxurious, with a tastefully done interior of soft gray leather and burled walnut. As the limo slipped away into traffic, she turned and waved to Bianca and Eddie and all the rest, who were cheering—or jeering, given their individual levels of cynicism—as they watched her go. She stripped off the gloves as soon as she was beyond Bianca's scope.

All well-equipped limos had ice buckets. In this one, a freshly opened bottle of champagne nestled into a bed of crushed ice. A thin trail of vapor curled from the bottle's neck, inviting her to partake. Lara reached for the crystal flute, then decided that she was tipsy enough without aid. Tonight she'd need her wits about her.

A florist's paper cone rested on the seat beside her. She picked it up and peeled back foil and tissue. Calla lilies. Beautiful. They were strong flowers, sleek and smooth and assured.

"Me, too," she said, stroking a lily, glossy on one side, soft on the other. "For tonight, me too."

A minute later, she realized that the limo wasn't leaving the East Village. She'd expected to rendezvous with Daniel at an expensive restaurant, but instead they were pulling up to an area of typical side-by-side row houses, the fronts flushed a rosy gray in the dimming light. The process of gentrification had recently struck. Or possibly stalled out. Most of the houses were nothing special—grimy two-and three-flats, showing their age. Several had been renovated and upgraded with freshly painted trim and handsome matching urns at the stoop.

The limo circled twice, looking for a parking spot. A flotsam of vehicles clogged the streets. Even the illegal spots were taken, though the fire hydrant would soon be clear because one unlucky soul's car was being towed.

"Ma'am, I'm sorry," the driver said at last, giving up on his only possibility—six empty feet between an oxidized red Trans Am and a rusty Buick. "I'm going to have to let you out on the street."

"That'll do," Lara said, smiling at her pretentions. So

much for Cinderella's stylish arrival at the ball. "Just point me in the right direction."

"I'll do better than that." Disregarding traffic, he put the limo in park and stepped outside. Lara hurriedly scooted across the seat as horns blared.

"Move the effing car," yelled a burly, tattooed guy, obviously practiced at leaning on his horn and flipping the bird simultaneously. Not a talent singular to New Yorkers, but one they'd clearly perfected.

Despite the increasing chorus of complaint, the chauffeur insisted on escorting Lara past the trash at the curb and up the steps of her destination. He rang the doorbell, muttered an apology, then raced back to the limo just in time to shoo away a wino with his eye on the silver ice bucket.

Which was why Lara was laughing when the door opened.

Daniel—*Daniel Savage,* she thought with pleasure—smiled at her, his eyes burnished like pewter in the soft glow of the entry light.

"You came," he said. "I'm so pleased."

She sobered, puckering her lips into a flirtatious moue even though she was kinda sorta awestruck inside. "What girl refuses a limo?"

"And you're so very beautiful," he continued as if mesmerized, "I think I'm forced to kiss you."

Her eyes widened, but in the next instant she was in his embrace and his lips were on hers, kissing the pucker right out of them. It happened too fast for her to react. No time to savor the flavor of his warm mouth. No time to absorb the woodsy, masculine scent of him. No time to appreciate the sensation of being pressed against his wide, hard chest.

He kissed her quickly but fully, and then he was drawing her inside the close, dim entry of the brick row house and she was looking around, gaze darting like a chickadee, landing everywhere but on his face. The dark woodwork needed refinishing. A jagged crack ran though the only window—a small, square, stained-glass panel near the door. The limited space was crammed with mailboxes, crumpled takeout flyers, inline skates, hats, jackets and a bike frame that had been stripped of its wheels.

"You live here?" she said, incredulous, his kiss burning on her lips.

"A humble abode, but mine own." To one side was a long narrow staircase that turned back on itself when it reached the second floor. On the right a door opened off the foyer, emanating light and warmth and cooking smells. Daniel shut the front door and herded her toward the open one. "Let's take our kisses privately for a change, shall we?"

She arched her brows. "I'm making no promises." But her body said otherwise. It had reacted instinctively to his.

He put his hand on her shoulder, pausing her at the threshold. "You don't have to do anything you don't want to."

That's just it, she thought. *I* want *to do it. I want to do...*

She looked into Daniel's molten eyes. *Everything.*

"Then no dishes for me," she joshed, her throat too dry to laugh.

His hand skimmed to her waist. "I never make my guests do dishes."

"Even if they stay all night?"

"Hmm..." He smiled slightly. "If you're planning to stay all night, then I guess you *can* help me." His mouth lowered to her ear and with a flick of his tongue against her lobe he set her teardrop earrings swinging. "To make the bed."

She shivered, sliding him a provocative glance beneath lowered lids. "If that's to be the case, Daniel, I'd much rather help you *un*make it."

4

LARA'S CAPTOR SLIPPED a blindfold over her eyes, instantly turning her titillation to raw vulnerability.

She shifted toward the warmth of the fire, curling tighter, her arms twined over her naked breasts. The sensory deprivation was startling—electrifying. Her pulse drummed in a frantic rhythm. She mustn't allow this. The man was a stranger. All she knew was his name, and the ease with which he'd seduced her with a long look, a single, coaxing caress.

But she didn't know if she could trust him.

Was that why she was so excited?

"LARA?" Daniel said, not for the first time. "Your drink?"

She looked at him quickly, dragging her unfocused gaze away from the tame flickering of flames in the gas fireplace. "Yes, thanks," she said, taking the glass of sherry. His eyes lingered on her face—curious, contemplative, but knowing.

Then he was way ahead of her. She truly had no idea what to expect next. *I don't know him,* she thought, finding the lack of familiarity deeply intriguing. *He could be anyone. He could do anything.*

Exactly.

She smiled to herself as she turned away to survey the modest apartment. It was small, made even smaller by the bookshelves that lined opposite walls of the...library? Living room? She wasn't sure. There was no window or sofa, only two big, deep armchairs, upholstered in an amber leather so old it was finely crackled and worn at the seams. A pair of starkly modern copper floor lamps, tilted at cranelike angles, were positioned beside the chairs. A nubby rug and a low round table of dark mahogany filmed with dust and stacked with multiple editions of the *New York Times, Wall Street Journal* and *Garden Design* completed the seating arrangement.

She did a double take. *Garden Design?* Other than a potted orchid constructed with a bamboo trellis and a crinkled tie of raffia, there were no plants in sight. But there was a lot of *stuff*—running shoes, balled-up socks, an open briefcase, a small terra-cotta urn filled with rocks, a spilled pile of spare change. Camera lenses were scattered over the bookshelves like objets d'art.

Daniel saw her looking. "Maid's day off," he said, plucking a pair of fingerless gloves and a roll of masking tape off one of the chairs. "Make yourself at home. Hope you don't mind clutter."

She'd pegged him as a neat freak. Wrong again. "Unless you go for minimalist design, it's hard to keep a small place uncluttered. I know—I lived in a Chelsea broom closet for nearly two years."

"A broom closet?"

"Seemed like." The chair creaked beneath her. "How much space do you have?"

Daniel cocked his head to indicate a closed door behind them. "There's the bedroom and connecting bath. Heading toward the back, we have the dining room slash foyer and kitchen. None of them larger than twelve by fourteen."

"Then you're not claustrophobic...."

"One day I might knock down a few walls and convert the building to a single-family living space, but for now I rent out the two upper-floor apartments. I'm a bachelor with modest needs. This suits."

"You own the building?" *And you foresee yourself with a family?* she silently added, sipping the smooth sherry to distract herself from a distinct sinking feeling. If Daniel was looking for Miss Right, he'd soon find out she was only Miss Right Now.

"Yes."

Her gaze caught on his hands. She imagined them on her body, on her thighs, opening her with a sure touch. *Miss Take Me Right Now.*

"I have a country house," she said. Awkwardly.

"I know."

"How..."

"Did I track you down?" He leaned back in the chair, his legs, clad in black trousers, outstretched and crossed at the ankles. He looked completely relaxed yet ready to spring into action at her slightest movement.

"You managed it very quickly." She held herself still, offering only a slow sweep of her lashes as she looked him up and down.

With his dark tousled hair and chiseled face, he was gorgeous in the firelight. His shirt was gray with a silvery sheen, the cuffs unbuttoned and rolled to his elbows, the soft, touchable fabric emphasizing the hard body beneath it. His eyes were alert. Nearly luminescent, it seemed. The man exuded sex appeal. Effortlessly. He'd tapped straight into Lara's darkest desires.

"Camille..." he said softly, a faint smile curving his lips. He'd shaved fresh for tonight.

She watched him, unblinkingly fascinated, holding still at the calm center of her swirling desires.

"I banked on you being one of the artists whose work was promoted at the restaurant opening. Tamar recognized Kensington Webb's name, and after that, finding his gallery was a simple matter. The receptionist gave you away with a little coaxing. But I'm afraid now they're hoping for a lucrative corporate art sale to Bairstow & Boone."

She conceded with an incline of her head.

"Why Camille Claudel?"

"A whim," she said.

He seemed skeptical. "Is that so?"

She lowered her lids. "Then you know who my father is."

"It came up during the search. I may not be an art maven, but even I've heard of Ian Gladstone. Isn't he having a major retrospective at the Met in a month?"

"Five weeks. The first of November."

"You must be proud of him," he said, sounding vaguely envious.

She shrugged. "Yes, my father's professional accomplishments are impressive. It's a lot to live up to."

"Are you trying, with your work in stained glass?"

"Certainly not in my father's eyes. Like many others, he considers stained glass mere craftwork."

Daniel winced. "You should have told me outright that the piece in the restaurant was yours."

"I wanted your honest opinion."

"My opinion is that you're very talented."

"Thank you."

"For what it's worth, coming from a layman."

She rubbed her thumb over the stem of the rounded glass. Her father's moods had swung according to the latest critiques from the professionals, even though he swore they were a bunch of idiots. It was an unstable way to live; she'd vowed to avoid it in her own life as an artist.

"Your opinion is worth a lot to me," she told Daniel. "I try to keep my priorities straight."

"You're too generous. I'm a nobody." He shifted forward in the chair, looking like a very important somebody to Lara. His smoky gaze was fixed on her face. She assumed he was feeling as drawn to her as she was to him—and that excited her. She crossed her legs, barely able to sit still.

Daniel continued. "Was your father there last night?"

"Good God, no! Ian Gladstone wouldn't be seen at such a common, crowded event."

"Doesn't he know his daughter's light shines above the masses?"

She shook her head, amused by the very idea.

"Do you often go by an alias, Camille?"

"I told you, that was a whim."

"Not an escape from your famous last name?" Daniel probed. "Having read Camille Claudel's bio, it occurred to me that you share—"

She interrupted. "It was for your benefit. I was playing a game."

His chuckle was lazy, resonant. "And still are?"

Her heart beat faster. "Cat and mouse," she said with a provocative smile.

He shook his head. "Chess."

"Mmm. That sounds...calculating. I prefer spontaneity."

Daniel stood. "I'm a planner and a plodder, myself." He stopped beside her chair, bending to take her chin in his hand, tilting her face up to his. "And my plans for you, Miss Gladstone, are quite involved."

Her eyes widened. "Do I dare ask?"

His thumb brushed across her bottom lip before he let her go. He straightened with an exhale, thrusting a forked hand through his hair. "After last night, I have no doubt that you dare anything."

Lara was relieved when he dropped the subject, begging her pardon before going into the kitchen to do something vital to their roasting dinner. She sat silently for a few moments, worrying at her lower lip, bringing her heart rate back to normal. Finally, to distract herself from further thoughts of both her complicated relationship with her father and the dark thrill of beginning a less complicated one with Daniel, she got up to prowl the bookshelves. Except for a row of classics by Dickens and Proust, she found mostly nonfiction—thick gardening tomes, gorgeous photography books, adventure stories set in Arctic oceans and South American jungles, biographies of Great Men. Many of the books were well used—leather bound and handsomely old, as if they belonged in a grand paneled library.

So Daniel read. He cooked. She nearly stumbled over a golf club. He sported. But there were no photos of family or friends, no mementos of his private life, very few decorative objects. All right, then. He was the messy but functional type, like so many bachelors. Which meant that he probably only cooked because he liked to eat, not for the joy of experimenting with exotic spices and sensuous flavors.

But wait. She was jumping to conclusions again.

Lara retrieved her sherry glass and went in search of the kitchen. It wasn't a lengthy search. A battered oak table had been shoved against the wall in the entry-dining area. It was heaped with more reading material, but no place settings. The next room was the galley kitchen, lined with tall, glass-fronted cupboards. She caught Daniel in oven mitts, pulling a big black skillet from the oven. Meat sizzled. "There's plenty to choose from if you're a vegetarian," he said.

"I'm a carnivore." There'd been no choice, growing up around Ian Gladstone. Her father had chomped on his cigars and his rare roast beef, laughing at the pale vegan milksops who populated the art world. "May I help?"

"Yes," Daniel said gratefully, not bothered in the least that she was seeing the kitchen in total disarray—the crumpled skin of an onion, the gloppy mixing bowl that sat in the ironstone sink. "Would you check the asparagus? Getting a full-course meal on the table all at once is tougher than I thought."

She lifted a lid and found the steaming vegetables. "You don't usually cook?"

"I try to. On the occasional weekend. But rarely for guests."

"Why did I get so lucky?" she asked, feeling jocular. There was something about sharing a kitchen with a man that defused the sexual tension.

Daniel spooned black bean sauce over the roasted pork. "Because now it's your move again. And I'd rather you make it in private."

"My move? You're certain?"

"I gotta tell you, I'm charged, waiting to see what you'll do next. Perhaps I can start a collection of your dainty unmentionables."

She giggled. She *never* giggled, but this time she giggled. Purely a nervous reaction. To compensate, her nose went up in the air and she said dryly, "I'd rather not repeat myself."

"Even better." His velvet tone reminded her that the sexual tension could flare up again at any moment.

The glass-doored cabinets made it easy for her to find a serving dish. She arranged the green stalks of the asparagus on it and looked at Daniel for direction. "The garden," he said, nodding toward a pair of open French doors. Candlelight flickered.

"The garden," she repeated, but inside she was wondering. *My move?* He was leaving the next step up to her? She wasn't sure she wanted that. Couldn't he just sweep her off her feet and be done with it?

Which was terribly postfeminist fairy tale of her. Although intellectually she should know better, in her fantasies she still wanted to be overwhelmed by passion through no fault of her own. It was all about surrender. Surrender to a strong, commanding man.

And here was Daniel, letting her guide the way. She should be pleased by that. It was what she'd said she wanted—to make a choice, to set the rules, to play the game, all at her own behest. Knowing that, however, didn't stop her craving.

Her craving to be taken.

Wildly.

Wickedly.

Savagely.

What did Daniel think? She watched him from the doorway, the ceramic plate beginning to warm her palms. He was giving nothing away. He couldn't be as easy to please as that. Sure, on the surface he was taking it casual, putting on no pressure, but a man didn't send a limo and cook a romantic candlelight dinner unless he planned to get...dessert. She'd certainly given him reason to believe she would be amenable. Even aggressively amenable.

She turned and went into the garden. Another small space, the courtyard was walled with crumbling red brick and filled with healthy green plants. It was a charming surprise, a quiet pocket of paradise in the teeming city.

She set down the plate and looked around. If a garden

could be masculine, this grotto was it. There were few flowers or colors. Lots of ornamental grass with tall wheatlike spikes or fuzzy plumes. Ferns and hostas thrived in the deep, shadowy corners. A rigid row of shapely junipers thrust toward the gray, clouded sky.

"Your garden is charming," Lara said as Daniel came outside with the main course on a platter. A marble-topped butcher's table had been set for dinner with fine china and old family silver. She remembered the gardening books and magazines. "You're the man with the green thumb?"

"Yeah." He actually looked sheepish about it.

"I'm in awe." A trickling sound drew her attention. Tucked among a thicket of lady ferns, a thin stream of water spouted from a stone lion's mouth into a low cement trough. Both it and the brick wall were damp and green with moss. "How incredibly charming. It's like opening a door and walking into a fairy-tale illustration."

Daniel nodded. "I needed a refuge from the city. There are times the crowds and noise get to me."

"Where did you grow up?" She'd been trying to place his accent—subtle, but there. A very slight twang. He was not a native New Yorker. She imagined him romping in the countryside with a younger brother and a dog named Skip and a mother who grew vegetables.

"West Virginia," he said. "Extremely modest beginnings. Not like you."

It was true that she'd had all the advantages—and disadvantages—of her father's wealth, fame and position. Good schools, European vacations, important connections. Although she'd done her best to go it on her own since she was sixteen, she was pragmatic enough to know that this was impossible without making herself completely anonymous. Certainly it had been the Gladstone name that had persuaded Kensington to represent her. She'd chosen to believe that her work had enough merit to stand on its own, regardless.

Lara approached the table. She picked up a piece of the silver, heavy with a family crest. "I'm not sure I believe you. I'll bet you're from one of those grand old families who hunt foxes and shoot skeet at their country estate. Modest only in a traditional, old-money way."

Daniel laughingly shook his head. "My father hunts now and then—rabbits and squirrels. Think Elmer Fudd, not Prince Charles."

Her head cocked. "Really?"

"My dad worked the coal mines, when he worked. My mother was on the line at an egg factory until her back went bad. My brother—" He stopped with a shrug. "I don't come from money. I have no pedigree. And I don't hide it. Does that matter to you?"

"Yes."

"Oh." His eyes became cool as rainwater.

"It matters because now I know what kind of man you are," she said. Admiration grew inside her as she stepped close enough to touch him, even though she didn't. "I'm even more impressed. You've attained success without the advantage of being born with a silver spoon in your mouth. That's something to be proud of." Playfully she tapped the spoon against his chin.

He took it from her, allowing his fingers to brush across hers. Every time he did that, her desire burned a little hotter. At this rate, dessert would be Lara Gladstone flambé.

"Straight from the flea market," Daniel said, referring to the spoon. "I like old things. They have a history."

She'd picked up his scent again—faintly woodsy, definitely masculine. She fought the urge to bury her face in his shirt and sniff. "Hmm. Gardening, photography, golf, antiques. You're a Renaissance man."

"I have help," he said, brushing shoulders as he reached past her to replace the spoon. Her breath caught short. The movement had brought his mouth so close to hers they would be kissing if she leaned in and angled her face slightly to the side....

A shrill call from above split the mood in two. "Yoo-hoo. Yoo-hoo!" Daniel straightened.

Lara looked up. The black metal tracery of a fire escape zigzagged up the back of the apartment house. Two men hung over the railing at the second-floor level, smiling big enough to show their molars. One put a hand to his mouth and semaphoned, "Yoo-hoo! Danny-boy!"

The other giggled. "We do hate to interrupt..."

"The help," Daniel said to Lara with a wry grimace. He took his hands off her waist, looked up and waved. "Hey, there, guys. Thought you were at the movies."

"Stew forgot his glasses. He can't fully appreciate Keanu's dimple without them."

"The dimple in his *posterior,*" called Stew.

"Naturally," said Daniel. He nodded from them to Lara. "Stan and Stew, my upstairs tenants. Guys, this is Lara. Lara Gladstone," he added softly, giving her real name a special spine-tingling emphasis.

They called hellos back and forth. "Honey, you look fabulous," Stew said. "Very Audrey."

"Vintage Givenchy," she explained with a smile, fingering the row of metal studs that set off the bodice of the simple A-line minidress.

Stew flipped a hand. "*Love* those studs with a capital *L.*"

"And the spike heels and chains," said Stan. The pair

nudged each other, chortling. "We had no idea that Danny-boy went for the kinky stuff."

"Not for lack of asking," Daniel said, waving them away.

"You two kids have fun," the middle-aged duo called. "Don't do anything we wouldn't do!" The metal platform clanged as they climbed back inside their window more noisily than they'd climbed out.

Lara looked at Daniel, her smile widening with delight. "Never mind that," she said. "We're still left with plenty of room for error."

His brows went up. "I wasn't planning on making errors."

"Well. That's a relief."

They studied each other's faces. The air between them crackled with tension and anticipation. "You'd better sit before I go back on my word," Daniel said at last, stepping around her—without touching, this time—to hold out a chair.

She took her place and unfolded a large linen napkin onto her lap. Tiny sprigs of herbs and ferns and ivory tapers in a small ormolu candelabra dressed the table. Whatever his upbringing, the man had style. Or enough smarts to take Stan and Stew's aesthetic advice.

"What word would that be?" she asked as he served, spooning up some sort of fruit or vegetable chutney.

"I promised myself not to kiss you again."

"Why?" Did she sound plaintive?

"Because the next move is yours, remember?"

A chess game, she remembered, recognizing again that she wasn't one for maneuvering behind the scenes. She would have to be open with him about her expectations. Or lack thereof.

"Before we can play—" she sent him a flirty look out of the corners of her eyes "—we must set the rules."

He placed a filled plate before her, making her taste buds water for more than his kiss. "As a woman who dislikes authority, you're terribly set on making up some rules."

She lifted a bite of the tender roasted pork to her lips. "It's been my experience that men need boundaries. They're unruly creatures, otherwise."

"And you like to keep us under control?" he said, pouring wine, a deep red Burgundy.

Suddenly dry mouthed, she grabbed her glass before he'd quite finished—a few drops of wine splashed across the marble tabletop. She drank, watching Daniel's bemused expression, then apologetically mopped up the spill with her napkin.

"Control issues?" he said, one side of his mouth tilting higher than the other.

Blindfolded, she was at his mercy.

Lara blinked several times in succession, trying to banish her churning fantasies and formulate a coherent response. How to ask for what she wanted? Shouldn't he just...know?

Daniel leaned closer. Put his hand on her arm. Good grief. His palm radiated warmth like an electric stove burner.

"Which of us needs to be controlled?" he asked, his quiet voice settling inside her, bone deep.

"Both," she said. She rubbed her lips together, tasting a hint of the tart wine. "Neither. I want— I want—"

Daniel's small, sexy smile returned. "I want," he mimicked. His fingers closed on her arm, leaving no doubt what he wanted.

"I want you," she blurted. "I want an affair. I want to

break the rules, not make them. And I want..." She bit her lip.

"A commitment?" Daniel guessed, and neither his grip nor his straightforward gaze wavered.

"The opposite," she said.

"Not a one-night stand?"

"No. I want an affair. But not a *love* affair. A—a—" She stopped and looked across the garden, going for a serene expression even with her emotions in turmoil. "I hadn't expected to be discussing this over dinner."

He took his hand away and settled back in his chair. Irrationally, she felt abandoned. She picked up her fork, but concentrating on the food was impossible when all she could think of was Daniel Savage. Daniel—stalking her, capturing her, holding her so tight against his body she was overwhelmed by him, absorbed by the sheer power and mass of him. She would be begging for it when finally his mouth took hers....

"I want a sexual affair."

Daniel's utensils clattered against the plate. His head came up, like a beast sighting its prey.

"No commitment, just sex," she said.

His nostrils flared. He had her scent.

"Pure sex."

Go ahead and pounce, she told him silently.

He didn't move, but he stared at her for so long she became warm and even a little dizzy. She laughed in defense. "Now's the point where you sweep the dishes off the table, throw me down on top of it and demonstrate the advantages of *impure* sex."

Deliberately he sipped wine, set aside the glass to unfold a napkin, touched it to his lips, dropped it onto the table—all without taking his eyes from her. She became more composed, even if her knuckles were white from gripping the arms of the chair. She'd said enough. She'd made her move. Let him choose the next step.

Daniel licked his fingers and snuffed out the candles one by one by pinching the wicks. When he was finished, the scent of wax and smoke was thick in the air and her eyes flew again to his face only to discover that he was still watching her. Simply watching her. His expression indecipherable but fascinating. A restless excitement zipped through her veins.

"Checkmate," he said.

HE TOOK IT SLOW. Slower than she wanted. Hell, slower than *he* wanted.

Soft music drifted from the house. He teased her mouth with his as they danced, swaying ever so slowly in small circles on the stone patio. Every time she reached for a deeper kiss, he withdrew exactly at the point that would leave her wanting more. Each time she relaxed, he kissed her again, licking her lips with soft flicks of his tongue until she parted them—then not delving any deeper. This went on and on until she was trembling in his arms, ridden with pent-up desire but still unwilling to reveal her innermost thoughts.

That was when he said, "Tell me what you want."

She shook her head.

"Tell me," he coaxed.

"I did," she insisted.

He put his mouth near her ear. Lipped the lobe, making her shiver. "I need details."

Her shoulders hunched. "It's pretty basic. Insert tab A into slot B. You know the drill."

He tightened his arm around her waist to keep her dancing. "Uh-uh...nope. That's not what you want."

With a sound of frustration, she tilted her head back

and scrutinized him through narrowed eyelids. "Since you're so smart, why don't you tell me?"

"I think you want it all." *But don't know it yet.*

"You're so wrong. *All* is exactly what I don't want. Unless you mean—" she nodded toward the house "—in the bedroom."

"Okay," he said, giving up on true insight for the moment, "tell me about your fantasies. What's your idea of a hot sexual affair?"

She dropped her gaze. "I already told you. I'm a...gameswoman."

"And what's your favorite game?"

Her body brushed against his. He could feel the tight beads of her nipples through her dress and it was making him wild. If she didn't talk soon, he was going to turn into a ravening beast and take her without an iota of skill. Just pure, raw, animal sex.

"I like slow teasing," she said with a fleeting smile. "You're good at that." A pause. "And I like it fast and hard and furious." She shrugged. "With the right person, I like it all."

He considered her words, suspecting she was still holding back. "But what's your *favorite* game?"

She stepped out of his arms. "That would be my own grown-up version of tag, Daniel. Winner take all." She edged farther away, angling toward the open doors before she turned and quickly tapped him on the arm. "You're it," she said, and took off into the house, shutting off lights as she ran.

He rubbed his hands in preparation, allowing her a lengthy head start.

Winner take all? Suited him.

He'd never been bested yet.

5

Three weeks later

THEY'D COME FULL circle.

She was in the woods near her house. The autumn leaves shimmered around her, glorious colors, yellow and red and golden brown. It was quiet, but she was not alone. There was a man. A dark, hungry man. He was stalking her. She must flee. Yet even as she ran until her heart was bursting, deep inside she knew...she knew...

She wanted to be captured.

Captured, Lara thought, shuddering with fear and excitement. And this time it wasn't a fantasy.

Daniel didn't need to speak—he held her mesmerized with only the force of his eyes. After a long moment, she shook herself, letting out a small whimper as she began to inch backward on the tree branch.

Even though she was far out of reach, he made a sudden lunge. She shrieked, losing her balance and falling forward. Only lightning reflexes prevented her from pitching off the branch entirely and crashing straight into her pursuer's waiting arms. Knuckles whitening, she handcuffed the branch, straddling it with her legs dangling among the leaves of autumn gold.

"Daniel Savage! You—you sneak," she accused. His handsome face laughed up at her. "You snake, you toad, you *mole.*"

"Cunning as a fox, darling. Stealthy as a wolf. Need I point out which of us is treed?"

Lara broke off a twig and threw it at his smug smile. At his continued low laughter, she twitched her skirts to rearrange them, trying to retain some modesty despite the awkward position. "I may be treed, but you still haven't captured me."

"Not yet," he said with a growl, dark eyebrows arching at her carelessly tossed dare. She was in no position to effect an escape.

She was his.

He told her so as he began to climb. "I hunted you." Easily he pulled himself up from one branch to another. "I chased you." Until he was on a level with her. "I treed you." He had only to step around the trunk to grab her. His face loomed among the leaves, a taunting smile appearing with a slow, sensual ease. "And now you're mine. Remember, it's winner take all."

Lara's pulse had kicked up yet another notch. She stared at Daniel, wide-eyed, motionless and seemingly compliant. His body swung around the trunk. He crouched beside her and reached out—

At the last possible instant she swiveled around, flipping off the branch like a gymnast. He caught her hand just as she released her grip to find another from a lower perch. Her fingers slithered out of his. He scrambled to recapture them, but she was gone, dropping through the golden leaves to another limb. For a second she hung by her arms, gathering courage, then released her grip and plunged the final ten feet, landing in a crouch on the soft, thick pad of dry leaves and loam.

"Never underestimate a Gladstone," she taunted Daniel, her upturned face seeking his. His eyes narrowed. She blew him a kiss. Then she was off.

Lara whooped with excitement as she ran, her long strides devouring the dirt path sprinkled with rusty pine needles, sailing over the minor obstructions of gnarled roots and protruding stones. Daniel, her hunter, her savage hunter, was not far behind, his footsteps thuddingly, thrillingly closing the gap between them.

She emerged from the cool green tunneled path into a sunshine world of long grass and warm earth. The scarlet and orange fringe of a border of tall sugar maples blazed vividly against the turquoise sky. At the far edge of the meadow's wide swath of pale gold grass was the clutch of evergreens that cloistered her small house. The peak of the steeply angled roof jutted among the treetops; a wisp of white smoke wafted from the fieldstone chimney. She sped toward the haven it promised.

Out of the corner of her eye she saw Daniel leave the forest. She pushed harder, lungs bursting as she cut through the long grass like a scythe, fast but not as fast as her pursuer.

Soon he was on her heels. The instant of knowing he was about to catch her was almost worse—or perhaps even better—than the reality. She screamed with pure exhilaration.

They went down together in a tangle of limbs and clothing and torn grass, gasping as their bodies jarred against the ground. She rolled free, but he grabbed at her skirt, then her leg, holding on even when she kicked. She twined around him, supple as a sapling, and wound up astride his supine body. The wind blew her hair across her face, but her gleeful shout of triumph was unmuffled. She straddled him, taming his bucking body between her squeezing thighs.

Panting raggedly, they ceased the struggle. Lara sat tall and brushed her hair back, gloating over Daniel's position beneath her. Unperturbed, he tilted his square chin up, watching her beneath half-lowered eyelids as his hands slowly crept up the supple fawn-colored leather, lacings and fringe of her moccasin boots. Her pioneer getup, he'd called it, teasing her for plotting the chase.

He'd reached her knees. She blinked in consternation.

"Yes, my darling, you're right to wonder." He was amused. "Who has captured whom?"

She might have bolted then, but his hands had disappeared beneath her skirt and closed on her bare thighs with a grip of iron. Inescapable.

Without warning he reached up, catching the waistband of her cotton panties and yanking them down so violently they ripped away from her hips. The sharp tearing sound and the sudden knowledge of her naked vulnerability shocked Lara, then thrilled her. She melted inside.

Daniel knew. "I told you," he murmured, his voice smoke and steel. "You're mine." He jackknifed up to a sitting position and buried his face against her throat and neck, moist with perspiration. His tongue darted out and licked across her collarbone like the first, flickering flame of an incipient conflagration.

Desire kindled. Lara pressed her body into his, upper arms resting on his shoulders as she cradled his head in her hands. He was kissing her neck, her throat, making deep, soft, animalistic moans. Her pulse skittered unevenly.

Lust coursed between them, rapid as a river. Dashing through the woods, she had known what would happen when she was captured. That knowledge and the wild flight itself had honed her desire to an arrow point so sharp it easily pierced the veneer of her remaining reserve. They had been seeing each other for not quite a month now, always on weekends—a month of teasing, seductive advance and retreat before each cataclysmic joining. They'd played with each other's minds, building their attraction to a fever pitch before there was no option but to put out the flames.

Today, what had started as a walk in the woods had become a chase, a challenge to “catch me if you can.” As Daniel knew, this was her favorite kind of game. They'd even played it out their first time together, when he'd caught her in his darkened bedroom and tossed her onto the bed and had his way with her.

Into the flame once more, Lara thought. Daniel's hands were at her waist, the fabric of her skirt bunched under his palms so her bottom was exposed. The sun was warm on her bare skin. There was a rich, erotic pleasure to be had in such total abandon. She was helpless to resist its spell. Verbally she and Daniel had played at the game of captor and quarry all week. Beneath the laughter and the taunts was a passion that could not be ruled.

Nor contained. Daniel made that clear when his hand slid swiftly up between her thighs. Without ceremony he dipped two fingers inside her. The move was bold but not unwelcome. She was already wet with anticipation, ready for their joining—as he'd known she would be.

The muscles in her thighs tensed in response to the intimate caress, lifting her up onto her knees. She cried out, the words incoherent, their meaning not. His fingers slid deeper, the heel of his palm pressing hard against the very pinpoint of her desire.

She sucked air through her flared nostrils, throat working frantically as uncontrolled gasps escaped her open mouth. “Oh,” she panted. “Oh, please. Daniel. Please don't stop.”

Her hips rocked with an instinctive rhythm as pleasure lulled her in its seductive embrace. With a swish of long hair, her head lolled forward and she drew her sultry gaze across his face like the sweep of a veil.

All her tension had transferred to Daniel. His face was drawn, an obvious raw, animal hunger laying bare his usual socially subdued handsomeness so she saw the unvarnished truth of the real man: fierce, honest, powerful, sexual, savage. His eyes glowed like coals, burning with an intense inner heat. His stare was scorching.

Her whisper sounded like a sigh. "Savage..."

He took her mouth with his lips and tongue as his fingers had taken possession of her body. Without hesitation—with total command. Her spine arched, bowing backward under the pressing assault. She felt suspended, afloat, bathed in the intense, humming pleasure, anchored only by the burning connection of her lover's hand between her legs and his mouth on hers. He kissed her deeply until she had completely surrendered her will to his.

He laid her down in the long grass. She closed her eyes for a moment; glaring spots of light, afterimages of the early October sun, burned on her inner lids. The dry grass, cool spongy moss and warm earth cradled her as she preened under Daniel's gaze, peeking up at him through slitted eyes.

His dark brown hair was tousled and wild. Tiny twigs and bits of dried leaves were sprinkled in it and across his shoulders. The sleeves of his chambray shirt were rolled up over sinewy forearms. Tanned and roughened with curling hairs, they rested on his thighs, framing the blatant bulge of the erection trapped behind his straining fly.

Nervously she wet her lips, thinking of reaching forward to unzip him so that he spilled heavily into her waiting hands. She pressed her thighs together, trapping the folds of her skirt and old-fashioned petticoat between them as she squirmed in the grass, inching backward.

Above them a raven glided soundlessly through the vivid sky. Daniel sat back and watched as she propped herself up on her elbows. Two tiny creases appeared between his knitted eyebrows when she slowly, provocatively traced one forefinger over the scoop neckline of her dress, dipping down into the swell of her cleavage. She hooked her thumbs in the patterned red cotton and pulled down, revealing more and more flesh until her pebbled nipples sprang out and her breasts were cupped within the wide neckline, nakedly exposed. His lips parted, revealing a hint of gleaming white teeth.

Sharp popping sounds punctuated his heedless wrench at the snaps of his shirt. She measured the gap he'd made, studying the stripe of muscle-ridged torso. In response she began to pull her skirts up, the frilly edge of the petticoat grazing her bare thighs. He exhaled, a gust of air whistling between his lips. She tightened her thighs, the skirt bunched at her waist.

"Go on," he said.

She blinked and he repeated his order, softly, but unmistakably demanding. "Go on. Open your legs for me, Lara. Let me see my prize."

Obedient to his potent spell, she followed his bidding, parting her thighs as the knowledge of her own female power surged through her. He responded with a deep growl. She opened her legs another inch, filled to the brim with daring and desire. No room for modesty.

Watching him watch her, she was both amazed and aroused by the raunchiness of her actions. Perhaps a tad worried. She'd made herself open, vulnerable. Was the picture she presented to him erotic or debauched? Or both?

His eyes devoured her. Whatever he thought, he wanted her more now than ever before. Relieved, she let out a sigh and lay back, turning her face up to the sky.

"Still no piercing," he said, touching her with a light, questioning fingertip.

She caught her breath. "I—I prefer to go natural."

"I like it."

She peered at him through lashes struck gold by the sun. "Savage," she whispered huskily. "Take me."

His gaze flicked over the wanton display of her body, lingering at the dewy thicket of honey-brown curls. He rubbed his glistening fingertips together. "You're ready."

She shivered, humming her assent.

His body blocked the sun as he moved on all fours to hover over her. "Look at me, Lara," he commanded, and she did.

His face was stark from holding back his deep need. She felt it rolling in waves off him, mingling with her own yearning hunger.

"You're my captive. Mine," he said, distinctly emphasizing each word. He'd learned her fantasy well. "To do with as I please."

She was impudent. "Then do it already."

He chuckled and lowered his head. "As I please." His lips touched hers. "When I please." Went lower. "Where I please." The tip of his tongue flicked one of her erect nipples.

She moaned in frustration, lifting her hips off the ground to brush against his rock-hard erection. He pressed one palm against her belly, forcing her down.

Before she could react, he was all over her, his hands and mouth at her breasts, fondling and squeezing and laving them, plucking one nipple with his fingers, sucking the other deep into his mouth, pressing teethmarks into her smooth, firm flesh. "Dammit, Daniel," she said, twisting under his skilled caresses. It was more than any woman could take and remain still. He couldn't expect her not to respond in kind! She hissed an oath and stretched out her arms, gouging her fingernails into the earth to clutch at its physical reality. If she couldn't touch him, she might lose her mind.

The sweet torture went on and on. She murmured his name, distracting him so she could reach down and stroke him, finally managing to unzip his fly. He cuffed her wrists against the ground, not allowing her to caress him even while his own fingertips and tongue slid over her bared skin, tweaking, nipping, stroking, driving her to the edge but not quite over it, teasing her until she was writhing, her body running with sweat.

Just when she thought relief would never come, his palm slipped between her thighs, opening them to his own. She dug her heels into the ground, tilted her pelvis, and said, "Please, now," unable to stop herself.

"Now," he agreed, his eyes darkening to slate as he took a small packet from his shirt pocket and quickly sheathed himself. He spread her legs even wider, nudging one of his knees beneath her bottom to tilt her up so that the first thrust brought him halfway and the second lodged him deeply within her. The sensation was riveting. She arched beneath him, her head twisting in the grass. Her lips opened. She would have gladly screamed her pleasure across the sky, but he took her mouth in a carnal kiss that smothered the sounds of her sudden, overwhelming climax to a whimper. She had to settle for clutching at him greedily, twining her legs through his as her muscles quivered and her entire body shook in release.

Tenderly he brushed his palms through her tousled hair,

kissing her face, murmuring sweetly, so sweetly. She closed her eyes, floating in bliss. Such a gentle man.

The complacence came too soon. His hips had suddenly swiveled, making a piercing contact that shot upward through her nervous system, so acute it was painful. She choked back her surprise and came shockingly to life, surging to meet him, her gritty, grass-stained palms clamped upon his shoulders. His thrusts became deeply penetrating. Bracing herself, her body opening like a flower in the heat, she accepted all of him, the sensation exquisite and brutal, glorious and rough and rapturous all at once.

Daniel's face above hers was cast in stark planes and chiseled bone, his eyes as deep and hot as a volcano. Pursuit of his own satisfaction consumed him, and Lara found it strangely exciting to be taken in such a way. She pushed her hips off the ground to meet his thrust, only to be slammed back down under its force. Fighting to catch her breath, she settled for hitching up her legs and wrapping them around his waist, lowering her hands to the taut, flexing muscles of his buttocks.

His frenzy, his male need, was mesmerizing. She couldn't look away, even when her second climax erupted with a furious intensity. He let himself go then, too, and they turned to lava together, burning, melting, flowing over and through and into each other with a heat that seared their souls. She hadn't expected to feel so much, so fast. Helplessly, she whimpered and clung as he ground against her, shuddering with the last pulses of his release. They heaved ragged sighs, racked by the fury of their coupling as they collapsed into each other's arms, bodies weak with utter satiation.

Minutes passed. Lara lay quiet, almost believing that she could feel the world spinning beneath her. Mounds of whipped-cream cumulus clouds moved through the sky. The raven glided by again, oblivious to the humans far below, posed among the crushed grass in a lover's tangle of twisted clothing, tumescent flesh and slowly deepening breaths.

She started to pull down her skirt, but he stopped her, sliding one hand along her hip, pushing the limp cotton back up to her waist. He stroked the slick, smooth skin on the inside of her thighs, then tugged at the damp curls between them.

"Yeow," she said, like a cat, and drew her leg up, throwing it across his hip. She snuggled against his chest, pushing her nose beneath the flap of his open shirt and inhaling the tang of his skin. She purred with pleasure, loving his smell. During the weeknights without him, she'd wear this shirt in bed to bring back the scent of sun and sex and Daniel.

He was tracing her hairline with tiny, licking kisses. Both his hands reached around and squeezed her derriere. "Just the way I always wanted you," he said with a laugh. "Bare assed and purring like a kitten."

She lifted her head to look him in the eye. "Don't gloat too much." She bared her teeth and lightly scraped her nails down his chest. "I still have claws."

"Big, bad she-cat," he teased.

"You know it, handsome."

She was surprised by how hard it was to keep her voice playful when her emotions were engaged. Maybe she'd been wrong to draw their game out for so long. What was supposed to be purely sexual had become…

Lara bit her lip. She could call it making love. But she didn't have to be *in* love.

Did she?

That wasn't what she'd promised Daniel. It certainly wasn't what she'd promised herself.

Disturbed by her turn of thought, even more alarmed by the sappy feelings drenching her cynical heart, clouding her brain, she pressed tighter against Daniel and reached between his legs to find his warm, softened penis. Cupping him intimately, she squeezed with slightly too much pressure just because he needed to be taught a lesson. Despite her surrender to lust, she wasn't anyone's pet.

Maybe the lesson was for both of them.

"Watch it," he said, but she saw that his eyes were unworried. He was relaxed and lazy, perfectly willing to allow her any liberty she cared to take.

"I could beat you in a race *now,*" she observed. He had one shoe on and one shoe off, with his jeans tangled around an ankle.

"You'd have to let go first."

She squeezed again, her fingernails lightly scoring the underside of his phallus. Was she imagining it or was he exceeding her grasp? She laughed to herself, noting that his eyes were no longer quite so sleepy. "Not so quick, Savage," she replied. "I do believe I've got the upper hand."

"So to speak," he growled.

"So to speak," she agreed, raising up on one elbow. She leaned down and kissed him soundly, her hair falling in a wavy curtain around their faces. She sucked softly on his lower lip, then tongued the shallow cleft in his chin. "Mine," she softly taunted, and peppered tiny kisses over his mouth, his jaw, his throat.

"I thought we'd settled that question to both our satisfaction. Literally."

She crouched over his outstretched body, her hair

sweeping across his bare chest as her mouth traveled lower. She outlined his navel with her lips and he groaned, the muscles in his midsection jumping as her tongue swirled around and around.

She sat up, tossing back her hair. "You had me," she reminded him airily. "*Took* me. Marked your territory like a savage."

His gaze drifted to where her bare breasts bulged over the neckline of her dress. Love bites mottled the pale skin around the dusky pink areolae. "I guess you could say that," he replied tightly, not quite able to draw a full breath.

His shaft had grown between her palms, was now swollen and rigid. She looked down, her lips curling, and began to stroke him, a bit roughly, almost…savagely. And when she had him panting, thrusting his hips off the ground, ready to burst, she stopped.

Daniel's eyes were screwed shut. "So do it," he said through gritted teeth, his voice hoarse and almost unrecognizable.

Lara was very aware of her heart, beating with an urgent demand against her chest. She no longer felt soft, weak and sentimental; she felt…in control. Her tongue flicked out to touch her salty upper lip. Fulfillment of their physical longings could be easily attained. If she chose to ignore how it might affect her traitorous feminine feelings.

"Lara," Daniel crooned. "C'mon, Lara…."

When she lowered her head and sucked the ripe velvet head of his penis deep into her mouth he said it again, writhing. *"Lara!"*

Relentlessly she drew on more of his rearing length. He reached down to cradle her against his groin, but she caught his hands, holding them away from her bobbing head, the reversal of power inciting her daring. Up till now, she hadn't fully understood the need to be the equal of his mastery.

Before very long, mindful of his impending climax, she raised up, smiling at his suitably glazed expression. Releasing his hands, she wiped her chin with the back of a wrist. He groaned in frustration. "Don't quit yet."

She shrugged, and drew a finger over the slickened length of him. "I haven't decided if I should let you come."

"I'll decide for you." He'd crossed his arms beneath his head, seeming to be casual and uninvolved…except that his voice sounded raw and his erection stood prominent between them, pulsing against her palm. "Lift your skirts." He thrust slightly upward, nudging at her thighs. "Take a ride."

The fink. That's what she'd *meant* to do, imagining the position would give her control. She wouldn't put it past him to have deliberately reversed her intentions!

Tilting her head thoughtfully, she tightened her grip in recompense. "I don't take direction well."

He panted. "You'd better do something quick or it will be too late."

All right. I'll tempt you into giving me what I want. She released him to crawl over him on all fours, letting the tips of her breasts tease his heaving chest. "Who are you to say? I'll do as I please with you, Savage." She peeked at his hardening expression through her lashes, then licked at his mouth, the tip of her tongue teasing his. "Just as slo-o-owly as I want."

Though there was no warning, she knew what was coming. His hands clamped on her waist and he tumbled her off him as easily as a doll, pressing her facedown in the crushed grass, holding her in place with his weight. When she'd ceased her token struggle, he lifted her hair away from her neck and opened and closed his mouth on her nape, biting her lightly. The alpha wolf.

"Too late for slow, you little tease." He reached between them, yanking feverishly at her skirts.

She wriggled as though trying to escape. He snaked an arm beneath her, using her own movements to raise her hips off the ground. Kneeling behind her, one hand pressed between her shoulder blades, he tossed her skirts up over her back to expose her lower half. A hot rush of intense, secret pleasure inflated her, making her bare bottom lift provocatively beneath his searing gaze. "Higher," he said, holding her shoulders down. Berating herself for accepting—no, *craving*—the erotic submission, she got her knees beneath her and arched her back, her heartbeat like thunder, her lips moving soundlessly against the scrape of the dry grass. *Please, please, please....*

Daniel gave a raspy chuckle as his hand slid over the curve of her haunch. "So you do take direction." He moved into position behind her, the flared head of his erection poised at her inflamed cleft. "Feel that?"

She could only moan. *Yes,* she felt it—intrinsically. She was beholden to it.

"You want it, don't you?"

Perversely she shook her head, her eyes closed tight as she rocked against him, trembling, waiting for him to plunge all the way. She wanted him to engulf her.

"Yes, you do." He pushed slightly inside her. "And to prove it, *you'll* have to do the rest." He stroked her upraised bottom. "While I watch. It's a very—" his voice broke "—arousing sight."

"I can imagine," she muttered.

"Should I describe it? Since you can't see?"

"Please don't." She twisted to peer over her shoulder.

He'd risen behind her like the satyr she'd always known he was, his hand possessive on her hip, the fingertips pressing into her soft skin.

"Don't say anything," she begged, knowing she couldn't withstand much more. He was right—it was too late to take her time. Already her muscles were painfully clenched from holding the intimate position. The urge to thrust backward and impale herself on him was incredibly powerful. She had to do it, even if that meant she was as susceptible and willing as the rest of the female sex....

"You look—"

"Arrgh." With a desperate growl, she rose onto her arms, thighs and buttocks flexing as she pushed back, her body taking over, brazenly eager to consume his thrusting erection.

He sighed, sinking into her. "Ahh. So tight. Will I fit?"

She answered with her body. The resulting slow, deep penetration was exquisite. Shamelessly she rocked her hips against him, arching higher, opening wider to accept every filling inch of him. They met and melded in a slippery, intimate embrace—hand in glove.

As nature intended, Lara thought through the wild, stabbing pleasure of moving together in the instinctively sexual flux and flow. Daniel's hands gripped her hips even tighter as he pounded into her, the pace becoming staccato as the pressure built. Her bones dissolved in the heat; her entire body shook and shivered, on the brink of prostration until she locked her elbows, determined to take all that he could give. She wasn't weak. She would not collapse.

But...the savagery of it. The piercing pleasure. *Oh my, oh my!*

He touched her pleasure point, stroked it, adding fuel to the flames. At the last instant, as she began to climax in wave after convulsive wave, he pulled out and turned her swiftly around so she sat in his lap, facing him as their mutual releases broke over them like the surf. She felt a vague resentment, but then was too lost in the aftermath of swirling sensation to grasp why.

She collapsed in his arms, so shaken by the power of their mating that her tongue fumbled. "What—why did you—um—do that?"

"Out of condoms."

Her head dropped against his shoulder. "Oh." *That's all?* Her world was still wavering out of focus and he was together enough to remember they'd already used the only condom? Knowing she should be grateful for his practicality, she couldn't help wondering how he stayed so unaffected. Was she the only one in danger of losing herself?

"Also..." He stroked his palms over her back in a very loving way.

She lifted her face, surprised.

He looked into it, unafraid. "I wanted us to end like this—face-to-face."

"I see." She blinked, becoming aware again of their location when the breeze whiffed through her hair. Even though the day was growing colder, the tight physical connection she'd made with Daniel here in the grass seemed to keep them close and warm and safe. But as the shock to her body lessened, she also began to notice other desires, other emotions, those that she'd used passion to suppress. Familiar, now. And only growing stronger. She shuddered. All part and parcel of the insidious weakness that made her want to curl up in his manly arms—happy, satisfied, completely trusting.

Daniel was watching her mutinous expressions. Probably reading her every thought. She lowered her lids, not ready to give him that, too. She would have no defenses left.

He held her close, kissed her, and said, so tenderly she ached, "You've surrendered your body, Lara. When will you let me into your heart?" Wordlessly she twined her arms around him and pressed her cheek against his warm neck, knowing he didn't expect an answer. Not yet.

6

LARA GLADSTONE CONSIDERED herself a fortunate woman.

Her twenties had been turbulent—a time of restlessness and searching. Around two years ago, Bianca had shocked those who knew her by announcing her impending motherhood, sending Lara, especially, into a tailspin that had brought about her own epiphany. If even Bianca, the diva of Avenue B, had given in to the urge to nest, what about herself? Early one morning, arriving at her cramped closet on West 24th after another late night, she had stopped to ask herself the eternal questions: *Where am I going?* And *What will I do when I get there?*

She'd showered the street grit off her skin and crawled into bed as the sun came up. By the time she'd drifted off to sleep beneath the wan sunlight that filtered through her smudged skylight, the grinding, clanking, shrill racket of the waking city echoing in her ears, she'd made a decision. Fame and fortune weren't necessary for her happiness; nor was the frenzy that surrounded them. What she truly wanted, despite her father's dire predictions of unavoidable failure, was to do good work in a calm environment. To be respected as an artist, not as a minor celebrity—a party girl with a famous last name.

Soon, recalling glorious summers in the Adirondacks, she'd given up city life for her country cottage. She'd given up men too. Mostly by default—there weren't many single men available locally, except those few who were beating the bushes for likely wives. It had been easy to turn down oily Pete who lived above his gas station and considered a wife a handy provider of clean socks and regular sex, Harold the weedy mycologist who wanted a woman to partner his expeditions into the swamps, and desperate Hank, the stocky hunting guide whose ex-wife had taken him up on his bluff to seek custody of their four children.

Perhaps she was an anachronism, but the single, solitary life suited Lara. She had her house, her friends and family—if at a distance—and her art. As of this weekend, she even had Daniel Savage.

All that she lacked was love and marriage.

No loss, she said to herself. Love was as ephemeral as a handful of water. How many times had she seen friends struggling to hold on to a love that trickled through their fingers no matter how they tried to save even the smallest drop?

No such fool was she. Better to open your fingers and reach for something more substantial, more attainable, more *real.*

Like a solid career, an inviolable home, regulated weekends with a beautifully proficient lover. That was plenty for any woman.

Lara watched Daniel from the corners of her eyes, smiling to herself. Yes indeed. She was a fortunate woman. A satisfied woman.

Extremely well satisfied.

Pleasurably aware of her sore muscles, she lolled on the couch, toying with the fragile stem of the wineglass Daniel had filled from one of the bottles he'd brought from Manhattan this morning. Since their first dinner together, when they'd struck the parameters of their relationship, their encounters had fallen into a pattern—she tantalized Daniel with words, he seduced her with food and wine and hot branding kisses that left her aching for more.

There seemed no reason they couldn't go on like this indefinitely. Aside from her one small moment of emotional weakness, which wouldn't happen again.

She'd learned to be disciplined, that way.

Lara savored the tang of the wine on her tongue as her eyes followed Daniel around the kitchen. He padded silently back and forth over the slate floor, making the final preparations for their dinner, wearing the new burgundy silk dressing gown she'd bought, for their weekends together—a good investment now that their compatibility was established. The contrast of refined silk and raw, potent masculinity was captivating.

She and Daniel had walked back to the house in the October gloaming, their arms wrapped around each other, so reluctant to let go they'd showered together, laughing and relaxed because their week-long sexual tension had been broken. Now Daniel's hair was almost dry, springing up in thick untamed curls at his forehead and nape. It had grown in the time since they'd met and she liked the look—less civilized than his previous no-nonsense Street clip.

She fluffed her own hair. Still damp. Finished with her wine, she set the goblet on the stone slab coffee table and stretched her bare legs across the cushions. She adjusted the front of her caramel-colored cashmere robe.

"Savage," she murmured, cutting her gaze toward Daniel as he made a clatter out of whisking something in a deep metal bowl.

His head came up. "What did you say?" he called across the open rooms. During renovations, she'd had a few walls knocked out of the old family cottage and the transformation was dramatic.

Her only answer was a ripe chuckle.

He sipped his own wine, coolly measuring her with a level stare that set the fine hairs on her forearms prickling. Finally he shook his head with fond indulgence. "You look like the cat that ate the canary."

"Mmm." She licked her lips. "Didn't taste like *canary.*"

"Wicked girl."

She chuckled again, letting the lower half of her robe fall open as she drew up her knee, arching her foot to bring definition to her calf muscles. "And you love it."

An odd look flitted across his features. "I love—" He stopped to concentrate on the salad dressing, adding a pinch of dill. "I love it, yes," he finally agreed.

A sense of something out of order tickled at Lara's languid satisfaction. She smoothed her palms across her forearms, stroking herself much as Daniel had when he'd massaged lotion into her grass-prickled skin after the shower. Was he having second thoughts about their arrangement? But he'd always seemed so...contained. She'd thought she'd finally found a man capable of conducting a civil, discriminating affair.

She looked toward the row of windows that framed a spectacular view of Coppercrown Lake. Although presently the sight was obscured by the purpling dusk, she could hear the lap of waves against the large, jagged rocks that lurked in the wedge of earthy blackness beneath the cantilevered deck. A loon's cry echoed across the water, eerie and lonely in the twilight.

Before Daniel, she'd been alone most nights like this. The isolation in itself hadn't bothered her. She'd relished it, in fact, having figured out that though noise and companionship were easy and fun, silence and solitude were better for her inner self.

Still...

"I'm glad you're here," she said to Daniel.

"Our first weekend at your house as lovers," he said.

"Yessss." She stretched. "As lovers." There was no reason for the word to bother her.

It had been her experience that men often scoffed at love as if it were a purely feminine hearts-and-flowers preoccupation and somehow beneath them, but then became rather distraught, and often downright angry, when they couldn't produce the emotion in her. So far Daniel had been perfectly willing to discard that side of things, in accordance with her one rule. She did hope he wasn't changing his mind.

Casually she said, "Just as long as we understand that calling ourselves lovers is..." She hesitated, searching. "Merely a convenient term."

He was watching her with the level, considering gaze she'd come to know well. After a full minute, he gave a sharp nod. If she had expected him to protest, she'd been wrong.

Suddenly Lara swung her legs off the sofa, her emotions doing a one-eighty. Damn, now she was disturbed by his easy acceptance of the situation! Since when was she so irrational?

She rubbed her arms. Okay. Sometimes feelings weren't consistent. She could admit it. Clearly, even though she was plainspoken about not seeking or needing love-with-a-capital-*L*, some part of her wanted Daniel to be so enchanted by her he couldn't help but offer it.

She frowned at the thought, even as she recognized its absurdity. But she truly didn't want it "all," as they said—she only wanted a lover. A discreet, undemanding lover who expected no more—or less—from her. That he be the flesh and blood embodiment of all her darkest fantasies was icing on the cake.

Perhaps what they needed was another label.

Lara rose from the plush sofa. Daniel stepped from the kitchen with a steaming casserole dish. They met at the big farmhouse dining table, set with an eclectic array of rustic stoneware and handblown glass.

"Are you my master?" she asked, slanting a mischievous glance at him from beneath a wing of sun-streaked hair. She flicked it aside with a turn of her wrist, taking the seat he held out for her.

He bent to place his lips against the curve of her exposed neck, nudging aside the deep hooded collar of her robe so it slipped down to bare her shoulder. His tongue slid along the slope of her shoulder until reaching her taut biceps, which he bit—none too lightly. She batted at him with the napkin she'd snapped out of its artful daffodil configuration. "No fooling, Daniel. I want an answer."

He moved to the other end of the table, his silky robe parting enough for her to see a slash of his furred chest. He sat and plucked the daffodil out of his goblet, looking at it with amusement, for Lara was an artist even with a scrap of cloth. "Am I your master? What brought this on?"

"Answer, please."

"You want to play another game?" he asked, eyebrows arching. "Master of the hunt? Master and maid?"

She shook her head. "As in master and mistress, Daniel." Putting her elbows on the table, she steepled her hands under her chin, waiting to see what he'd say.

"I see. You're not asking if I'm your master. You're asking if you're my mistress."

"I suppose. But not the kind who wears black leather and brandishes a whip." She grinned. "Alas."

He picked up a gilt-edged box of fireplace matches and began to light the candles in the center of the table. "You, Lara, are my lover. It's as simple—and as complicated—as that."

"Mmm...yes," she said, though her murmur was tinged with dissatisfaction. She reached toward the center of the table and lifted the cover off the dish of lamb stew. The mingled scents of the bouquet garni wafted on its steam. "But doesn't the word *lover* connote a certain feeling of—" Her gaze sought his. "Can we correctly be called lovers if we're not actually in love?"

"It's not like you to quibble over syntax, Lara." He blew out the match and a spiral of smoke rose above his head like a question mark. "Unless you're having qualms about our arrangement?"

"Not at all." She was coolly imperious, her defense whenever she felt unsteady in her position.

There was a subtle change in his expression. "Then why the worry over labels? Have you suddenly started to care about society's opinion on the proper progress of our relationship?"

Tossing the curly endive salad, Lara didn't answer at once. It wasn't society that worried her. It was the Gladstones. No wall of privacy could keep them out forever. Her aunt lived nearby; her mother was back in the country as of this week; her younger sister, also a New Yorker, was the nosy type, already asking questions about Lara's mystery man.

"It's not society who'll come knocking on the door," she said with a sigh. "It's my family. And I don't want them...mixing in. I want this—us—to be kept private."

"Then I'm to forever remain a secret?"

"Not a secret. Just separate."

"Why?"

"I've told you why. And you agreed."

"That was just to get into your pants."

She choked.

He laughed. "Don't you know that a guy will agree to anything if sex is the result?"

"But—but—you can't mean—"

"I'm kidding," he said, amused by her terror.

She patted her chest. "You're a businessman, Daniel. We struck a deal. I expect you to hold up your end of the bargain."

"You have complaints?" He cocked an eyebrow. "So soon?"

"I didn't say that."

"Because you seemed like a satisfied customer this afternoon. Thoroughly sated, in fact."

Lara took a long drink of water, her face going hot as she remembered how wantonly she'd offered herself to him on her hands and knees. "I have no complaints," she said, amazed by the prissy sound of her own voice when she'd proved she was anything but.

She waved at him. "You're distracting me."

His smile was wicked through and through. "You've been distracting me for weeks."

"We're off the subject."

"The subject was our deal." He got up to retrieve a second bottle of wine from the granite-topped island that separated the kitchen from the open living and dining areas. "Our pleasure deal," he added in a slightly mocking tone.

"We agreed not to let others be involved."

"I don't need a ménage," he said, squinting at the corkscrew. "One woman is more than enough when the one woman is as inventive as you. You nearly ran me ragged out there in the woods.''

She tried not to smile. ''I thought you were a serious man.''

The cork popped out of the bottle. ''I used to be.'' He trailed his fingertips across her bare shoulder as he refilled her glass. ''You bring out another side of me.'' His hand slid inside her robe. Lightning shot through her, stalling the breath in her lungs. He rolled her nipple between two of his fingers until it was tightly puckered.

She moaned at the back of her throat. A guttural sound. Was that her?

''Go—go back to your seat,'' she croaked, making herself push his hand away when she wanted to clasp it to her breast. ''We're having a conversation.''

He set the bottle down. ''All right. If you're sure.''

She wasn't, but she shooed him anyway.

''Tell me,'' he said, taking his seat, obviously amused by her reactions, ''how are your parents?''

She blinked. ''My parents? How did you know they—''

''I read the newspaper. They've arrived in the city for your father's retrospective. I believe you mentioned it, weeks ago.''

''Uh, yes.'' Idly she pressed the tines of her fork to her thumb. ''They're quite well, thank you.''

''You've seen them? When? Not last weekend. And you didn't let me know you were in the city any other time.''

''I—'' The tines bit deeper, turning her thumb bright pink. ''No. I haven't seen them yet. I suppose I'll have to.''

Daniel ladled out the stew. Silently.

Did he expect an introduction? Lara wanted to avoid that, if possible, although there was no avoiding her father's fame. Ever since *Time* magazine had put Ian Gladstone on their cover and labeled him America's Picasso, even those whose only exposure to art was reading the cartoon pages were familiar with her father's crusty *Old Man and the Sea* visage.

"You'll be needing an escort for the big show," Daniel said.

"No. That is, Kensington Webb has asked to be my date. He's eager to do it." *Too eager.*

"Then I *am* to remain in hiding."

She winced. "If you insist on calling it that."

"Lara Gladstone's clandestine lover," he mused. "Her dirty little secret. I suppose I can live with that."

Her dirty little secret. The way he said it was stirring. For a moment she closed her eyes, imagining Daniel coming to her in the night, right there at her parents' house, under her father's nose, the one man Ian Gladstone couldn't influence or intimidate…

No. Her gaze shot to Daniel's face. "You wouldn't want to meet him anyway."

"Him?"

"My father. He's a beast."

"What about your mother?"

Delphine Gladstone was a good woman, but one who'd chosen to subsume her own potential in support of her husband's. "You wouldn't want to meet her either." Lara shook her head. "She'd want to know when we're getting married."

His lips quirked. "When are we?"

She tossed her hair. "Ha!" Aimed her fork at him. "I'm catching on to your ways, Danny-boy."

They ate in silence for a few minutes, their eyes sending flashing signals across the table. Lara thought she'd nipped the subject in the bud, but when Daniel spoke again, his tone had changed. "What do you have against marriage, Lara?"

She studied her food while searching for a pithy answer and settled on "the cost," which came out less pithy than she'd intended.

"What does that mean?"

She tore apart a piece of sourdough bread. "You want the story of my parent's marriage?"

He shrugged. "They're still married. It can't be that bad."

"Ha," she said.

He knew what she meant. His parents were still married—co-dependent ever after. While he had no intention of using them for a model, that hadn't stopped him from believing that a good marriage was possible. Lara was being narrow-minded. But she'd learn.

"They met in Paris in the fifties, both of them starving expat artists," she said airily. "Matching garrets and berets and all that jazz. Terribly romantic, as my mother tells it. Within months, she'd given up her own art to devote herself to my father's. Buying his bread, mixing his paints, procuring his models, selling his drawings on the street. They both carried American passports, but she was half French—she had connections at the galleries. And my father used them. By the time they returned to the States, he had a valuable reputation and an international following—thanks to my mother."

"In part. I assume he also had his own talent."

"Oh, yes, he has that." She tilted her chin. "The talent's his ticket through life. My mother lives to make Ian Gladstone's ride run as smoothly as possible. No matter how little he respects her efforts, and how badly he treats her."

"Or his daughters?"

"Shelly's his pet. She knows how to play him." Lara's face darkened. "Whereas I checked out. Along about the time he told me I'd never be a great artist, and if I couldn't be great I was wasting my time. Same thing he told my mother, only she believed him."

And you didn't, Daniel thought. His heart swelled with pride. *Gutsy girl.* No wonder she had such a ferocity and bravado. "What does he think of you now?"

Her eyes sparked. Her chin went up another notch. "I told you. He thinks of me as a craftsperson."

"Has he seen your work?"

"That wouldn't matter. He'd seen my mother's work and still encouraged her to give it up."

"Maybe it wasn't..."

"Up to par? Maybe not. But that's not the point." Her burning gaze had switched from his face to a point beyond his shoulder. He turned in his chair and saw she was looking toward the fieldstone fireplace. At the painting leaning on the rough wooden mantel beside a large mirror.

Daniel drew the napkin out of his lap. "Your painting?" he asked as he approached it.

Lara came up behind him. "My mother's."

"Oh." It was a watercolor. A semiabstract street scene, colorful and lively, but tentative in execution and dated in style. Even he could tell that.

"You don't have to say anything. I know it's not—" she took a deep breath and threw out her hands in a sarcastic gesture "*—Great Art.*"

He touched her shoulder. She slid her hands into the pockets of her robe. "Then maybe your mother knew too."

"Maybe, but I've seen her face when my father is parading his act before a journalist or, worse, another of his bubbleheaded nude models. And I've seen how wistful she gets over her old paintings. There are regrets.'' Lara spun around, throwing her hair away from her face. ''I don't want regrets. And dinner's getting cold.''

She sashayed back to the table, sending him a narrow look. ''You're psychoanalyzing me.''

''It's your eyes. They withhold all your secrets. I want to know what's going on in there.''

''I'm a simple creature. I want food, shelter, comfort and—'' she flicked her tongue at him ''—really good sex.''

''With no strings.'' He went back to the table, wrapping and belting the damn slippery robe a little tighter. Lara watched him with a saucy little smile that made the corners of her eyes tilt upward. If she'd had whiskers, they'd have been twitching.

''Then we're understood,'' she said.

Hardly. Apparently she had no inkling of the feelings he'd developed for her. He had no doubt that if she knew, she'd be running fast in the opposite direction. Although he'd caught her this afternoon, it seemed that catching her emotionally was more of a challenge.

Elusive Lara, he thought, looking across the table at her, admiring her reckless beauty. Was her elusiveness the quality that most intrigued him? Or had he fallen for the entire, complicated package?

One day soon he would have her—really have her, body and soul.

Have her, hold her, love her. *And never let her go,* he vowed with a sudden, sure decision.

Even if that meant breaking all her ''rules.''

He remembered the slick satin heat of her kiss, the erotic invitation she'd whispered in his ear—*If you catch me, you can have me*—just before she took off running through the woods.

What she didn't seem to understand was how very much she wanted to be caught.

7

"You have to take hold gently..."

Daniel's eyes narrowed. "As if I didn't know that."

"...slide it in..."

"Mmm. How's that?"

"Good." Lara licked her damp upper lip. "Now you can rub. Carefully."

"In and out?"

"You're scrubbing too hard. You'll break it." Exasperated with his big clumsy man hands, she took away the narrow brush and fragile cracked-crystal bud vase.

He let his hands splash down into the hot sudsy water. "Can't you give me something easy to wash, like a plate?"

"We have to do the vases first." She swiped the back of her hand over her forehead and started working the slender bristle brush inside the vase. "If I don't get every speck, bacteria will—"

Daniel kissed her cheek, moistened from steam, his nose nuzzling her ear. He nipped her lobe, sliding the tip of his tongue along the inner pink curves of cartilage. The fine tendrils that had escaped her upswept hair tickled his nostrils; he snorted a blast of warm air into her ear.

Lara laughed and squirmed. "Let go of me."

His hands inched around her waist, dampening the wrap belt of her cashmere robe. "I have to take hold gently..."

Moving to stand behind her, he reached around to ease open the knot.

"Why don't you start loading the dishwasher?"

He parted her robe with the flat of his hand. "Slide it in..." The tip of his thumb slipped into the indent of her navel. "Rub gently..."

She said, "Really, now, stop that," but her hips moved instinctively.

He splayed his fingers against the soft curve of her belly, spanning it from hipbone to hipbone as his palm moved slowly downward. "If you let me, I promise not to break it."

She stiffened. "Oh, lord no."

"Not quite the reaction I'd hoped for, but we can work on—"

"No, Daniel. Look." Lara pointed a sudsy, rubber-gloved finger out the window at Coppercrown Lake. In the dark, a large, wooden canoe was making its ponderous way toward Lara's dock, the prow slicing silvered vees into the green-black water. "That's Teal."

"What's teal?"

"Teal Gladstone, my father's sister. She lives on the other side of the lake. And even worse, it looks like she's got a full fare." Lara tossed the brush into the dishpan. "I can't believe she'd do this to me."

"Teal?"

"Shelly. My sister. That's her in Teal's canoe, or I miss my guess. Along with her two little boys. They're hellions—she can't control them."

"Company? This breaks the rules," Daniel said measuredly, knowing Lara wasn't going to like it. He'd already figured that by keeping him separate, she was keeping him a fantasy.

"How could she?" Lara stripped off the yellow rubber

gloves with an irritated snap. "She knows I wanted this weekend to be private."

"Shelly?"

"Aunt Teal. And Shelly, for that matter."

"Maybe we'd better..." Daniel gestured at her half-open robe, and the nakedness it revealed. Lara let out a shriek and flew toward the open wood and wrought-iron stairway. He followed more leisurely, enjoying the view.

They were out at the dock within minutes, haphazardly dressed, but in time to greet the unexpected guests as their canoe slipped against the pilings with a thump. "Hold her steady," Teal Gladstone said. When Lara reached for the rope to secure the canoe to a cleat, her aunt tugged at the fraying brim of a shapeless straw hat, pulling it lower over downcast eyes. "Sorry, kiddo. I'm not staying." With her chin, she indicated her passengers. "But they are."

Lara muttered through her teeth. "How can you do this to me?"

Weather-beaten and sixtyish, Teal Gladstone wasn't the type to make apologies, Daniel figured. Sure enough, she shrugged her plaid-flannel-clad shoulders. "Not my call." Her unsparing gaze traveled over Daniel in his incongruous button-down shirt, rumpled chinos and sockless, untied chukka boots. She zeroed in on his eyes and seemed satisfied when he held the stare. "This your man?" She grunted. "He'll do."

Lara rocked back on her heels. "Teal Gladstone, Daniel Savage."

Although Daniel was helping the two boys scramble out of the canoe—they managed to exit with only the toe of one sneaker and the bill of a baseball cap dipping into the water—he nodded and extended a hand to Teal. "Nice to meet you."

She shook like a man. Bright green eyes, set in a face

that was as creased as old brown leather, assessed him at a second glance. She muttered a short hello.

The two boys had wrapped themselves around Lara's waist and legs, jittering and jostling and chattering all at once. Daniel turned to the very self-possessed young lady seated in the middle of the canoe, bandbox perfect with her fingers laced around the handle of the designer purse set upright in her lap. "And you're Shelly Gladstone?" He offered his hand.

She giggled. "Oh, my." Dimpling, she tucked the purse into the crook of her elbow and let him help her out, her sandy blond ponytail swinging to and fro when the canoe lurched in the water. "Ooh," she squeaked, clutching at Daniel's forearms as she stepped onto the dock. Smiling prettily, she released him and smoothed her pale yellow linen trousers. "It's actually Mrs. Michael Robinson," she explained, leaning closer to add in a whisper, "but I'm getting a divorce."

"Oh. I see."

"These are my boys, Michael Junior and little Toddie." Shelly Robinson pointed discreetly into the canoe, flashing another dimpled smile. "And there's our luggage."

Obligingly Daniel lifted out the heavy cases, making a neat stack of them on the dock until the boys barreled into the pile, knocking the pieces across the gray planks willy-nilly. A round hatbox rolled into the lake. Teal fished it out, the leather handle looped around the blade of her oar.

"Mikey! Toddie!" Shelly squawked, ineffectually tugging at the sleeves of the sweater tied over her shoulders. "Please, boys! Don't you want to behave yourselves?"

"Give me a hand, men," Daniel said before the boys could supply the inevitable answer to their mother's question.

Lara chimed in. "Why don't you two take the hatbox and this satchel and carry them up to the house?"

"It's kinda dark here," the younger, towheaded one said, looking at the dense, impenetrable forest that loomed around the house.

"Fraidy-cat—betcha I beat you!" The older boy, all of eight, freckle-faced and rambunctious despite a formal school uniform of navy blazer and tan slacks, grabbed the dripping hatbox and raced his brother up to the lamplit deck. Their thudding footsteps and excited whoops echoed across the water.

"Careful, Toddie, honey," their mother called. "Wait for me."

Lara put out her hand. "Shell? What's going on?"

"My life is such a mess!" Shelly stamped one foot on the wooden dock. "Why couldn't Dad have stayed in Italy?"

"Oh, boy. Tell me what happened."

Already absorbed in their conversation, the two sisters waved at their taciturn aunt and began to walk toward the house. Teal thrust her oar against the dock, propelling the unwieldy boat into the lake. Daniel watched until she and the ancient dowager of a canoe merged with the darkness, her paddle dipping almost silently into the silken water. Then he gathered up the rest of the cases and followed the women to the house. This was going to be interesting.

"You know how Dad is," Shelly was complaining. "He said my boys—my sweet babies—were too noisy and rude. He said his creativity was stifled with them in the house, even though there's scads of space. He was working himself into one of his awful tyrannical moods and I would never subject my boys to *that*, so, well, what else could I do? We had to move out."

"But all the way to the Adirondacks?"

Shelly flapped a hand at the large moth fluttering around her head. ''I don't see why not. We had nowhere else to go. Anyway, the boys love it here, and—''

Lara interrupted. ''What about school?''

Shelly's ponytail flounced. ''Michael says he can't pay the tuition *and* my temporary support payments. What a bunch of hooey. The school insisted I come and get Mikey until his tuition is caught up, which was so humiliating, but does my selfish husband care? Of course not! What could I do but come here, to my family? I wasn't going to put my precious babies into *public* schools, not in New York City.''

Suddenly she stopped and glanced back at Daniel. ''Oh, gosh, sorry. You don't want to hear about my terrible problems. Even when they've caused me to disturb your...'' She tilted her head, eyes widening as they absorbed Lara and Daniel's disheveled appearances. With pursed lips, she glanced at her sons, dangling over the deck railing in the dark. ''Your little, um, *weekend*.''

Shelly smiled, showing small, even white teeth. ''I did try, Lara. I went to Aunt Teal's cabin first, but, well, you know how it is there.''

''Aunt Teal has an outhouse!'' Michael Junior shouted. ''It was whack!''

''The boys started dropping things into the—down the, um, opening, and so, what with pumping our own water and no telephone and only a cranky generator for electricity...'' Shelly paused expectantly, peeping at her sister through her lowered lashes.

Lara shook her head, but fondly. ''How long did you last?''

Shelly giggled. ''Nearly an hour.''

''You're welcome to stay here with me. For a while.''

Lara sounded dutiful until she smiled at the boys. "For as long as the two little monsters behave."

"Then we won't be here but five minutes!" Shelly laughed gaily and trotted up the stairway to the large, triangular deck. She held out her arms to gather in the boys. "Come along, my darlings, let's go inside where it's warm. Doesn't the old cottage look grand since Aunt Lara renovated it?"

"Does it have DSL?"

"And Crispy Coco-Crunch?"

Shelly simpered. "I'm sure we'll make do. In the Adirondacks, one must be prepared to rough it."

Daniel put down the suitcases and slid his fingers through Lara's. "This ought to be fun," he whispered.

She bared her gritted teeth. "You say that now..."

"Hey! Look, Todd, Aunt Lara's holding hands!" Michael Junior flung himself at the railing and pretended to wretch over the side. *"Eee-yick."*

"DO I HAVE TO GET into this?" Grimly Lara sliced through a banana. The boys had insisted on a bedtime snack; after fifteen minutes of spineless negotiations, Shelly had gotten them to agree to peanut butter and banana sandwiches, cookies and juice.

Daniel laid slices of seven-grain bread on the plates and picked up a butter knife. "Not if you don't want to." He dipped into the peanut butter jar. "Keep me in the dark, feed me a load of garbage, I don't care."

She had to laugh. "Okay, so I'm being as inflexible as my father. I just don't want to mess up what we have."

"What do we have? Except a situation—a relationship—that seems darn selfish and secretive if it inhibits you from opening your home to your own family."

Lara's heart gave a jolt. She swallowed. "Is that how

you feel,'' she said flatly. Her voice was low and tense. ''Is that what you think of me?''

''No.'' Daniel sighed. ''Not really, but...maybe a little.'' He put his arms around her waist and squeezed—a conciliatory gesture. ''Baby, the truth is that I can't thrive as your dirty little secret mushroom.''

Grimacing despite his teasing, she raised her gaze to the ceiling, where the boy's footsteps pounded back and forth, sounding like a herd of buffalo. When her first instinct was to cringe at the thought of them getting into her neatly organized closets, or the studio with its potentially dangerous glass supplies, she realized that Daniel was right. Despite her previous declaration of self-satisfaction, she wasn't altogether pleased with herself. She'd become too closed off. Not only as it concerned her affair with Daniel, but with regard to her life in general. Better to be open and generous and giving rather than physically indulgent but emotionally stingy—like her father. Why hadn't she noticed she was heading in that direction?

Deciding that there was no harm in being slightly more forthcoming, she launched into an explanation. ''After Shelly recently separated from her husband, she took up residence in our parent's Manhattan brownstone while they were out of the country. They usually stay at their house in Umbria for six months, till the end of November, but they came back early this year so my father could prepare for the museum retrospective. I guess you heard the rest.''

''And it's very kind of you to let Shelly and the kids stay here. Even though it interferes with our weekend.''

She shrugged and started laying slices of the banana over the thickly spread peanut butter. ''My nephews are troublemakers, but lots of fun. They were here for two weeks this past summer and we went on loads of adventures."

Daniel asked casually, "Should we cancel our plans for next weekend?" For the time being, they'd decided to alternate weekends between the city and the country.

Regardless of her recent revelation, Lara wasn't going to obligate herself to hostessing chores when she had better things—better men—to do. "No need. I'll still be coming into the city. Looks like I'll have to work out some sort of compromise between Shelly and our father, anyway, unless I'm willing to put up with the Swiss Family Robinson indefinitely."

"Then you're the family peacemaker."

"Not really. Oh, perhaps. Shelly's his pet, so usually she turns on the charm to get her way. If that doesn't work, it's dramatics and whining. I've learned how to deal with dear old dad in a less emotional and manipulative way." By turning off her feelings. Lara had once thought that was a good thing. But now she wondered. Since Daniel, lack of feeling no longer seemed to be an admirable character trait.

He sliced the sandwiches into halves. "I would imagine that eventually Shelly will find her own place."

"Yes, you might imagine," Lara said dryly, but she didn't want to get into *that* can of worms, so she grabbed the plates and told Daniel to bring the cookies and juice, chop-chop.

"IT'S NOT PROPER in front of my boys." Shelly's voice was shrill, insuring that her sons would feel the same way because they were likely listening behind the closed bedroom door. "Honestly, Lara. How could you suggest that I allow..." Emphatically she shook her head. "No, it's not proper."

Daniel touched the sleeve of Lara's robe. "Look, don't worry about it. I can sleep on the couch."

Lara crossed her arms, being stubborn. "This is my house, Shelly. I make the rules."

"Why don't we go downstairs?" he suggested, trying to move the sisters along the hallway, out of listening range of the Robinson boys' bunk room.

Shelly pivoted, her blond ponytail swinging like a metronome as she jounced down the steps. "Well, I'm the one who's in charge of my sons' moral development! I don't want them asking questions about why a strange man is sleeping in their beloved auntie's bed."

"Okay," Lara suddenly conceded. "You're right. Daniel and I won't reveal our illicit relationship."

Instantly the sparkle returned to Shelly's smile. She winked at Daniel. "It's only for one night. I'm sure you understand my position."

"Actually, I do." He inclined his head in a bow, but from the light in Lara's eyes, she'd seen the mischief in his expression. "I'll comport myself as a true gentleman."

"You won't have to sleep on the couch," Shelly said. "The boys would be thrilled to have you share one of the bunk beds. As long as you don't mind the bottom—Mikey and Toddie have claimed both of the tops."

"On occasion I even prefer the bottom position," Daniel said, too gravely for Shelly to be sure of his meaning.

Lara arched her brows, trying not to laugh. "Not so great a view, though."

His glance skimmed her torso. "But I get a good angle of whoever's on top."

Shelly snickered. "It sounds like you mean…"

Lara blinked, all innocence. "What?"

"Never mind." Rolling her eyes, Shelly whispered to

her sister, "You know, it wouldn't hurt to play hard-to-get now and then."

Daniel was meant to overhear. "Camille doesn't play games," he said deliberately. "At least...not *that* kind."

Lara shot him the evil eye and tipped her nose up into the air. He laughed to himself. There was nothing to be said in her defense and she knew it. Mentally he rubbed his hands with dastardly glee. This *was* fun.

"Camille? You're not still identifying with *her,* are you, Lara?" Shelly rolled her eyes again, then shrugged and turned toward the curved staircase. "On that weird note, I think I'll go up to bed." Cheerily certain of her pampered position in the household, she'd ensconced herself in the best guest room like a diamond ring nestled in a velvet box. At the landing, she paused to peer over the wrought iron railing at Daniel. "Let me just pop into the boys' room to tell them to expect a bunkmate," she simpered, and he began to suspect she wasn't as vacant as she appeared. Hell, it was apparent that she knew *exactly* what she was doing. "You'll want to turn in soon so you don't disturb their sleep," she added. Having trumped all possibility of nocturnal shenanigans, she waggled her fingers at their upturned faces. "Good night, all!"

"Sweet dreams," Daniel said under his breath. He looked at Lara. "Now that your sister has made certain I'll have a very long and frustrating night, she's certain to sleep like a baby."

"You poor thing. Cut off for all of twelve hours."

"Does that mean we get to have a quickie sometime tomorrow before I drive back to the city?" He touched his fingertips to her smooth abdomen, one thumb sliding under the edge of her cropped T-shirt. The other hand slid around to the small of her back to draw her closer. The sunshine-and-soap scent of her skin was exhilarating.

Breathing it, he could understand what might prompt a man to cash in his portfolio and take up the country life. Aside from the thrill of natural sex in the great outdoors.

Lara was demurring. "I don't see how..."

"Try. Otherwise I'm cut off for all of one hundred and forty-seven hours—"

"Approximately," she inserted, laughing at his facility with numbers. Beneath his palm, her skin was prickling with arousal.

"Possibly longer, if I don't get to see you next weekend. You might be too busy with your parents." He dragged the T-shirt up over her rib cage, his fingers moving unerringly to her breasts. In their haste to dress she'd skipped her bra, and he wasn't a man to let that detail go unappreciated. "Now that we've done it, I can't imagine going too long without having you again, and again, and again," he whispered, feeling himself swell with anticipation. His need for Lara was a force too powerful to deny. Having her once, no, twice—well, three times, counting the shower—wasn't nearly enough. He ran his thumb back and forth over her budded nipple. "Can you?"

She sagged bonelessly against him. "We have no choice."

"Yoohoo! Don't get sidetracked, Daniel—the boys are expecting you." Shelly's trilled warning drifted down to them from the balcony. "Good ni-ight!"

Lara dropped her forehead against his shoulder and moaned. "It's bad of you to tempt me this way. I hate you, I hate you." She panted. "Why don't you sneak up to my bedroom?"

"But that would be improper."

"Sinfully improper." She raked her teeth over the

cords in his neck and pressed a wet kiss below his ear. "Which is why we'll keep it to ourselves."

He squeezed her breast. For such a long, lean woman she was very squeezable, so he did it again. Hot, liquid need sluiced between them, submersing any thoughts of setting a good example for her nephews.

"Wicked, wicked girl," he said, licking at her mouth until it opened. She twined her arms around him and they shuffled toward the stairs, pressed together in a hungry embrace.

Daniel lifted her onto the first step. Still kissing, he peered upward through one slitted eye. Hand-hewn treads spiraled into the open second level like the spine of a dinosaur's petrified skeleton. The original cottage had been a humble two stories, with the bedrooms tucked under the eaves. Lara had expanded the attic into an expansive studio, opening the front of the house to a steep ceiling with a network of riblike beams.

It took them several minutes to get up the stairs. But as soon as they reached the top and began creeping toward Lara's room, the bunkroom door shot open. "Where're you going, Uncle Daniel?" said Michael Junior.

Toddie stood behind his older brother, rubbing his eyes. "Yeah. Where you going?"

Daniel stopped dead. Lara pulled away, tugging at her shirt, soothing her puffy bottom lip with her tongue.

Daniel cleared his throat. He turned his face toward the boys. They smiled hopefully. "Uh, I was just saying good night to your Aunt Lara." He looked at her with regret, reluctant to let go of her hand. "Good night, Aunt Lara."

She stepped over and cradled his jaw in her palms, fingertips patting gently on his cheeks as she pursed her lips and smacked the air near his mouth. It was sheer torture, having her so close but not being able to grab her.

"Sleep tight." Off her upturned palm, she blew a second and third kiss to her nephews.

"Don't let the bedbugs bite," Toddie said, dopey with sleep.

Michael's eyes were bright with interest. At eight-and-a-half, he probably already knew more about sex than his mother would deem proper. Daniel remembered his own burgeoning curiosity at a young age. Damn. There was no chaperon more alert than a curious boy.

Daniel waited a couple beats for the blood to stop thundering in his veins and then he turned to usher the boys back to bed. "Isn't this a treat. I haven't slept in a bunk in years." They left Lara in the short hallway, her eyes going soft as she watched Daniel take Toddie's hand. When she saw him looking, she gave a startled smile and quickly dashed off to her own bedroom.

TWENTY MINUTES LATER, he was still staring at the underside of the top bunk in the dark, trying to distract himself by thinking of anything but Lara. Although he'd shared a metal bunk with a college roommate for two years, this particular bed was dredging up an old memory of his lone excursion to summer camp. At age ten, his good grades had won him a scholarship to a four-week course of a math and science camp in Maine.

Suddenly he was remembering the smell of dank towels, stinky sneakers and piney walls, the sound of giggles and rustling candy wrappers in the dark, the whine of mosquitoes hitting the screens, the snuffles of the homesick boy in the next bunk. Even at ten, Daniel had been too tough to admit to homesickness. Mostly because he hadn't had much of a home life to miss. He'd returned from camp on a bus, all excited to show his parents' his insect collection and handmade book of pressed leaves, but their lackadaisical "humph, yeah, that's real nice" reactions had been typically disheartening.

Camp Skowhegan. That was it. Daniel smiled wryly in the dark. With his usual single-mindedness, he'd dumped out the bugs and leaves and dismissed the camp from his thoughts. Surprising, then, that the memories were suddenly so vivid. Must be the similarities. Only in those days his feet hadn't hung over the edge of the bunk and he wasn't yet familiar with this damnable itch of wanting a woman tucked in close beside you....

With a soft groan, he rocked from side to side, trying to work himself into a comfortable position on the thin mattress that was clearly not meant for a grown man. He flung off the blanket and plucked at the waistband of his boxer shorts, tenting the fabric. Better. In his present circumstances, he couldn't abide even the slightest scrap of cotton on his flesh. There was only one touch he needed, and the woman who could provide it was out of reach for the duration. When he'd tried to sneak out at the fifteen-minute mark, Michael's voice had piped up in the darkness, "Can you get me a drink of water, Uncle Daniel?"

Blast. Forget ten—he was sixteen again. Good old sex-on-the-brain sixteen, raging with hormones, gnawingly hungry for what he'd only imagined. Lucky he hadn't known a girl like Lara when he was still a virgin sixteen. He'd have gone stark raving mad for her. Even a few years later, when he'd channeled his energy into making it through school, she'd have been a major distraction. He'd bet that she was nothing like the usual private-school princesses who'd seemed so frivolous to him at Harvard. Lara would have been tall and skinny and untamed, seething with an artistic temperament and a desire to succeed that matched his own. For him, success meant security. For her, it apparently meant independence.

Did that mean they couldn't come together? Not with any permanence?

Every muscle in Daniel's body clenched at the thought. He didn't see how he was ever going to make it to morning.

LARA SAT AT THE TOP of the stairs, her nightgown and her clasped hands pressed between her thighs. Her hair hung in her face as she rocked slightly front to back, crooning softly in her throat.

This was ridiculous. She should be forcing herself to snap out of it. No, she should have had better control than to succumb to such a bad case of heartsick longing in the first place. Why, it was only a matter of hours since she and Daniel had last made love!

If it was just sex, you wouldn't be needing it so bad.

"I need..." she whispered, staring across the space to the tall windows that framed the dark lake shimmering in the moonlight. "I need Daniel." *I just want to feel his arms around me. All night.*

Which was as much as she was willing to admit.

Scaredy-cat.

No. Opening herself to more than that was what would make her weak. Look at her mother, at Shelly. They relied on their husbands, not themselves, which put them at the mercy of their flimsy wedding vows. Flimsy to their partners, anyway. To women, the bonds of love and marriage were as good as shackles.

Lara nodded to herself, ignoring the messages her body was sending her. Because that was the trap. That was how they got you—turning you to mush, making you think about cozy homes and cuddly babies and how good it would be to have someone to rely on.

She was too savvy to be trapped. The relationship she'd

set up with Daniel was ideal. Being apart during the week made them appreciate each other all the more. They weren't stifled by each other's constant presence. The heart grew fonder, and all that. Too much togetherness would inure them to each other. And really, in the end wasn't it almost always the woman who wound up being taken for granted?

So they were fine as they were. The interruption by Shelly and her sons was temporary. After they went, Lara and Daniel could go on as they'd started.

No strings.

No bonds.

No shackles.

Lara touched her forehead to her knees, telling her body to behave itself. It would be a lot easier on her if all this longing and craving was only for sex rather than something infinitely more complicated. Better to be *taken,* than to be taken for granted.

Just the same, it was going to be a very long night.

8

"GEE, YOU'RE CRABBY this morning."

Lara scowled at a Cheerios circlet adhered to the side of a bowl. "I am not."

"Reminds me of Dad," Shelly said.

Lara set the bowl in the dishwasher rack and said nothing.

"The artistic temperament, I suppose," Shelly persisted. She licked at the jam spoon. "Being just a regular person, I have to blame my moods on PMS." She pointed the spoon out the window, where the three males were "fishing" off the dock with fishhooks, strings and sticks. "I wonder what's Daniel's excuse?"

"Maybe that he slept on a child-size bunk."

Shelly grinned. "*Did* he?"

"He did." Lara closed the dishwasher door. "All night long. And soon he has to leave."

"Aha." Her sister's tone was arch.

"Don't *aha* me, Shelly." Lara grabbed a sponge and started spraying the countertops with antibacterial cleaner. "You knew what you were doing."

Her sister giggled, maddeningly. "I had my boys' unsullied innocence to think of."

Lara wrung out the sponge. "Daniel's behavior was above reproach." She scowled again, mostly for show. "I hope you're happy."

Shelly answered with another giggle. "Jeesh, you're

crabby this—'' she started to repeat, when the sponge hit her in the face. She shrieked and snatched up the sink's spray attachment, squeezing off a good douse of water before she realized that Lara was halfway out the door.

''Darn it,'' she said, nearly slipping on the wet slate as she followed her older sister outside. Growing up, Lara had always been one step ahead; the only thing Shelly had done first was marriage and babies—at which, Lara, typically, expressed no envy or regret.

Out on the dock, the day was memorably lovely, a perfect slice of autumn with its crisp air and endless deep blue sky. The mirrored surface of the lake reflected the fading tapestry of the trees in a watercolor stillness marred only by the squabble of rust-colored mergansers flipping their tail feathers as they bobbed in and out among the rushes. The vestiges of Lara's fitful mood lifted, and even Shelly, the unabashed city girl, gazed at the beauty around them with appreciation.

Her sons were more interested in the occasional slender silvery minnow slipping through the clear green water around the pilings. ''This stupid stick's no good,'' Michael said, wrinkling his freckled nose as he tossed aside the make-do fishing pole. ''I need a Big Blue Troutmaster 2000. That's what my dad uses.''

''Yeah.'' Toddie discarded his pole, too. ''Let's go visit Aunt Teal and dig for worms in her compost. Betcha we catch a monster fish at her secret fishing hole.''

Although Lara might have begged off such a family outing, Daniel spoke first, almost eagerly. ''Good idea,'' he said, and to Lara in a whisper, ''Quick, get the canoe.''

She wasn't fast enough; Michael ran to the overturned canoe and helped flip it into the shallows. He clambered aboard. ''I want to ride with Uncle Daniel.''

''Me, too, me, too!'' Worried about being left behind

with the women, Toddie jumped into the canoe with a big splash. Michael sputtered a complaint as his brother hoisted himself headfirst over the side. Their mother scattered her fussings and scoldings like birdseed.

Daniel launched the canoe, then jumped aboard. "You two sisters'll have to take the rowboat." Dipping the oar into the lake, he shrugged regretfully at Lara. "Maybe we can switch passengers on the return trip."

Michael waved, pleased with the present arrangements. "My mom's scared of boats. You shoulda heard her squeal when I rocked Aunt Teal's canoe."

"Yeah, and when we splashed her she yelled. Like this." Toddie's shrill ululations carried over the water as the canoe coasted into deeper water.

"Maybe I'll stay here," Shelly said.

"Aw, come on, Shell. I'll row." Lara stepped down into the squat wooden skiff. "You weren't always such a Miss Priss. Remember how we used to race each other from Teal's cabin to the Adamses' cottage at Sunfish Inlet? Once or twice you nearly beat me."

Fussily Shelly settled herself on one of the rowboat's plank seats. "Only because there was a cute cousin staying with the Adams twins and I wanted to get to him first." Pouting, she watched her sister untie the boat. "But I never did."

Lara could no longer remember the name of the boy who'd ducked her in the middle of the lake and given her her first underwater kiss, but then she was concentrating more on catching up to Daniel. Pulling hard on the oars to make up for their late start, she glanced over her shoulder and called to the canoe's occupants, "Race you!"

"Race you! Race you!" echoed the Robinson boys' happy voices, already far ahead of the slow-moving rowboat.

Shelly glanced at the churning water and folded her arms with a sigh. Now she was maddeningly placid. "You'll never catch them."

Between huffs, Lara challenged, "Not without help."

Unconcerned, Shelly tapped her fingertips on her elbows, admiring the view across the lake. Finally her competitive sense got the better of her—as Lara knew it would—and she moved surefootedly to the center seat. "Shove over," she said briskly. "Give me that oar."

Within a few strokes the sisters were again a team, as in their youth when they'd conspired to beat the other summer residents in various water races. Until adolescence had turned Shelly boy-crazy, they'd been the Gladstone Girls against the world. And sometimes in cahoots against their father.

"Watch out, men," Lara warned. "We're gaining on you."

Daniel was not overexerting himself and Toddie was paddling only with his hands, but Michael took the challenge seriously from his position in the canoe's prow. His oar dug into the water with much enthusiasm but little skill. Even so, the canoe pulled steadily ahead. Michael gave a war call, lifting the oar over his head in triumph. "*Last of the Mohicans!*"

Lara laughed. A fleeting memory of Daniel chasing her through the woods shot an extra spurt of adrenaline into her own stroke. It was clear they were going to come in a very sorry second place in the half-mile race. Coppercrown Lake was narrow, but more than three miles long, with an irregular shoreline that twisted and dipped, offering privacy to the small number of cabins and cottages built around it. Lara and Teal Gladstone were the only year-round residents, so the lake had grown exceptionally quiet with the close of high season. Even the gabbling ducks spoke of the arrival of winter.

"Why the big secret about Daniel? What is it between you two?" Shelly asked abruptly, letting her oar flop while she used her fingers to comb her hair back from her face. The canoe of exultant males was already rounding the bend toward Teal's cabin. "Could you finally be involved in a serious relationship?"

Good question, Lara thought, knowing it was one she didn't necessarily want to answer, even to herself. After ten more strokes, though, Shelly was still waiting for an answer. The boat had swung around in a lazy arc.

Lara chose her words carefully. "We are involved."

"Said the cat to the cream." Now that they had no chance of catching the canoe, Shelly wielded the oar with less vigor. Her one-year-older sister's love life had become of far greater interest. "What I want to know is..."

Lara tensed.

"Are you in love with him?"

Lara gave one extremely hard stroke and dropped her oar. It bobbed in the oarlock as she undid the sleeves of the sweatshirt tied around her waist to swab the perspiration dampening her nape. "What do you mean?" she asked quietly, slumped with her elbows on her knees, dabbing at her hairline.

"What do I mean? Isn't it obvious, even to you?"

"Oh, well, love," Lara scoffed. Yet her voice caught in her throat.

Shelly's lips curved into a smug smile. "I knew one day you'd turn out to be as susceptible as the rest of us."

Lara straightened. "I didn't say I was in love." She blinked. "I am not in love!"

"Mmm-*hmm.*" Shelly was being pompous, in the especially irritating way that had always gotten under Lara's skin. Certainly that must be why she felt so itchy all of a sudden. And hot.

"Now you'll find out," her sister gloated.

Lara leaned over the side of the boat and splashed water on her face. "Find out what?"

Shelly took hold of both oars and stroked in a perfect, smooth rhythm. The small boat drew inexorably toward Teal's dock, where Daniel and the boys were waiting.

"Now you'll finally know why most women want to marry—are in fact *eager* to marry." Shelly was gleeful at the prospect of above-it-all Lara feeling humbled by an uncontrollable emotion. "I'm so glad I was on hand to see this day."

"You're way over-dramatizing," Lara muttered.

Daniel must have misinterpreted her expression as he helped her out of the rowboat. "Is this okay?" he asked, gesturing toward Teal's cabin.

She stared. In putty-colored chinos and a red henley with a broad white stripe that contrasted sharply with the tan of his skin and the dark mahogany color of his hair, he was vigorously handsome. Riveting, in fact. His eyes, curious and alert, were the color of a moonlit pond. She feared that she'd plunged beyond her depth. She, who prided herself on gliding through even the most dangerous waters without a care.

"I—I think so," she said, not really able to focus on the question of Daniel's involvement with her family. "Let's try to keep it light, shall we?"

He shrugged. "You're making the rules."

And he was breaking them, she realized, whether he meant to or not. It worried her, but she wondered. Did she want him to? Or not?

"Help me up, boys," Shelly was saying. Michael Junior and Toddie took her hands as she gingerly stepped from the unstable rowboat to the ancient, weathered dock. "Oops, careful with your old mom. I don't want to get wet."

"Nonsense," Lara said, linking arms with Shelly. "You're all of twenty-nine and as sprightly as a monkey. You had Mikey when you were just a baby yourself. You still look like a teenager." Lara knew this was what Shelly liked to hear, and it served well to divert her own confused emotions.

Shelly winked at Daniel. "I was a child bride. Only nineteen when I married."

"'Cause she wanted to get away from Grandpa Gladstone," Toddie said, comically sober, nodding wisely as a judge.

"Out from under his thumb," Michael added.

Shelly was flustered by their revealing statements. "But don't forget I was in love with your daddy, too. That's what's most important." She glanced at Lara. "That's why people get married."

Shelly's oldest son grabbed hold of her words. "Then why are you getting a divorce—"

"Divorce?" Toddie's voice wobbled.

"Um, Daddy and I are only separated, Toddie, honey." Shelly ruffled his white-blond hair, searching for a nonthreatening explanation. "It's sort of like we're on a vacation!"

Lara kept quiet even though she wanted to tell Shelly not to mislead the boys about the circumstances. While the truth could be harsh, it was always easier in the end. Then again, she couldn't see her sister toughing out an actual divorce and the usual subsequent downturn in lifestyle. And, knowing Shelly, it was even possible that she *did* consider the separation from Mike Robinson a mere vacation. Or a strike. She was probably angling for a renegotiation of a marriage that had become too much work. Shelly wasn't good at being neglected and taken for granted.

"Hello, below!" hailed Teal, emerging from the trail that wound up through the forested hillside behind the cabin. She wore another of her plaid shirts, cargo pants and hiking boots, and carried the walking stick that had seen her through many seasons of tramping the wilderness of the Adirondack State Park.

Michael and Toddie ran up the trail to meet her. Teal Gladstone and her traditional storybook log cabin had always held a special appeal for children. As a girl Lara had often been her aunt's summer companion for long hikes and overnight canoe trips; as an adult she'd returned for more of the same as often as possible. When she'd moved from the city, there'd been no other place she wanted to go. The rest of the family had insisted that life in the remote wilderness was bound to drive her as crazy as Teal, their avowed eccentric. At times during the harsh winter months when she was snowed in and suffering a bad case of cabin fever, Lara was liable to agree. Her antidote was a visit with Bianca or a short jaunt to a warm clime for a delicious sun-soaked reprieve.

Her staunchly independent aunt was accustomed to the lack of conveniences and the unreliability of those that had been installed in her old-fashioned cabin over the years. Though Lara's house across the lake offered ready comfort, Teal preferred to do for herself—she tinkered with balky generators, warmed frozen pipes, canned her own produce and was a demon for snow shoveling and wood splitting. Ian Gladstone called his sister a tough old buzzard, to her unspoken pleasure.

On such a glorious autumn day as this, however, the amenities of the large old cabin seemed finer than any a luxury hotel could offer. The group of six sat at a plank table on the fieldstone patio, drinking Teal's homemade apple cider, admiring the lake view, commenting on the colorful foliage and briskly refreshing air.

As Lara warily watched Daniel and Teal size each other up, she came to realize that her lover and her aunt had much in common. Both exuded a confidence that manifested itself in a calm demeanor and impeccable posture. Yet there was no social puffery or slickness about either one. She valued their opinions. Envied their individuality. And aspired to a similar composure and certainty.

For instance. Had she been entirely secure, there would have been no reason to keep her relationship with Daniel strictly private.

Perhaps she'd only been greedy. She hadn't wanted to share him.

A good excuse, but she knew that wasn't it. What she'd worried over was that once introduced into the equation, the dynamics of her family would begin to impact on the fragile balance of her and Daniel's equality.

She twisted restlessly in her chair. Her lashes lowered as she turned to gaze out over the glittering lake. A sunny breeze ruffled the water, making the red and orange autumn leaves spiral like confetti once it reached land. Toddie ran to catch a perfect specimen. Teal sent Michael after the shovel. Lara's lids quivered as Daniel's brooding gaze panned over her, as bright and hot as the light of a copy machine.

She looked at him. When his dark eyebrows raised a notch, something inside her rippled with awareness. She crossed her legs and rolled her neck and rubbed her palms over her forearms.

"Gosh, Lara," sniped Shelly, "you're as twitchy as a dog with fleas. Worse than an eight-year-old."

Teal chuckled dryly. ''She's got the fall flibbertigibbets.''

Daniel moved his foot so the toe of his boot touched Lara's ankle.

Shelly glanced slyly from one to the other. ''I don't know that it's got anything to do with the season.'' She sugared her tone. ''I think maybe Lara's in lo-o-ove. Sweet savage lo-o-ove.''

Lara jumped, as much at the flash of Daniel's eyes as her sister's needling. ''Honestly, Shell,'' she said hotly. ''Mind your own business.''

''You teased me mercilessly when I got my first boyfriend.''

''I was fourteen!''

''Touchy, touchy,'' Shelly said in a singsong voice.

Lara pressed her fists against the table as she stood. ''I'm out of here.''

Teal shook her head at the spat, saying with an easy tolerance, ''Sisters.'' Having dismissed their sibling squabbles in a word, she went to meet Michael and Toddie in the garden, where they were to dig for worms in the compost pile.

Lara glared down her nose at Shelly and extended her hand to Daniel. ''C'mon, I'll show you the view from up top.''

''Aren't I invited?'' Shelly asked plaintively, grinning at Daniel.

''Certainly not!'' Lara stomped toward the path without looking back. She didn't care to look at Daniel either. He was bound to think her reaction extreme. Possibly amusing. But if he actually saw her face he'd know that she'd taken Shelly's teasing far more seriously than it merited. He'd begin to get *ideas*.

This was exactly why her rule against family interaction had been perfectly reasonable.

He said not a word as they climbed the hill. The steep path cut through lush balsam firs, sugar maples clinging to their colored leaves, silver birches showing a network of bare black twigs. He kept hold of Lara's hand even when they had to duck the extended branches. She laced her fingers through his and felt herself relax. Daniel, at least, accepted her limits.

The trees thinned out at the top of the ridge, where rocks had heaved up through the topsoil. She brought him to a granite outcropping that overlooked the whole of Coppercrown Lake. It glistened like a ragged length of blue satin ribbon unfurled across a gaudy shag rug.

"This is the crown." Lara's extended finger followed the outline of the jagged rock lookout. She waved at the hillside's steep spill of golden browns and rusty reds. "And I guess there's the copper."

Wordlessly he took in the view, then said softly, "You're lucky to live here."

Could he ever—? Lara shook her head at the involuntary question, knowing that asking was beyond her boundaries. "Tell me again when winter hits," she said instead, but that led to another realization, and this one was a shock. Suddenly she was assaulted by a sense of impending loss and loneliness as never before. She, who was so proud of her loner status.

It was undeniably disturbing. And scary.

Their silence was broken by the tiny birds hopping among the trees, calling *chickadee, chickadee-dee-dee* to one another. "You know," Daniel ventured, "we won't see each other as often once winter arrives."

"I know." Incredibly, she already missed him. An aching hollowness yawned inside her. Surely her heart would cave in. "I guess I haven't wanted to think about it." She hadn't planned for their attachment to grow so strong.

"Whenever the roads are clear, you can come to Manhattan, maybe by train..."

It wouldn't be the same, but she nodded anyway, pressing her fingertips to his.

"...and stay for as long as you like," he concluded. He stepped closer, murmuring into her ear with a voice as deep and soft as a fur rug. "I'd keep you all winter, if you'd let me. Keep you tucked into my bed like a bear in a cave. We could hibernate together, waking only to make love." His lips moved dancingly across the slope of her cheekbone as his words mesmerized her. "Loving and sleeping, sleeping and loving..."

Lara pressed her mouth onto his. Their kiss was tart, like wild apples. She moved her tongue into his warm mouth, then out, teasing the tip across his softening lips. "Mmm, baby," he moaned, dropping his hands to her fanny. "Baby bear."

She chuckled in her throat. "Believe me, I know exactly who's been sleeping in my bed."

He pulled her hard up against him and nuzzled her hair. "No one, last night."

Their mouths met again. Lara sank into Daniel's kiss—it was bittersweet, searching, hungry. His tongue caressed hers and the tingling sandpaper pleasure of it turned her intentions inside out. "I know I'm greedy," he murmured, "but I want you all the time. Tell me you'll come to see me next weekend when you're in the city." His lips moved against hers. "Promise you'll come to me."

"I will." She was ready to agree to anything. Almost anything. "I promise I will." Desire seeped through her bloodstream, insidiously seductive. She couldn't fight it, and right now couldn't see any need to. They'd only just begun, and already she knew that Sundays would always be like this. Aching. Hollow. She wanted to absorb everything about Daniel, each taste and touch and thought and word, fortifying herself for the coming week. When they came together it was earthshaking. Likewise, the thought of parting wrenched her heart.

And still you insist on keeping him compartmentalized? asked the nagging inner voice. *If I don't,* she answered, *he will invade every space. He will take over.*

Daniel sucked on her lower lip, he kissed the tip of her nose. "Every day without you is going to be endless."

"Every minute."

"Then why are we going to part?"

Their eyes connected. "You know why," she whispered.

His stare seemed to reach inside and tug on her untethered heart. "Homes, careers...? Can't we compromise on all that?"

She shook her head, dismissing those concerns. "That's not it."

He looked away, beyond the treetops, up to the sky. "I know that you're not..." The silvery sheen of his eyes had clouded to dull gray. "You're not ready," he said heavily.

"Not ready?" Suddenly Lara was backpedaling, literally and figuratively. "Wait a minute, there, Daniel. What are you saying?" Feeling dangerously on the edge of losing herself as she pressed against the barrier of rocks, she didn't dare pause to let him answer. She had to hold on to her place. "It's not a matter of being 'ready.' Ready for what? We had an agreement, didn't we? There shouldn't be any question of *readiness.*"

"Of course." He was looking at her without visible emotion now, his intentions blinkered once again. "What we have here is only a bad case of the fall flibbertigibbets.'' He tried to smile.

Lara felt that his acquiescence came too glibly, but she didn't know how to protest without saying the words they were both avoiding. She thrust her hands into the roomy pockets of her madras pants. No. It was not necessary for further warnings against love to pass her lips.

They both knew full well where they stood.

Miles apart.

TEAL AND THE BOYS HAD GONE off to fish, and Shelly had already taken the canoe back to the house, which left Daniel and Lara the rowboat.

She sat directly across from him, shoulders squared, knees together, knuckles prominent where she gripped the plank seat. Her amber hair made an aureole around her serious face, wavy untamed strands of it rippling on the breeze. Brows drawn together, she stared silently at Daniel until he was glad of the rowboat, glad that he could put all his energy into pulling on the oars, the burn of his straining shoulder muscles a welcome distraction.

''This isn't the Olympics, you know,'' she said.

He grunted and put his head down and kept on rowing, blotting his mind with the rhythmic motion. When exhaustion dropped through him heavy as a stone and every cell of his body screamed for oxygen, he unclenched his hands, looked up and blinked dazedly. They'd gone far past Lara's house, all the way to the southern end of Coppercrown Lake. Cedars, browsed ragged by deer, lined the swampy shore. Lily pads floated in water shot with shafts of the noon sun, creating in the shallows a green-gold haze that was very nearly the color of Lara's eyes.

Her depths weren't shallow. They were murky with

doubt and fear. He couldn't think of a way to convince her that it was safe to trust him with her heart.

Every breath was a benediction as he dragged deep drafts of oxygen into his lungs. He scrubbed one hand over his damp scalp. He was panting with fatigue and frustration, but, man, he felt alive!

"We're at Sunfish Inlet," Lara said calmly.

When he finally looked at her he knew that she might never say what he wanted to hear, so he surrendered to her stubbornness and his own endless need and said, "Get yourself over here."

She notched up her stubborn chin, but a small smile twitched at the corners of her mouth. "Caveman tactics," she said, and he speared her with one of his long caveman arms and pulled her onto his lap. She came with so little reluctance he overbalanced and suddenly they were tumbled into the flat bottom of the rowboat, laughing, his legs and her rump up in the air. His skull had rapped the bottom of the boat, but he didn't care about anything except the delicious promise of Lara's lips coming down on his, her breath like warm cider, her sunny outdoor woman scent sinking into his pores and her breasts—oh, man, her breasts—full and round and mashed up against his chest.

Another of the things he loved about Lara: She could be elegant, contained and sophisticated one day, fun and sexy and ready to rock 'n' roll the next. But still somehow contained, he thought fleetingly, as his arms went around her and she took his shirt in her fists and pushed it up around his neck, her lips fastening hotly on one of his nipples. At the rake of her teeth all that blessed oxygen drained from his lungs, but soon he filled instead with pleasure and heat, enough to sustain him into the next millennium.

They kissed. And kissed again, both of them extravagant and eager.

Daniel tried to drag his mouth away, only to be lured lower by the smooth curve of Lara's throat. Muttering into her collarbone, he said, "This wasn't how I intended to..." Then, distracted by more important things, he forgot that he was speaking. Lara had sat up and was somehow managing to toss her hair and strip off her shirt in one efficient motion. Her breasts moved against the sheer nothingness of her bra in a way that was not precisely efficient but did serve to short-circuit every rational thought in his brain.

"We have to be together," she said firmly, looking down at him with her hands on her waist, elbows akimbo.

Daniel wasn't going to disagree, even though there was barely enough head space under the seat for him to nod. He inched forward on his elbows until his head and shoulders had cleared the plank, then peeled off his bothersome shirt and sort of curled himself into the confined space, all the while staring up at Lara in glazed approval. She was slender and strong and beautiful and fierce. A warrior in her own right. Nobody's conquest, but all that he could ever need or want—his match in every way. So how the hell did he convince her of that?

Not with sex: he'd tried that. But suddenly he was willing to try again because she'd skinned out of the blue-and-green plaid pants that looked like pajama bottoms and pounced on him with a wildcat's snarl, kissing her way up to his chest, making every muscle in his abdomen ripple and clench under the sweet, sucking pull of her mouth and the ticklish tracings of her hair and fingernails. Her pointed tongue licked between his pectoral muscles, making patterns on his skin. Then the top of her head smacked into his jaw and she said "Ouch," sliding her mouth crookedly over his as she tried to bring her knees underneath her and still have enough room to reach down and get both hands on his fly. He cradled her face on his fingertips, directing the position, his tongue flicking into her mouth. Each hair on his body prickled with arousal—even his follicles felt zapped.

Lara fumbled with his zipper in the swaying boat and there was pressure and then a welcome release that lasted only a second before her warm hand was stroking him, stroking him. "Stop," he gasped, and she said, "Too late," both arms braced on the seat behind his head as she lifted herself up. He sucked in his breath in anticipation; she'd never been so...single-minded.

"We have to be together," Lara said again. And then she lowered herself onto him, her eyes losing their focus for a second or two before her chin snapped up and she tossed her head, flinging her arms wide, a triumphant Amazon astride a charger.

At the sudden hot shock of her descent, Daniel's head had jerked back involuntarily, cracking the base of his skull against the edge of the seat. And still he felt no pain, being more than occupied by the way Lara's left breast had popped out of her bra—had she *planned* that?—and the deep enveloping pleasure that was so intense he had to close his eyes and lay his head down on the bottom of the rowboat to regain his faculties.

His ears filled with sloshing sounds. In tandem with the slow rolling movement of Lara's hips, the rowboat was rocking gently from side to side, lapped by water. He groaned and shifted, discarding faculties right and left as male instinct drove his hips upward in desperate need of the relief offered by her wet, clasping heat.

"Lara," he groaned.

Her eyes glittered. She pressed her palms against his

expanding rib cage. He wrapped his hands around the gunwales, gritting his teeth, every muscle stretched tight as they surged into each other, the pressure welling, welling, until Lara cried out with pleasure. She smiled then, and slumped forward, lipping kisses over his face, her sweetness oozing over him like a puddle of warm syrup. And still it wasn't enough for him. This time, he wanted more.

She sat up and swung her head back, the slick pouting curve of her lower lip glinting in the sunshine. "I'm getting splinters in my knees," she said silkily, eyes narrowed to indolent slits.

"What a shame." Panting, he peered out from beneath the seat. "I think you gave me a concussion."

With a slow, ripe chuckle, she swiveled her hips. "Too bad."

"C'mere." He wrenched himself up, gathering her into his arms and rearranging their position until he was seated properly and she was seated in his lap—improperly. "Is this better?"

"Mmm...better," she hummed. "I can kiss you."

He kissed her first, a dizzying fusion of lips and tongue. A terrible yearning overtook the lust that he'd used in place of his true desire, and suddenly he was impelled by the confusion of emotion into doing the unthinkable.

He lost control.

Hands on her hips, mouth pressed to her flushed cheek, he spoke without thinking, the words coming purely from the heart. "I've fallen in love with you, woman," he said, then turned his face and kissed her again—possessively, bruisingly—pretty much daring her to deny the truth as suddenly his body spasmed in a magnificent, painful release.

Turning her head away, Lara closed her eyes and said only one word, a word that was far more painful than sex in a rowboat.

She said, "No."

9

DANIEL STOPPED. He wanted to continue until she was so filled with him, so much a part of him, that his need would become hers. But for the first time, unimaginably, making love to Lara didn't feel right. And he knew that it was no way to convince her that she was wrong.

She pulled against his encircling arms, their slippery flesh clinging as if her body knew more than her brain. "No," she said in a dull monotone, battering her fists against his bare chest. "No. No. No."

"Hush." He grasped her wrists and held on even when she struggled. "Don't say that again."

She turned her head and looked askance at him through her disheveled hair. "No," she said deliberately, her voice infused with both reproach and confusion. She pulled free and raked her hair back from her face. Defiance hardened her expression. Blind defiance.

It was over. Something in Daniel that had been strung as tight as a barbed wire fence snapped. "All right, have it your way," he said, seething with frustration and pain. He put his hands around her waist and abruptly set her away from him on the opposite seat. Her mouth opened and closed in silent shock.

He looked at his empty hands, turning them over as though he didn't recognize whose they were, amazed at their slight tremble. He clenched them. "Forget I said...what I said. Pretend this didn't happen."

She dragged her shirt on over her head, stabbed her legs into the madras pants. "It's too late for that."

"Probably." *Was it over?*

She rubbed her eyes. "But we had an agreement!"

"No, you had an agreement. I had a lover." Despite everything, he hoped he still did. "And Lara?" He waited for her to look at him. "It *did* connote feelings of love."

With care, she held herself still and straight, as if she might shatter if she didn't. "Nevertheless, we had an agreement." She hesitated, and he could tell she would do anything to avoid direct reference to the *L* word. "I don't get you. It's men who are supposed to want this kind of thing—a sex thing—" Her lids lowered as she wonderingly touched one fingertip to her lips, a gesture that told Daniel more than her words.

"Oh, I do," he said.

Her eyes flashed. "Sex without commitment," she went on frankly, underestimating both of them. "Incredible sex. Hot sex. Sex on demand that's also no-demands sex."

"Believe it or not, there are still one or two men out there who think there's more to life than *s-e-x.*"

"Sure. There's cars and booze and sports and strippers. Not necessarily in that order."

She wasn't going to make him smile that easily, not with the scattershot of her noes still stinging his pride.

"I want more," he said. "I always have." He honestly had, in a vague, sometime-in-the-future way. It was only since meeting Lara that all that encompassed "more" had seemed not only desirable, but imminent.

She'd certainly dashed *that* to pieces.

"I warned you not to ask." She'd turned to stare unseeingly at the bobbing lilies and the button-topped rushes clogging the shoreline. Her glance slid sideways, then flicked away again. "Would you put on your shirt? I can't have this conversation if you're half-undressed."

He'd have stripped down to his birthday suit and stood up and posed like George Washington crossing the Delaware if it meant that she'd be too flummoxed to remember her noes. Fat chance of that, though, so he zipped up—very carefully—and found his wrinkled henley on the bottom of the boat and pulled it on. Nervously Lara combed her fingers through her hair, her face shadowed with dark thoughts. *Damn.* A man felt real proud to have his declaration of love provoke such a negative reaction.

He arranged the oars in the locks, glancing up now and then at a white cottage with a screened porch that was half-hidden among the evergreens. "I hope no one's home, or they got a real eyeful."

"The Adamses left a month ago."

So there were no witnesses to his ignominy. Good, but it wasn't as if the moment wouldn't live in infamy all the same. Stunned by his unaccustomed failure, he operated by rote, making an experimental circling of the oars. Feelings of inadequacy were rising to the surface—old memories from his childhood. He ignored them. "Are we stuck?"

They'd shimmied the boat into the middle of a patch of clinging lily pads. Lara kneeled in the bow, her pert, plaid-clad behind waving in the air as she reached overboard. Glaring at it made Daniel feel fractionally better. "Keep rowing," she said, so he had to quit glaring and turn around to row. With a disgusted "ugh," she pushed aside one of the slimy aquatic plants.

Eventually they reached clear water. The green shallows deepened color, the surface of the lake corrugated by the sighing wind. Lara returned to her seat at the stern and tried a smile, long strands of hair blowing across her cheeks. "Smooth sailing from here on out."

"Don't count on it."

She glared. "Don't blame me, Daniel." When he met her eyes, she looked away, squinting across the lake toward home, and said more softly to herself, "I had it all figured out. This wasn't supposed to happen."

He brooded. "Sorry I spoiled your neat little scenario by expressing an honest emotion."

"It's not like you haven't enjoyed the status quo."

"Too much for your taste."

She flicked her hair back. "Don't make me out to be a heartless bitch." Her eyes were stormy, almost passionate, or so a man less rejected than Daniel might have thought. "I have feelings for you. Of course I do."

"Feelings."

She hesitated. "Strong feelings."

"But I'm forbidden to bring up the possibility that these strong feelings might approach love."

Lara closed her eyes. There it was again, that word. That pesky, disturbing, *loaded* word.

She just couldn't bring herself to believe in it as optimistically as the rest of the world. Love to her meant a blind devotion to wrong-minded precepts that had never accounted for human nature. It meant sacrifice, piety, loss of freedom.

Other kinds of love she could handle. Even when they weren't easy, like the complicated, double-edged love-hate she felt for her difficult father, or the instinctual but exasperated love of her mother and sister. Loving Teal and her nephews, her work and house and land and the higher power of their creation was easy in comparison.

It was only romantic love that her heart absolutely refused.

Yet, before Daniel, that refusal hadn't been such a struggle. He'd provoked emotions in her that even undefined were strong enough to make her question her beliefs. And somewhere inside, she'd known all along that once hearts were involved he wasn't a man to be satisfied with a less than total commitment. She'd just never imagined that it would happen so fast.

One little word. So simple, so complicated. A word that demanded so much. Too much. Lara gritted her teeth. She was too mulishly independent—and just plain scared—to surrender.

But she didn't want to lose him. Desperately.

She opened her eyes. Daniel was still glowering as he rowed. "Lara Gladstone, you are the most infuriating, confounding, complicated woman."

"Even to myself," she said.

"Tell me why."

"If I knew—" She gave a short laugh.

"Go on," he coaxed. "Tell me."

She shook her head. "You ask too much."

He snorted. "I've asked nothing of you until today."

"You—have." Her breath caught. *Every time you touched me, you asked me to surrender my heart. With every caress, every kiss.* A strange hunger, worse than the moony need that had kept her up all night, grew stronger within her. "You have asked a lot of me...silently...in bed...."

"Back to sex again?" He sounded hard.

"No! I meant more than physical."

His voice softened. "I knew what you meant, I'm just surprised that you did."

"I'm not made of stone."

"Seems we've got a role reversal going here." He laughed dryly. "And I'm not particularly liking my role."

"Ah." Lara tipped up her chin and surveyed him through narrowed eyes. "Then you begin to understand my position."

"Not entirely. There is the possibility of establishing an equal partnership."

"Happens all the time," she said with scorn, thinking of her parents' marriage, all take on one side and give on the other.

"How very cynical of you."

"Tell me I'm wrong," she challenged. The longing inside her made her realize that at least part of her wanted to be wrong. She wanted a reason to give in to him, to let herself go…to fall in love.

But the ironic aptness of the phrase—*give in to him*—stopped her cold.

"My parents have been married for nearly forty years. They seem, uh, satisfied with each other." Daniel frowned, obviously searching his mind as the boat slowed. "And I'm sure there are other couples…"

"Wherein the husbands think the relationships are fifty-fifty," Lara said. "Check with the wives and get back to me."

"You know what they say. Sometimes it's fifty-fifty, and sometimes it's twenty-eighty. It's all supposed to balance out in the end."

"But the problem is it never does."

He squinted one eye. "Does that mean you wanted to row this boat half the way home? Fifty-fifty being your standard?"

She flushed. "Fine," she snapped, and moved over beside him. "I'll row. I have no problem rowing. Just don't let the sight of me flexing my muscles send your fragile male ego into a tailspin."

He chuckled. "Oh, don't worry your pretty little head about that."

"Very funny." She knew he was purposely needling her now, pricking at her overblown outrage. Still, he hadn't proved her assertion wrong. And even though he couldn't, he clearly expected that in the end she would capitulate to it. The nature of her feminine biological imperative would seal her fate.

Enough! She stabbed the blades of the oars into the water and flicked them once, spraying Daniel with droplets. "Refreshing," he said. She responded with a tight smile.

If she could have kept up her temper, she might have been okay. But the problem was that as she rowed, Daniel's body—his overweening male bulk, she told herself crossly—was in the way. He stretched his arms, flexed his fingers, sighed with satisfaction, and didn't budge an inch except to lean farther back and put his arm behind her when she swung the grips of the oars around and nearly clipped him in the family jewels. She smiled at him again, meaning it to be nasty, but the smile came out too loose. She could feel it relaxing her cheeks and her throat and the hard knot of tension below her solar plexus. Every time she pulled back on the oars, her tingling arm brushed his side; each time she pushed forward, her knuckles ran the length of his thigh. She blew out a loud breath and tried not to notice. Which of course made her so aware that every touch reverberated right down to her toenails.

It was a test, she decided. If she could make it to the dock without going all girly and gushy inside—well, maybe just outside—then she could withstand anything. Even their impending goodbye.

She might have done it, too, if Daniel hadn't put his hand over hers on the oar and started rowing with her.

The gesture was all too symbolic. And this time her smile was genuine, suddenly, nonsensically, as giddy and loose as if her heart had taken wing and was doing loop-the-loops across the sky. He loved her. She hadn't asked for it, didn't want it, but all the same—*he loved her.*

She turned her head and there was his face, such a few inches away that it seemed natural to lean her forehead against his. "I'm so sorry. What you said…rattled me. I don't know what to do." She sighed. "As you can tell, I have issues."

This time Daniel had the smarts not to push her for explanations. He didn't even speak. He just moved in a little closer and touched his lips to hers, skimming them with a goodbye kiss that was as light as a fluffy curl of duck down floating on the current.

COLORED BITS OF GLASS WERE arranged in a complicated pattern on Lara's worktable. Their design had been inspired by images of springtime reflecting in the lake. A lovely pink gold glass, a hammered purple and chunks of milky whites formed wavy streamers among the translucent blues and greens of cathedral glass and curved slices of a gorgeous rippled aquamarine. Tall vertical panels representing the other seasons were already completed and framed in lustrous satinwood. When the fourth piece was finished the panels would be hinged together to form a large standing screen.

Lara squinted, blurring the loose pieces of glass into a kaleidoscope of color. The Summer panel was a study of striking blues and golds, an impressionistic depiction of sunlight dancing on the water. Spring would appear softer, rippling with the blossoming pastels of renewal and promise.

Today she wasn't satisfied with the effect. Frustrated,

she pushed away from the table, swiveling on her stool to face the opposite direction, trying to lay the blame on her usual dilemma. She never knew, until the entire piece was soldered together and could be surveyed in the light, if her design had been entirely successful. There were still a hundred hours of painstaking work between now and then. It was an anticipatory process of creation that she usually relished.

Not lately. It had been forty-eight hours since Daniel had left on a frustratingly incomplete note, and still she couldn't work worth a damn. She'd tried cutting. Every scrape of the blade on the glass had grated on her nerves; every cut felt wrong. After shattering a piece of expensive "ice crystal" glass she'd finally given up.

Foiling, the process of wrapping copper tape around the edges of each piece of glass, was mindless work. Too mindless. Her thoughts had been free to wander endlessly over every nuance of Daniel's words, and her own disparaging responses. She told herself she should have seen what was coming, should have handled it better, should have been cool enough not to let it get to her!

She shot up from the stool and paced around the open studio, past the balcony that overlooked a section of the angled living room and around to the wall of windows that filled the triangular peak of the roofline. Far below, Michael and Toddie were readying the canoe for another trip across the wind-roughened lake to Teal's cabin.

Shelly was queening it on the deck, stretched out on a wrought-iron chaise longue, a glass of fruit juice at her elbow and the cordless telephone in her lap. She was on and off the phone a dozen times a day, calling her husband on one pretext or another, getting advice and updates from her circle of girlfriends, and on occasion taking a message for Lara—all of which Lara had ignored because they weren't from Daniel. In between calls Shelly twittered at her sons, interrogated her sister about her love life and complained about being marooned so far from civilization because of her unresponsive husband.

Even if it hadn't been a good excuse to see Daniel again, Lara would have been eager to get to New York. She intended to deliver Shelly and her sons to whoever would take them—preferably Shelly's husband, but their father would do—and then turn up on Daniel's doorstep, hat in hand, essentially. She would offer him a compromise.

In the past few days of heavy thinking she'd come to see that it wasn't necessarily *love* that she was afraid of. Indeed, she'd been loving Daniel all along—admittedly without realizing it—and had managed to stay her own person. Ergo, that must mean it was *marriage* she was opposed to.

Absolutely. Marriage. She'd draw the line at marriage.

As long as Daniel hadn't done something silly like go to Tiffany's and buy her a ring, they might yet work the whole thing out. They could still be together.

In love, yes, perhaps, but not in marriage. No way.

Did that make any sense at all, or was she merely grasping at straws, justifying her weakness because she'd already surrendered?

Lara touched the windowpane. On the dock below, Shelly was buckling Toddie into a bright orange life vest. Preparing for a bumpy ride.

THE NEXT DAY, the sounds of Aaron Copland's glorious *Appalachian Spring* filled the attic studio. Making a decision about what to do about Daniel had given Lara the measure of peace that enabled her to concentrate on work. She flitted around the long table like a firefly, agile fingers darting out to nudge at various pieces of finely cut glass, rechecking their fit as she thumbtacked them in place. Her pleasure expanded. The hundreds of colored bits, sharp edges and smooth curves alike, meshed as precisely as a jigsaw puzzle.

She stepped back, gaze roaming over the unfinished panel, then allowed herself a small sigh. If only "love" turned out to be as easy a fit!

There was a rap at the door. "Yoo-hoo," Shelly said from the other side, sounding so cheerful her afternoon call to Michael must have gone exceedingly well. Perhaps she would work out her marriage on her own. "Lara, I've got a surprise visitor for you! Can we come in?"

Thinking *Daniel,* Lara hurried over to throw open the door. Her hopes sank. "Kensington. Damn. What are you doing here?"

Kensington Webb raised one supercilious eyebrow. Shelly slid her hand around his elbow protectively. "Honestly, sis, what a greeting."

"Pardon me," Lara said, even though her first response had been perfectly honest, if not appropriate. "Hello, Kensington. To what do I owe the unexpected pleasure of your visit?"

Shelly sniffed. "What else can one expect when one ignores one's phone messages?" She smiled up at Kensington, clearly smitten with his elegant good looks and impeccable manners. He was tall and lean and beautiful, a silver-haired Caravaggio in a pinstripe designer suit.

Kensington cocked his head. Light caught on the fringe of silver hair that capped his noble bronzed brow. "No need to fret, dear girl. I've learned to tolerate such treatment from my stable of artists. How fortunate that it's advantageous to my gallery when creative urges come before social niceties." He laughed politely.

"You're too kind," Shelly said, playing up her sisterly role for Kensington's benefit, but shooting mean little darts at Lara with her eyes. She edged into the room. "And I'm sure that Lara intends to invite you into the studio, seeing as you've come so far."

"How could I refuse?" Lara moved aside grudgingly. She was covetous of her private space. She didn't want just anyone fingering up her works-in-progress. Trying not to scowl about their invasion, she went to shut off the music.

Kensington studied the panels leaning against the windows facing the lake. He murmured over the intricate cuts made from the icy blues and clear, crackled art glass that represented Winter. A wordless gesture of appreciation greeted the complicated, colorful water and leaf patterns of Autumn. "What can I say?" he said, clasping his hands in line with his tie. "Magnificent!"

Lara hung back. She'd been with Kensington Webb long enough to know that it was not love of art that motivated his compliments, but love of his percentage of their worth. Nevertheless, his business sense and suave salesmanship enabled her to make a good income, so she owed him her thanks for that, at least.

"The Spring panel will be finished and framed in another two weeks," she said. "Plenty of time to be included in the show." She was to have a one-woman show at Kensington Webb Galleries in November. Kensington, with an unerring instinct for publicity, had rescheduled the show's original January date to coincide with Ian Gladstone's retrospective at the Met.

The art dealer moved to overlook the cork-surfaced work table, examining the pieces laid out on the paper pattern of her design. He touched a piece of moss green glass with his fingertip. "Hmm. I see this quartette as the centerpiece of the show. We'll set the screen on a spotlighted dais before the windows at the front of the gallery...hmm, yes, it will be marvelous." He pursed his lips, calculating. "I believe I can rouse interest among the important collectors. Your prices will skyrocket."

Shelly's eyes widened. "Lara's opening doesn't conflict with my father's retrospective, does it? I have a stunning new gown for Dad's event, and a cute new hat I can wear to Lara's thingie. I wouldn't want to have to choose between them."

The apparel or the shows? Lara wondered, but Kensington looked at Shelly with appreciation. "You will rival the artwork with your beauty. But not to worry. I've set Lara's opening party for the weekend after Mr. Gladstone's gala. The invitations have already gone out."

Shelly simpered. "Oh, goody! Then I'll get to dress up and show off twice."

Kensington's smile was as glossy as a prestigious auction catalog. "I shall be agog with anticipation." When his eyes swiveled around to Lara, she could see that he'd shed all thoughts of Shelly in a blink. Typical. She dredged up a pleasant, if detached, expression. By now, Kensington knew not to trifle with her.

"Tch-tch, Lara, dear, you really should have returned my telephone calls. However, despite the rigors of the long drive north, I'm not displeased to have this opportunity to view your work in its natural habitat, so to speak." Kensington's discerning gaze swept along the slanted ceiling with its hand-hewn beams and multiple skylights. "You've managed to carve out a nice little space for yourself here, among the treetops. And look at that lake—it's marvelous. A truly inspirational location."

Lara murmured a polite agreement. Despite Kensington's pretty words, she doubted that he understood her source of inspiration. He wasn't the type to, say, roll around in a meadow or "tour" the lake in a rowboat.

Shelly laughed gaily. "But it's also miles away from Starbucks!"

Kensington chuckled. "There is that."

"Lara's on the verge of turning into a hermit, tucked away out here in the boonies. Or so I thought until I met her weekend, ah...visitor." Shelly puckered her lips, hesitating for just a moment. Lara glared at her, to no avail. "Daniel Savage," Shelly intoned.

Kensington's interest heightened. "Daniel Savage?"

Lara's body tightened. She didn't want to share her confused feelings for Daniel with these two any more than she wanted them cluttering up her studio with their curiosity and insinuations.

"Lara's little secret," Shelly said mincingly. "Her sweet, savage lo-o-ove."

"I had no idea." Quietly Kensington studied the pink mottling Lara's cheeks. "I'll have to see that this mystery man gets an invitation to your show," he said, quite stiffly, even for him.

Lara didn't answer, but Shelly was willing to tell all she knew. "He's a financial analyst with Bairstow & Boone. On Wall Street."

"Really." Even though Kensington didn't smile, he seemed to make a conscious effort to return to his usual glib self. "This little visit has already been worthwhile, and we've yet to discuss business." He looked at Lara expectantly. "There are several details about the show..."

"Yes. I can give you a few minutes." *Now that her concentration was shot anyway.* "You'll stay for dinner? I've promised my nephews tacos, I'm afraid," she warned, amused at the thought of Kensington dripping hot sauce on his pristine white French cuffs.

"What a generous invitation. I haven't had Mexican in ages." Kensington favored Shelly with a playful glance. "It'll be fun."

The happy curve of Shelly's lips was punctuated with dimples. She took his arm to lead him downstairs. "Oh, I'm sure it will, Mr. Webb." Her pretty oval face turned up to his like a sunflower basking in the sun.

His smile was brilliant. "Call me Kensington, my dear."

LARA TOOK A BASKET of Aunt Teal's garden tomatoes from the windowsill and picked out a half dozen of the ripest. Shelly was browning the ground beef and Michael was grating three kinds of cheese at the island counter. In the living room, Toddie had the job of entertaining their guest over glasses of red wine and Hawaiian punch. So far, Kensington seemed amused.

"He's really cute, even with that silver hair," Shelly said under the cover of the sizzling meat. "How old is he? Has he ever hit on you?"

"Early forties," Lara said, evading the second question. "And I warn you, he has a very intimidating ex-wife. Hans from the gallery calls her Valerie the Valkyrie."

"Who cares, as long as they're divorced."

"But you're not."

"Yet." Shelly put down the wooden spoon and went to wash her hands. "Yech—I'm all greasy. And I wanted to look good for—" She eyed Michael Junior and his triple mounds of cheddar, jack and Swiss. "For, ah, dinner."

"Be careful, Shell," Lara whispered. "Don't do something you're going to regret."

Shelly fussed with the gathered waistband of her long

floral dress. "I just want to flirt a little. Is there anything wrong in that?"

Lara shrugged and added the contents of a spice packet to the beef as her sister went to join Kensington on the couch. Shelly was an expert flirt. Men appreciated her coy smiles, batting lashes and feminine style of dress, even though as a married woman she was ultimately more style than substance. Whereas Lara—she looked down at her old brown trousers and pumpkin-colored rag knit sweater—had always been the reserved, simmering, slow-to-warm-up type. But neither a tease nor indecisive. She trusted her instincts about men.

She'd trusted them with Daniel. Still did, even though he'd breached her defenses without hardly trying.

Another reason she might as well go ahead and admit she'd fallen in love with him.

"Is this enough cheese?" Michael asked.

Lara came out of her reverie. "Gosh, yes." Hurriedly she spooned the spicy beef into white corn taco shells. Michael helped her add cheese and slide the pan of tacos into the oven to warm. She arranged the cold fillings and bottles of hot sauce on a tray and sent the boy off to announce dinner.

Kensington had the foresight to remove his suit jacket and roll up his monogrammed cuffs. Lara smiled across the table at him. She was liking him better now that he'd loosened up and even laughed at Toddie's silly Halloween riddles.

"What do ghosts and goblins like to eat?" she asked, once they'd all filled their plates.

"Greasy gopher guts." Michael Junior poked at his refried beans. He was scornful of such babyish jokes. "French-fried eyeballs."

"Uh-uh." Sauce leaked from Toddie's taco as he

stopped it in midair to concentrate on the joke he'd already told a dozen times. "It's booberry pie!"

"And ice scream," Lara added.

"Ice scream, like ice cream." Toddie looked to Kensington. "Booberry pie and ice scream. Didja get it?"

Kensington chuckled dutifully.

Shelly rubbed her palm across Toddie's thin shoulders. "My boys are treasures. Do you have any children, Kensington?"

"I'm afraid not."

Shelly tilted her head and smiled shyly at him from beneath her lowered lashes. "You should get some. And a wife, too."

Kensington dropped the remains of a crumbling taco on his plate and fastidiously wiped his fingers, watching Lara. "It's a thought."

She made a noncommittal sound, suddenly aware that the sky was darkening and they were hundreds of miles from New York City. Was Kensington hoping to spend the night? "Uh, we have ice cream or frozen yogurt for dessert," she said.

"Ice scream," said Toddie. "Chocolate, with sprinkles!"

Reaching out to spear a slice of tomato, Shelly brushed against Kensington. "None for me, thanks. I'm trying to keep my girlish figure."

He eyed her slender frame and said, with just the right touch of ribald charm, "Oh, I wouldn't worry. It doesn't look like it's going anywhere." Giggling, Shelly nudged him with her elbow.

Lara moved the remainder of the dinner hour along briskly, doling out ice cream and riddles and napkins and sprinkles, then accompanying the boys upstairs to get into pajamas and brush their teeth. Leaving them to an hour of TV before bedtime, she returned to discover Kensington and Shelly standing in cozy proximity out on the deck, pressed side to side in the corner, their elbows on the railing. Shelly's teasing laughter rose on the cool night air.

Lara hesitated. Should she interrupt? She didn't want to get into anything with the man herself, but her sister—all flirt, no experience—was playing with fire. Shelly had no idea just how smooth Kensington could be.

Lara decided to clean up the kitchen first. By the time that was done, it was almost too late to send Kensington home. She opened the French doors and went outside.

One of his arms was draped across Shelly's shoulders as he waxed eloquent about his extensive and valuable art collection. She looked up at him with a fixed expression that could pass for wonder, but that Lara recognized as glazed boredom.

"Hey, Shell," she interrupted. "Your sons are waiting for their good-night kisses."

Shelly grazed Kensington's shirtfront with the tips of her polished nails. "Excuse me for a moment, will you, Ken?" She made a sound of purring pleasure. "I'll be right back."

She went inside, not reluctantly. Through the double-height windows, both Kensington and Lara watched her toss a flirtatious glance over her shoulder and skip up the stairs, swishing her skirt as she went.

Lara faced Kensington with her hands on her hips. "Shelly has a husband."

"Not a very attentive one, by the sounds of it." The art dealer leaned back against the railing like a model in a Hugo Boss ad, his ivory shirt and platinum hair luminous in the dusk. "Pity."

"You're toying with her."

His teeth flashed in a negligent grin. "She's a cute kid."

"Leave her alone, Kensington."

He chuckled. "You'd better tell her that. I wasn't the instigator."

"Listen." Lara's voice lowered as she pointed at him. "Shelly married young. She's an innocent, really. All she does is flirt, so don't expect more." Her index finger stabbed him once in the chest. "I mean it. Stay away from her."

He clasped her hand between both of his. She tried to withdraw, but he held on tightly, lifting her fingers to his mouth. "A Gladstone in the hand," he murmured, and kissed her knuckles. "Is worth two in the—"

She slid her hand out of his grasp. "So there it is, at last. I've always wondered if it was my name and connections that you wanted, not me." She'd been suspicious of him from the outset, particularly when he'd tried to curry a personal involvement, but had overlooked his hints for an introduction to her father because, frankly, it worked to her advantage. Bianca had said that she'd be crazy to turn down Kensington Webb's representation. So what if they were using each other—that was how the world worked.

But suddenly Lara felt like a hypocrite. All the misgivings she'd put off rose inside her until she thought her brain would burst from too much heat and embarrassment and disgust. For all her avowed independence, was she only fooling herself? Was she wrong about *everything?*

Kensington drew himself up. "I said no such thing."

"As good as."

"No. You've misinterpreted me, dear Lara." The art dealer was oblivious, his voice as smooth and silky as cream. "I meant that as you've seen fit to reject my attentions—'' he eyed her with what she took to be an utterly insincere regret ''—I have to console myself where I can. And your sister is rather delightful.''

''Here I am,'' announced Shelly as she came breathlessly through the doorway. Her hazel gaze bounced between Lara and Kensington. ''What are you two talking about?''

''Kensington was just saying that he has to leave.'' Lara turned her back to Shelly and glared pointedly at him. ''Isn't that right...*Ken?*''

10

"I CAN'T BELIEVE you offered Kensington the guest room," Lara said with exasperation as she and Shelly changed the sheets on the bed. "You didn't do that for Daniel."

"Ken's taller, by about three inches."

Lara snapped an elasticized corner into place. "What does that have to do with it?"

"He wouldn't fit the bunk bed, and besides, I like tall men. They make me feel petite." Smiling to herself, Shelly unfolded the top sheet. "Anyway, how could you send him away at this late hour? Huh? Mom taught you to be a better hostess than that. And after he came all this way to see you."

"But I didn't ask him here, and there are hotels. I'm not in the mood to be...accommodating."

Shelly billowed the sheet; Lara batted it down. "Your attitude stinks, sis. Kensington Webb seems like a perfectly nice man."

"It's best if our relationship remains strictly business." *If it remains at all,* Lara added silently. Then she thought of her mortgage. Her emerging career. How success might finally make her good enough for her father.

"I'm not bound by your silly restrictions," Shelly said, being blithe. She was like their mother that way. Cheerful in the face of all opposition, as if refusing to acknowledge the ugly truth made it disappear.

"Oh, Shelly..." Lara sighed as she smoothed and tucked in the sheet. She was going to have to warn her sister about Kensington's motives, but it probably wouldn't matter. Shelly would believe what she wanted to believe. And when it came to men, she wanted to believe that they loved her. It did no good to point out that what she was really seeking was their father's approval.

Oddly familiar, no?

"He's very attractive, for an older man. I like him." Shelly shook a pillow out of its case. "I think he likes me. At least he notices me more than Michael does." Her head tilted contemplatively. "Are you jealous? Is that why you want to keep us apart?"

"God, no. I'm trying to look out for you."

"Oh, please. When it comes to men, I know what I'm doing. I know how to get my way."

"But this time you're playing for high stakes—not a date for the prom or a lenient curfew from Dad." Lara jerked the other pillow free. "Kensington is—" She stopped, biting back the words *out of your league*. Shelly would take that as a dare. "Won't you simply trust me? You'll save yourself a lot of grief if you stop now."

Shelly narrowed her eyes. "Says you."

They finished making the bed in silence. Afterward, feeling drained, Lara sat at one end and slowly gathered the used sheets and pillowcases into a pile. "Kensington is only after the Gladstone name," she said, trying one more time.

"No worry. Mine's Robinson." Shelly dismissed the concerns with an air bubble of a laugh as she moved from bathroom to bedroom, packing a few necessary items for her stay in the bunk room. "Really, what a bore. You *always* think people are reacting to Dad's fame."

"This time it's—"

Shelly made a yackety-yack motion with her fingers. "I don't need to hear about how Ian Gladstone's fame has been a blight upon your tortured artistic soul. All that has nothing to do with me and Kensington." A lipstick and a tube of mascara went into her makeup bag. She inspected herself in the mirror over the oak bureau, fluffing the ends of her sandy-blond bob. "Is it so hard to believe that he might want me for myself? I'm still an attractive person, aren't I?"

There was an underlying hint of neediness in her voice, making Lara wonder if her sister's marriage was truly in trouble this time, instead of being another tempest in a teapot. Given Shelly's facade, it was too easy to dismiss her as a pampered princess. Unless you knew firsthand how she had been trained to seek out her father's praise for being a pretty ornament.

Lara went over and hugged her. Shelly gave back a few pats, making a little sound of sisterly thanks before withdrawing—and turning straight to the mirror. Lara tried not to wince. Shelly had never been without a boyfriend, but then men finding her attractive was not the issue. Her need for constant approval was.

"Shell, honey..." Lara said cautiously, not sure how to dig deeper without bursting the bubble of her sister's pretty little rose-colored ego.

"What now?"

"You need to concentrate on your problems with your husband. Forget about Kensington."

"You need to stop telling me what *I* need. Michael's not here. Obviously he doesn't care enough to come after me and the boys. He'd rather work, as usual. I'm not even his wife anymore—I'm just a housekeeper and a mother." Shelly stroked her cheek in the mirror. "Ken says I'm an alluring woman."

"Sure you are. But Mike's not here, remember? Making him jealous won't work."

Shelly giggled. "I'm not actually going to *do* anything. It's enough to have someone interested again."

Lara picked up the wadded sheets and clenched them to her chest. There was one quick way to annoy her sister. "Whatever. But, you know…Kensington tried for me first."

Shelly's smile dimmed. While she didn't like being in second place in general, she was particularly competitive when it came to male approval. "You said you two are strictly business—"

"By my insistence."

"Oh, well, then. He was probably just trying to flatter you."

"Listen." Lara approached from behind, meeting her sister's petulant gaze in the mirror. "Kensington knows the value of the Gladstone name. He came on strong, wining and dining me, courting me for his gallery." *And more.* "Then, surprise, our photo shows up in a few gossip columns and art journals. 'Kensington Webb to represent the new generation of Gladstones…' That sort of thing. Next he's angling for an invitation to our parent's house in Italy. When I accused him, he swore that getting an introduction to my father was only a perk of our business agreement, not its raison d'être." Lara grimaced. "At the time I chose to believe him. Now I'm not so sure."

After a moment of silence, Shelly opened a drawer and rifled through it, keeping her face downturned. "But that's your story, Lara. You don't know how he feels about me."

"You're eminently lovable. Still, it's the fact that you're a Gladstone that's important to Kensington. Don't fall for his act."

Shelly nipped at her bottom lip. "You're too sensitive where Dad is concerned."

"*Dad* is a tyrannical, egocentric brute without a compassionate bone in his body, but that's neither here nor there."

"You see?"

Lara sat on the bed again, her shoulders slumped. "Yes, I see. It's true that I'm hypersensitive about being valued for myself, not my name. And it's also true that on top of being a brute, Dad's generous, entertaining and immensely talented." She lifted her head. "But none of that concerns Kensington's motives for playing up to you."

"Oh, *motives,*" Shelly said, resuming her blithe airiness. "You're always looking for motives. Well, I don't care what you say." She gathered up her things and flounced from the room. "I just want to have a little fun. I deserve it!"

After a moment, Lara followed. She dumped the sheets in the laundry hamper and set out fresh towels, then bumped into Shelly as they both came out onto the second level balcony. In the living room below, Kensington was rattling ice cubes—he'd discovered the drinks trolley. He raised a decanter of amber liquid and called up to them, "Care to join me for a Scotch?"

Shelly leaned over the railing, her eyes brightening with anticipation. "I'll be right down, Ken." She gave her sister a wide berth and bopped gleefully down the stairs.

Lara followed with less enthusiasm. Ugh, it looked like she was in for a long evening of playing chaperon. Served Shelly right. Turnabout, as they say, was fair play.

IT WAS NEARLY eleven-thirty by the time the house guests had been seen safely to bed. Lara closed the door to her bedroom, grateful there was still one space that was hers alone. The master bedroom wasn't huge, but it had a cathedral ceiling with the same honey-colored beams and rough white plaster walls as the rest of the house. To satisfy her sybaritic side, there was also thick wall-to-wall carpet in sage-green, a carved pine armoire that housed an entertainment center, and an overstuffed reading chair in a faded mulberry, moss and cream pattern of vines and roses. The adjoining bath was just as luxuriously appointed.

Lara took a quick shower, musing over how her solitude had so enamored her that the presence of four unexpected house guests seemed vaguely like an invasion. Suddenly it was easier to sympathize with her father's demands for peace and quiet—not that *she'd* ever throw a paintbrush at Michael and Toddie for making too much noise!

She put on a silk nightshirt, then climbed into bed and clicked the TV to David Letterman. He was sitting behind his desk saying something sarcastic about Hillary's adventures in the Senate. Lara plumped her pillows and settled in, resting her head against the padded, mushroom-colored velvet headboard.

Twenty minutes later, Letterman had dispensed with his first guest and was racing through a top-ten list of the World Series losers' excuses. Lara was wide-awake and sitting up in bed painting her toenails with an old, leftover bottle of vampy black-red polish—a hideous shade that she'd actually worn in her clubbing days.

Rain spattered the windows. She shut off the TV and slid out of bed very carefully, walking on her heels to the glass door that opened to a small Juliet balcony. She flung it wide and stepped outside. A gust of wind lifted her nightshirt, but there was no one to flash. The lake and forest all around were as black and devoid of light as her toenails. Fat raindrops made splotches on her taupe silk nightshirt and ran in rivulets down her bare legs.

She turned her face up to the sky, letting the rain splash against her face so she wouldn't have to admit that she'd begun to cry.

Where had her mood come from? Emotion was indulgent. So was crying. Sure, she missed Daniel, but by now she should have grown used to their separations. Although admitting that she might be in love with him *was* rather traumatic for her stoic, armored self, it certainly wasn't worthy of melodrama and tears.

She was too strong to cry, particularly over a man. Her mother, Delphine, shed a few discreet tears whenever Ian stayed in the studio all night with a new model. Wallowing in dramatics, Shelly had gone through three boxes of tissues during the first days of her marital split.

But Lara was made of sterner stuff. She was independent and self-assured.

Rain pelted her face. Just rain. She wasn't crying.

After another minute, she stepped back through the open doorway. Forget crying. She refused to be one of those pitiful girls who played by the rules only to end up staring at the silent phone waiting for a man to call. Or standing out in the rain filled with so much longing her fingertips throbbed with it.

"I am woman, hear me roar," she muttered bleakly, stripping off the damp nightshirt and finding a towel. "I decide my own future."

Remembering that she'd sneaked Daniel's chambray shirt out of the hamper and squirreled it away in the back of her closet, she slipped it on over her bare skin with a deep sigh of pleasure. Not as good as being held in his arms, but far better than the cold embrace of rain and self-pity.

She took the telephone off the nightstand and put it in the middle of the bed. Her toenails were a gluey mess, but she ignored them in favor of speed dial. God bless speed dial. She really needed to hear Daniel's voice.

His rough-and-thick-with-sleep voice. "Hello?"

Suddenly Lara was stricken. She didn't know what to say.

"Lara?" Daniel's senses had sharpened. "Lara? Please tell me it's you."

She cleared her throat. "It's me. Sorry I woke you."

"*I'm* not."

"Ohh. So I guess I might as well have called you three days ago and saved myself all this agony?"

"I've been waiting. Not patiently, but I've been waiting." He manufactured a laugh. "Do you see what a considerate fellow I am, giving you your space and all? Letting you make up your own mind instead of pushing my bossy male opinions on you?"

"Okay, okay, I get it. Thank you. And my tortured soul thanks you, too."

"I like the sound of that. Not that I want you to be tortured, but..."

Relief. He didn't hate her for being so...so...distant. She stretched out flat on the bed, one arm tucked beneath her head, the other holding the phone, elbow in the air. "You had every right to dump me out of that rowboat after what I said. I wouldn't have blamed you a bit."

"Ah, but would you have sunk? Or would you have floated?"

"What are you suggesting? If I sink, I'm innocent, and if I float..."

"Oh, you're definitely a witch, Lara. A sexy, slinky, very bewitching type of witch. You work magic with glass and I think maybe you've worked magic on me."

She hesitated, not quite ready to take the plunge into full intimacy. Better to work up to it. "Um, speaking of glass—as in stained glass—guess who's sleeping in the bunk room?"

"Not me, thank heaven."

"Shelly."

"Then who's sleeping in the guest room?" Daniel asked. Lara could hear him stirring in bed. She imagined joining him. She imagined being joined *with* him. "Whoever he is, he's getting the first-class treatment, huh?"

"First-class accommodations, but not first-class treatment. That's reserved for you." *From here on out.*

"Can I check in permanently?"

Lara caught her tongue between her teeth before she could blurt out a lifetime invitation. "We were talking about my guest. It's Kensington Webb. Remember him?"

"The guy with the gallery? The silver-haired, silver-tongued manipulator?"

She chuckled. Trust Daniel to be a keen judge of character. "Then you do remember him."

"Yeah." He sent a *harrumph* over the line. "How'd he arrive? Helicopter?"

"He drove, all the way, by himself. Which is why he's spending the night. Shelly refused to subject him to the Adirondacks at night with only a flimsy little Porsche roadster between him and the vast, untamed wilderness."

Daniel turned the word *great* into a sarcastic growl. "He must have really wanted to see you if he was willing to venture hundreds of miles out of Manhattan."

"Oh, it hasn't been so bad. I fed him tacos. Toddie repeated all his Halloween jokes and Kensington managed to laugh. Shelly flirted with him, he drank most of my Scotch and went to bed a relatively happy man."

For a moment, Daniel went suspiciously silent. "If

you've called me after midnight just to tell me that Kensington Webb's wearing my robe..."

"I wouldn't put another man in your robe!" Lara turned her head and smothered her laughter in the mound of pillows. It wasn't that funny. She was just so relieved to know that things were going to be all right between them. Now, if she could get rid of what felt like a lump of hot coal lodged at her center, she might even begin to relax and enjoy herself. But her need to make amends for her harsh reaction to Daniel's declaration still burned.

"So why did Kensington undertake the Adirondack trek?" he asked grumpily.

"I'm not sure. There were a few business details he wanted to go over, but most of that could've been done by phone or e-mail. I guess, since the show has been moved up, he wanted a look at the panel I've been working on, to check my progress. And maybe—" Her voice cut off. She was remembering Shelly chatting on the phone and taking down Kensington's messages, dropping hints about how nice he sounded whenever Lara glanced at the Post-it notes stuck all over the fridge. Kensington, being an erudite opportunist, had probably known exactly what he'd find when he arrived to gauge the Gladstone situation in person.

"And maybe?" Daniel prompted.

"I do believe he's realized that I'm not the only daughter who can arrange an introduction to Ian Gladstone, every art dealer's favorite wet dream."

"Oh." Daniel sounded relieved at first, and then concerned. "You mean he's going after Shelly even though she's married?"

"That's a gray area at the moment." Lara rolled over onto her stomach. "I can't blame Kensington entirely. My sister's sending off signals of availability—she thinks it's a game."

"Hmm, maybe, but I still say the guy's a manipulator." Lara could hear him punching a pillow and resettling himself. "Tell me again why you've stuck with his gallery."

"It's one of the best. He's advanced my career immeasurably." She went on to explain how conflicted she felt about staying with Kensington even though his likely purpose was to milk the Gladstone name for every drop of publicity he could. "But we have a contract," she said. Realizing she'd been pressing the receiver so hard against her ear it had gone numb, she unclenched her fingers and switched sides. "Plus—oh, heck, I admit it. I like being successful. Being a Gladstone might have opened the door, but my ego is big enough to believe that my work would have been recognized even without my father's name attached to it. Eventually."

"I'm sure you're right. I liked the piece that was displayed in the restaurant even before I knew who you were. Not that I'm a noted art critic."

"I remember," she murmured. "I remember your expression. It meant more to me than pretty words."

"But then you had to go and tell me your name was Camille, just to confuse the issue."

She closed her eyes, smiling to herself. "I didn't know you. It was a game."

"The Gladstone girls are good at those."

Her stomach clutched. "Apparently."

"But what started out as a game..."

"Yes."

"...has ended as a..."

"Yes?" *Not ended,* she thought. *Never ended.*

Silence welled.

Daniel filled it. "Love match," he said.

"Oh, yes," she whispered.

She'd been lulled by the easy flow of her tenderness for him. When she realized what she'd agreed to, she opened her eyes wide and clenched her teeth with a click, then just as quickly relented. And said into the phone, softly accusing, "Sweet talker."

"How could you not have guessed that I'd fallen in love with you?" Daniel's voice was gritty with emotion, and it didn't make him sound weak. Not in the least.

An impulse flared inside her to be as courageous. But so far their relationship was all impulse. She wanted to take this most important step more slowly. "How long did you know?" she asked.

"I always knew."

"Not from the first."

"From the very first. At least I think so. There was an instantaneous connection between us. You felt it too, babe, I know you did."

She inhaled sharply, even though he was right on the mark. "How could you tell?"

He chuckled. "It was obvious. I knew you wouldn't give just *anyone* your panties."

"Maybe I would. I had a wild streak, you know."

"Still do," he said. "But now it's only for my benefit."

"Are you gloating?"

"I'm basking."

"Don't get too comfortable."

"Not with you, that's for sure. You like to keep the pot stirred, don't you? Coming right out and telling me you didn't believe in love." He made a graveled humming sound that reverberated pleasurably in her ear. "How was I supposed to respond to that? Disagree and you'd disappear again. So I decided to take my time and convince you otherwise."

"Pretty sneaky."

"Yup."

"Oh, Daniel, you snookered me." She laughed shortly and flipped to her back, the telephone cord wound twice around her neck and shoulders.

"I hope that means what I think it means."

"It means that you made me fall in love with you—you rat." There, she'd said it. But her voice was thick and clotted and vulnerable. Taken aback, she cleared her throat and continued more saucily, "You snake, you weasel, you *mole.*"

"Give it to me, sweet talker."

"Ugh, I'd like to get my hands on you—"

He moaned theatrically. "Oh, baby, oh yeah."

She burst into laughter. "Not that way!"

"You sure of that?" he taunted, and she could almost see his naughty-boy wink.

"Well..." She sat up to unwind the snarled cord, her legs crossed beneath her.

"So, lover girl, what are you wearing?"

She looked down. "Um, if this conversation is heading in that direction, how does a red satin bustier and crotchless panties sound?"

He moaned with real pleasure this time.

"Studded black leather hot pants with a chain-mail bra?"

He pretended to choke. "Does that outfit come with a whip?"

"Wait, I know. What would you say if I wore nothing at all?" Her nerve endings fluttering with excitement. "Nothing but bare skin and a blindfold?"

He was breathing heavily. Not for pretend. "I could work with that," he said, "but honestly...?"

"I'm giving away a secret here, but then I guess it's

not the first one I've let slip tonight.'' She nudged the base of the phone aside and slipped her legs beneath the sheets, curling her torso into the lavish stack of pillows. ''The truth is, Daniel, I'm wearing your shirt. Ripe and unwashed.''

''My shirt.''

''The chambray one, from last Saturday, when we...well, there are grass stains on both of the elbows and one of the snaps has popped off.''

''Oh, *that* shirt. Thanks for reminding me.'' She heard his amusement. ''I chase so many wenches through the woods that I might have otherwise mixed-up that shirt with another one.'' He paused and said quietly into the phone, his voice sounding like he was practically kissing the mouthpiece, ''May I ask why you chose to wear that specific shirt to bed?''

Lara closed her eyes and listened to the pattering rain while she breathed in and out, enveloping herself in scents and memories. ''It smells.''

''Yeah, I believe we've already established that it's ripe and unwashed.''

''You know what I mean, Daniel. It smells like you, kind of tangy with perspiration and musky male skin. It smells like the forest, like sunshine in the meadow. Like sex...''

''And love.''

''Uh-huh. It smells like love, like making love.''

They fell silent for a long while, a silence that was not empty of meaning. Then Daniel sighed deeply and said in a wry tone, ''That was the best phone sex I've ever had.''

''Ooh, boy,'' she hooted, ''if you call *that* phone sex...!''

''Can you do better?''

She knew he was telepathically leveling her with his

measured stare. Daring her. "First tell me—exactly how much phone sex *have* you had?" she teased, tucking the receiver under her chin. She hugged herself out of sheer exuberance, rocking against the pillows with her bare legs drawn up to her chest. She wiggled her toes. She even chortled. "Okay. Let's do it. Tell me what you're wearing."

"This is really boring," he warned. "I'm wearing a washed-out pair of gray sweatpants that are so baggy they're falling off my hips and so short my shins show. You might call it Nerd Nightwear. Sorry."

"Nothing to apologize for," she purred. It was easy to imagine Daniel in those sweatpants. She could see the frayed cord at the waistband that drooped below his navel, drooped far enough for her to glimpse the vertical lines of muscles that defined his groin. *Uh-uh,* sorry *was not the word.*

"See," she said, "since they're so baggy and all, it's real simple for me to slide my hand down your stomach, my fingernails grazing your sensitive skin as I reach into the sweatpants and grab—"

"Easy..."

"Oh, my gosh," she breathed. "What have I found?"

"You're the one making all the moves." He panted in her ear. "Don't you recognize it?"

"Well, it's bigger than I expected..."

"Uh, thanks, I think."

"Why, it's a pocket," she said innocently. "But what's this in it? A condom? What should I do with it?"

This time she heard him groan from far away, as if he'd dropped the phone. "Do what you want. As you've discovered, I'm prepared for anything."

She raised her voice. "I can scarcely hear you." Her shoulders shook with silent laughter. "According to phone company regulations I must disconnect this call if you can't keep at least one hand on the phone."

There was a rasping sound as he brought the receiver back to his mouth. "Fortunately I'm ambidextrous."

"Hey, lover boy, I've been in a movie theater with you. You're *multidextrous.*"

"Let your fingers do the walking, to coin a phrase."

"Okay, whatever you say. My fingers are walking up your abdomen. Slowly, very slowly—"

"Hey, what about the rubber? You're sure those fingers aren't walking *down* my abdomen? Aren't we going to have *safe* phone sex?"

"Well, no, because I'm on top now, and that's where I'm sitting, you see."

He sighed. "That's good, too."

"So my fingers are walking up your bare chest...are you ticklish?"

"Why?"

"Because now I'm teasing your nipples." She licked her lips, making certain that he could hear the smacking sound of it over the telephone line. "Mmm, they're hard. Should I keep touching them? Does that gulping, fish-out-of-water sound mean that you like this?"

"I like it very much, but I don't want to be selfish. Maybe you should touch yourself."

"Myself...?"

"And tell me all about it while you do."

Lara kicked away the sheets and blankets and slowly lifted the hem of the chambray shirt. The thrust of her breasts popped a few of the snaps as she rolled against the pillow, drawing herself up tighter, her hand sliding over the curve of her stomach and past her ribs to catch the underside of one breast in her palm. She held herself firmly, crossing her arms, pressing harder, throbbing with need. "Can I pretend that it's you who's touching me?"

"We both can." She heard his bed creak. "Your skin isn't just soft, you know. It's...alive. Sleek and pliable, and I can feel your muscles moving beneath it. I want to touch all of you. Every inch, every hot, private, secret place."

She'd pinned the phone between her cheek and the pillow and clenched her fists against her breasts, her own voice caught in her throat as Daniel's words went on and on, so hot and provocative they made her breathless with desire. She wanted to feel his arms around her. She wanted to see his face.

"Your thighs," he said, strangled. "Your eyes, your tawny skin, like a lioness."

After a long moment she found enough voice to pick up where he left off. "I'm strong, but I know how to be soft. I let you turn me, push my back up against the pillows. My thighs are open. My arms, too, pulling you toward me..." She squirmed, digging herself deeper among the pillows.

"Make yourself ready for me."

Thoughts reeling, she followed his direction, her back arching, hips tilting, fingers fumbling, sliding, tickling, opening herself to the flowing desire. "I need for you to be here with me," she gasped into the phone.

"I'm there. I'm with you, deep inside you." Daniel's voice continued to speak directly in her ear even though her head no longer seemed tethered to her body. She was insensate, her veins swelling, thrumming. "Going deeper," he said, his throaty voice seething with a vow of lust. "All of you, all of me..."

"Together," she moaned, her body an arc of quaking pleasure. "Oh, yes."

"I love you, Lara."

She held the receiver to her lips, her eyes closed, their lids quivering. "I—I've never been like this with anyone before. I must be out of my mind, I don't know what—" *She did.* "No. Yes. I mean..." She wrapped herself around a pillow, the phone sliding from her limp grasp. She had to talk fast. "Good night, Daniel, and I love you, and I'll see you soon." *If there is any mercy in the world.*

The phone dropped. With a whistling sigh, she let her head droop against the disarray of the pillows.

She felt crushed. Completely spent, rocked to the core.

But she was happy. Sweet heaven on earth, she was happier than she'd ever been in her life.

Because of a man.

One man.

"But not just any man," she whispered to herself for reassurance. And then she fell asleep.

11

BEING ESCORTED into a cheap, cheerful, noisy Greek diner tucked away on a narrow street quite a ways northeast of the financial district had startled Tamar. Daniel saw the astonishment on her face before she schooled her expression to its usual cucumber calm. He'd taken her to lunch before, on special occasions, but always to a place like The Four Seasons or the Ivy Room—places that suited her.

She slipped into the cracked vinyl booth. "Couldn't get reservations?" The brow went up. "I would have made them for you, boss."

Daniel shrugged, unconcerned. "Spur of the moment." But he was grinning inside. Tamar was perplexed. It was a first.

A guy with hairy forearms and a stained apron wrapped around his thick middle leaned over the counter and flipped them a couple of plastic-coated menus. The diner was that narrow. "Give a yell when you decide," he said.

"Classy service." Tamar plucked at the fingerprinted menu with the tips of her nails.

"Is that a complaint?" Daniel had rarely heard her complain. No need. She said it all with an upraised eyebrow.

"I'm delighted," she said dryly. "To what do I owe the pleasure?"

"Does there have to be a reason? We're two friendly

co-workers sharing a quick lunch, that's all.'' He snapped opened the menu. ''I recommend the gyros. Messy, but good.'' Tamar would really loosen up if she had meat juice dripping off her chin.

Her nostrils flared. ''You've eaten here before? And didn't come away with botulism?''

''That *is* a complaint. Why, Tamar, how human.''

His assistant's dark red lips twitched once in warning. She grabbed the menus, stood halfway up in the booth to toss them over to the counter, and barked, ''One lamb gyro, one chee'buggah platter, and make it fast, Spiro.'' Then she settled in, as collected as ever after a small shake of her sleek black head. She laced her fingers together on the tabletop and looked at Daniel expectantly.

He let out a short laugh.

Tamar's face remained blank. Waiting.

''Let's get to know each other,'' he said.

She blinked. ''We've known each other for eleven years.''

''We've worked together for eleven years. We don't *know* each other.''

''What brought this on?'' A trace of suspicion.

''I'm looking at life from a new perspective.''

Tamar took a paper napkin from the dispenser, wet it with a pointed tongue and rubbed at a spot on the speckled Formica. ''So I noticed. You do realize that you wrote a report recommending a strong buy for Nortex, not Nortech? Nortex is the company that makes the cell phone that gives shocks.''

''Did I? I'm sure you corrected me.''

''Of course.''

''I've been distracted.''

''Yes, I noticed.''

''You already said that.''

"It bears repeating." She raised her voice to be heard over the shouts of a delivery man, the clatter of dishes, a hiss of steam. "I don't want another luncheon date like this one."

Daniel was certain now. "You're laughing at me, aren't you, Tamar?"

Her expression had remained placid, but there was a glimmer of humor buried in her dark eyes. "You've developed a hearing problem? On top of the attention deficit disorder?"

"Laughing inside," he said. "I can tell." He chuckled. "I know you well enough to tell that much."

She turned her head aside to brush a fleck off the sleeve of her gray cashmere sweater. The motion made her hair swing forward against her hollow cheeks. Her bottom lip had disappeared. She was biting it. "I know you very well, Daniel. I know you sneak off to this place every Wednesday for the blue plate special—you smell like garlic when you come back. I know why you hold your thumb and index finger against the side of your face—" she demonstrated, pulling her taut skin even tauter "—during boring meetings. It's because you're secretly framing photographs. 'Broker in Brooks Brothers and Desperation.' I know that you call your parents and write them a bigger check whenever there's a rural poverty story in the newspaper. I know why you *didn't* call them this past Monday the way you usually do. I know you arranged for the company to send some freelance work to your attic tenant. I can calculate within fifteen minutes at what point in the day you'll loosen your tie. And I know what you're thinking when you do—"

Daniel held up a hand. "Stop."

Tamar stopped.

It was probably the most she'd ever said to him in one

breath. And he wasn't exactly sure why he felt so uncomfortable. Maybe because she'd observed so much about him in the course of her job when he'd thought she cared only as far as the walls of Bairstow & Boone offices. Or it could be that she'd made him see he had more connection to the people in his life than he'd believed. He had been thinking that Lara was the reason his horizons had expanded to such proportions. But maybe caring for her—*loving her*—had only opened the floodgates.

"Do I have to eat a greasy cheeseburger to prove myself, or can I go back to the office now?" Tamar asked.

"Don't go," he said. "I'm thinking." The corners of her thin lips gave a tiny hitch, but he forestalled her. "And don't say you know what I'm thinking, even though I'm sure you do."

Arms crossed, she sat back and watched him.

His mind raced, collecting the little tidbits he'd picked up about Tamar Brand. More than he'd expected. From her favorite flower—calla lilies, which she'd ordered for the limo—to the name of her mother—there'd once been an emergency in the nursing home—to her secret obsession for all things Oriental.

"I know you," he said at last, and was rewarded by the flash of surprise she couldn't quite contain. Tamar hadn't expected *that*. Neither had he. He'd been prepared to pry some information out of her, then coax her into accepting a dinner invitation to his house—for her and the mysterious man who occasionally called the office. Just to see.

But now he didn't have to.

"I might not know you as well as you know me," he said, "but I know one thing. If you were in love with this Gabriel guy, it would show."

Spots of color flared in Tamar's cheeks. "That is absolutely none of your business."

"I'm overstepping my bounds, I know. Can't help myself. Lately I seem to want to send flowers to every worker in the typing pool and dance the tango with the lady from the newstand."

"Endorphins," Tamar scoffed. "The love drug."

"Try 'em, you'll like 'em."

"I can't talk to you when you're like this." She started to slide out of the booth.

"Why?" he said. "I'm happier than you've ever known me."

"Not on Monday."

It was true. On Monday he'd been a bear. Steamrolled by his weekend with Lara and all the issue her rejection had brought up, he'd barely been able to drag himself out of bed and had arrived late for work—the first time ever. He'd growled at the poor newsstand lady with the unfortunate mustache and the blackened tooth. Even the brashest traders had stepped lightly around him.

Then Lara had called in the middle of the night. And he'd become Fred Astaire. Mary freakin' Poppins.

Tamar stood and tapped the face of her watch. "Three days and counting to your next mood swing. Not for me, thanks."

He *would* be bereft if Lara left again after this weekend. There must be a way to convince her not to.

"You don't know what you're missing," he blurted to Tamar. Just on the off chance she might admit otherwise.

Tamar only smiled. Rather gently, for her. "I prefer an even keel."

That's for sure. "What about your burger?" he asked as she walked away.

"Use it to lube your bicycle chain."

Daniel decided to eat both their lunches. He was stocking up on energy. Lara would be in town tonight. She was having dinner elsewhere, but he'd had a message from her to meet him at eleven in a bar called Viceroy's, on Broadway. While he didn't know what she was expecting, *he* was planning to stake his claim in a way she wouldn't forget. Most likely she'd be having doubts about letting him too close. But this pendulum wasn't swinging back again. Not if he could prevent it.

Mood swings were for wusses.

LARA AND BIANCA DIDN'T get to settle in for a session of girl talk till the studio had emptied around six o'clock. Several of the usual crowd had wanted to order in a pizza and stay on for a gabfest, but for once Bianca had taken in the hospitality mat. Even Eddie wasn't going to come by till later, after he'd watched a repeat of *The Sopranos.* Eddie had once sold a pair of Italian leather shoes to James Gandolfini and he'd jokingly called himself "connected" ever since.

Accompanied by Michael Junior and Toddie, Lara had taken the train into the city. Shelly had driven with Kensington—a bad idea, but they weren't listening to her. She'd brought the boys to the Gladstones' city house, a brownstone in Gramercy Park, grateful to find that Shelly had arrived in one unadulterated piece. After a quick hello to her mother—the man of the house had already been sequestered in the studio—she'd come to Bianca's, where she was always welcome to stay.

Bianca's was home.

Lara started off the catch-up talk over tiny cups of hot, rich espresso. Eddie had recently bought an espresso machine at a restaurant supply shop and given it to Bianca for the *cantina.* "What's new? Has Eddie made any progress in getting you to marry him?"

"He's stopped asking." Bianca untied the yellow scarf she'd worn as a headband á la Sophia Loren. Her brow furrowed as she ran a hand through her hair. "It's strange."

"He's playing possum."

"You think?"

"I can't see him giving up." Lara paused. "Even though it's been about two years now that he's been asking. Ever since you started showing with Rosa." The little girl had finished her dinner and was burbling happily in a bouncy chair, patting at a jumble of bright mosaic tiles in the tray.

Bianca's scowl deepened as she slumped lower on the frayed-beyond-shabby-chic chaise she'd liberated from a Fifth Avenue curbside. The Upper East Side had the best pickings. "Maybe he's changed his mind."

"Nope. Eddie's faithful as an English sheepdog." Lara sipped her coffee. "But we all need to be thrown the odd bone."

"Uh..." Bianca moaned as she stretched. "No worry there. We still sleep together. On occasion."

Lara winced. "Still making those Saturday night booty calls?"

"Not exactly." There was a long silence while Bianca slumped, unmoving. Finally she sighed. "Can a couple lapse into a boring sex life even if they're not married?"

Uh-oh, thought Lara.

"Sweet Mary," said Bianca. "If I'm going to have the dull marital blahs, I might as well have made it official."

"Has Eddie really cooled? Or could it be that he's just sick of panting after you and getting only a few pats on the head in return?"

Bianca glanced at her, clearly troubled. ''He told me he'd love me forever. That he'd be here whenever I was ready. But now...''

Lara's stomach lurched. It wasn't the espresso. ''Oh, Bianca. What are you waiting for?''

''We've talked about this. I've never felt that *zing* of the heartstrings for Eddie. I mean, look at the guy. He's a schlub. Not even close to the dashing, romantic type I expected to sweep me off my feet.''

''But you knew plenty of those kind of men. Not one of them won your heart.'' Lara wondered if she should say it. She gulped and decided yes. ''No one has touched you the way Eddie has. Maybe you didn't fall head over heels in love, but you love him all the same. You should marry him.''

Bianca didn't protest. But she didn't agree. She looked at Lara with speculation and said, ''Hmm. Something's changed, *cara mia.*''

''It doesn't matter that Rosa's not his child,'' Lara said to distract her.

Affront flared in Bianca's eyes. ''Did I say she's not?''

''I was teasing. There's the red hair...'' Lara shrugged. ''Everyone assumes she's his, you know.''

Bianca lapsed back into her funk. ''I never wanted Rosa to be the reason we got married.''

''Is there a better reason, my friend?''

''True love,'' said Bianca, looking quite unlike the woman who used to insist men were like gypsy cabs—she'd ride one when she really needed it, but they weren't to be trusted.

''True love?'' Neither was Lara as skeptical as she used to be. But she wasn't ready to believe in happy-ever-afters. As far as she could tell, marriage was an unending proposition. ''Not hot sex?''

Bianca nudged her. "Isn't *that* more your and Daniel's style?" She perked up when Lara fell suspiciously silent. "Is that a look of guilt? Are you holding out on me?"

"Well. There have been...developments."

Bianca threw her hands into the air. The yellow scarf flew. "The plot thickens at last."

Lara chuckled lazily. "You're one to talk."

Rosa threw one of the tiny mosaic tiles. It made such a pleasing clatter, she threw the rest of them, her chubby little hands flailing. Like mother, like daughter.

"Make you a deal," Bianca said, kneeling to gather them up and drop them onto the tray in handfuls. Rosa chortled and tossed them off again. "I'll get serious with my Eduardo if you get serious with Daniel."

Lara was jerked out of her complacency. Her eyes opened wide. She almost upended her cup of espresso. "You don't mean that. We always agreed that marriage is too confining."

Bianca's back was turned. "A girl's got to change with the times."

"But marriage is the antithesis of change. Isn't it?"

Bianca hugged her knees, her head bowed, letting Rosa twirl a length of her hair. "Not necessarily."

"That's not what you used to say."

One meager stretched-out diamond of sunlight slanted across the floor from the kitchen window. None of the stained glass lamps had been turned on yet, so the living area seemed unusually drab. Lara was reminded that Bianca had been living in the same spot for fifteen years. She painted frequently, rearranged her furniture, traveled whenever she could—many weekends were spent at craft shows—but, still.

"What would you do if you married Eddie?" asked Lara. "Move to the suburbs?"

"*Dio mio,* no!" Bianca rose and snapped on several lights. The bright jewel tones of the glass shades sprang to life. "But it might be nice to..." She was unusually hesitant, sliding her hands up and down her jeans-clad thighs.

Lara reminded herself that she was supposed to be encouraging her friend into marriage. "To be a real family?" she guessed.

Bianca exhaled. "Yeah." She looked at Rosa with such a cherishing, protective, hopeful love in her eyes that Lara's chest filled with a desire to know what it was like to feel so deeply. She swallowed again and again, but the ache wouldn't go away.

"Then go for it," she said thickly.

Bianca tossed her hair off her shoulders, her face glowing with life and more warmth than even her lamps. "And will you?"

Lara tried not to look stricken. "Don't count on it."

She halfway expected Bianca to pounce on her, making fiery comments in Italian, poking and prodding and insisting in that laughing, contagious way of hers, but the other woman only smiled. Rather gently, for her.

She's really mellowed, Lara thought. *But not me.*

Not yet.

VICEROY'S TURNED OUT to be a small but posh lounge filled with club chairs and cigar smokers. The light was murky—below a long narrow panel of darkly colored stained glass, green curtains on a brass pole shrouded the only window. The bar was a solid hunk of carved cherry wood, fitted out with lots of brass and a row of padded leather stools with high backs. They swiveled. Daniel knew this because he turned toward the front door every time it opened. Lara was late.

He ate pretzels until his lips puckered, then ordered a second club soda. "Twelve stepper?" said the bevested, bowtied bartender.

Daniel shook his head. His only addiction was Lara.

A slim brunette in superfluous sunglasses slipped into the seat beside his and plunked her bag on the bar. "Guiness," she said with a vaguely British accent.

Daniel looked out of the corners of his eyes. Great legs. In short boots and fishnet stockings. The woman crossed them, slowly, caressing one shapely calf against the other. She didn't look at him. Her skirt was black leather and very mini; her matching jacket open to a silver top that hugged her breasts.

He stared straight ahead, wondering what her game was. Hard to tell these days. Lara better hurry up.

The brunette took off her jacket. Her shoulders were broad, tanned and bare. She took a cigarette out of a fresh pack and leaned over to the guy on her left to let him light it, sharing a flirtatious laugh. In the mirror over the bar Daniel could see that her breasts were high and round, but her face was indistinct, hidden by wings of sleek dark hair.

She was attracting lingering looks from the cigar smokers. The bartender set down her drink. He was dubious.

The suit on her other side said, "Let me pay for that, sweetcakes," but she'd already pushed a couple of bills across the bar.

"I'm not that cheap a shag," she told her admirer, and his eyes literally went *boing*.

Daniel swiveled for a closer look.

She held the cigarette at eye level, not smoking. Her lips and short nails were dark red. A pulse beat at the base of her long neck. She was being very careful about not looking at him.

"Sweet thang, you're gorgeous," said the suit, slavering openly. "How much?"

The bartender descended, flexing his forearms. "Take it outside, you two. This isn't that kind of joint."

"She's with me," Daniel said. He put his hand on her leg. She made a silken purring sound and leaned against him so that her breasts pressed into his arm.

"Yum," she said into his ear before closing her teeth on his lobe. Daniel reacted—with a sudden sizzling shock of electricity—though he didn't particularly want to.

The suit's face had gone red. "Hey. I saw her first."

The bartender pointed. "Outside."

The brunette slid a hand inside Daniel's elbow. "Do you think I look like a chippie?" she whispered.

"You look like trouble."

"Then..." She laughed lightly, tickling his ear. "Care to buy yourself some trouble?"

"I can get it free anytime I want to. I know a girl."

"Lucky girl. But they say variety is the spice of life." She put her mouth to his ear again and listed exactly what she was willing to do. At a certain price. He couldn't help it—a raw, primal lust scorched him, like a blowtorch aimed straight at his groin.

He grabbed her hand. She grabbed her jacket.

"Hey, lady," said the suit to their retreating backsides. "Come again."

"Not till I come the first time," the brunette replied, laughing, and Daniel wrapped his arm around her waist and gave her a boost out the door. She spun across the sidewalk, her arms swinging wide, her stiletto heels clacking against the pavement. The unsmoked cigarette went arching toward the gutter, the end lighted like a firefly.

Daniel whipped off her sunglasses. "What do you think you're doing?"

Lara's green eyes laughed at him. "It was just a game."

"You were playing with fire in there," he warned. "And I'm the one who'd be burned. I might have had to fight for your good name."

"If you'd paid proper attention to me when I first sat down…"

"I checked you out."

She put her hands on her hips. "British tarts aren't to your liking?" The leather skirt was stretched taut as a drumskin across her hips; the glittery tube top was the kind that made a guy think of how easy it would be to remove. Her eyebrows had been darkened to match the wig and her face made up with a paint box of cosmetics. She looked blatant and bold and sexy as sin in a trashy sort of way, but she didn't look like Lara.

"Where do you come up with these things?" he demanded.

"These things?" She cupped her hands around her breasts and gave them a hoist. They threatened to spill out of the silver top.

"Don't do that." Daniel looked up and down the street. A cop car was cruising toward them. He moved quickly to shield Lara from view. "Put your jacket on, for crying out loud."

She slipped into it, snuggling closer to his chest, singing the lyrics to "Bad Girls" with a breathy insolence. "You're nuts," he said, holding her by the shoulders so she couldn't get away and do something worse—like flashing the officer who was peering at them as he slowly passed.

Lara peeked past Daniel's shoulder and gave a little wave. As soon as the cop was gone, she grabbed his hand and pulled him into the shadowed inset doorway of the building next door to the bar. She clutched the back of his head and kissed him deeply, being so brazen with her tongue he became aroused in spite of himself. "Got any money?" she whispered into his ear, just before nipping at the lobe again. Her teeth seemed sharper than usual.

"No."

"Not even enough for a blow job?"

"No!"

"P'raps I'll give you a freebie," she said, her hands busy at his trousers, unbuttoning, unzipping. "I can do things to Mr. Happy that you've never dared imagine, luv."

"Lara..." He grunted as she plunged a hand down his shorts. "This isn't—" Her fingers were warm and skilled. He braced himself against the stone doorway. "Not here. You have to stop." He gripped her wrist, forced her to release his raging erection before there was no turning back.

"They can't see what we're doing." Her eyes glittered at him from the deep shadows. Her ripe lips were equally hard to resist, especially when she pouted them at him, making him think of how they'd look ovaled around his erection, while her dancing tongue worked in synchronization with the heat and suction of her mouth.

He steeled his will. "Anyone walking or driving by could tell." *Especially if she was on her knees.*

She rolled her hips against his. The friction was painful, and provocative. "Take a chance."

"I only take calculated chances."

Her head tilted speculatively. She gave an insinuating chuckle. "Then, tell me. What are the odds you can resist these?" With one tug she yanked down the tube top and her naked breasts popped out, shockingly pale in the dim light, centered by the tight pink buds that inevitably drew his heated gaze.

His mouth watered. He swallowed, trying unsuccessfully not to stare as he maneuvered her around so that his body blocked hers from street view. Looming over her, both hands on her breasts—to cover them, only to cover them, even though he might be squeezing more than strictly necessary—he threatened her in a low voice that tore at his throat. "And what are the odds that you'd actually go through with this blatant invitation, hmm? If I were stupid enough to be willing?" He rubbed her nipples with his thumbs—tempting both of them.

She bit her lip, no longer so giddy. "Um. I'm game. You know I'm game."

"Right here?" He pushed up hard against her and thrust a hand between her legs, cupping the damp silk of her panties. She was hot, all right. Hot, wet and ready. He began to think that maybe…if he kept his coat on to shroud their movements….

"Sure. Right here. Right now. Give it to me, Savage."

She'd thrown her head back. The words dared him, but not her flinty voice. He remembered in a cold, sobering rush that sex alone was not what he wanted from her. Doing it in a doorway was the antithesis of intimacy.

Maybe that was why she'd offered.

"Hold still," he said, tugging at her sequined top to cover her naked charms. And just in time. A group of pedestrians strolled by, staring a few seconds too long until Daniel's glare hurried them along.

Lara shimmied against him, wiggling her breasts into place, but also keeping his nerve endings clanging—a five-alarm blaze. Dammit. He clenched his jaw. Removed his hands. He absolutely was not going to let her distract him with cheap sex. Not when they were on the verge of something ten times better.

She kept wriggling. "That's not holding still," he said.

"I'm pulling down my skirt."

She bent forward to do so and he backed off, nearly stumbling over the step in his haste. He glanced along the empty block, then stepped farther away, damning the strength of her feminine wiles. He remained painfully aroused. Searching for distraction, he cast his gaze upward and saw the Viceroy's sign above the awning. "Why the hell did you want to meet at this place? Was it the word *vice* that confused you?"

Lara stepped out of the shadows, looking more subdued despite the come-and-get-it outfit. Maybe she was ready to speak to him on a serious level at last. Her voice remained tightly strung, even when she shrugged negligently. "My father sometimes comes here. And they commisioned the stained-glass window from me."

"Sounds like two good reasons *not* to make an appearance dressed the way you are."

"I was in disguise. No one recognized me. Not even you." She flicked at the dark brown wig. "Don't be such a drag. It was all for fun."

"I don't think so." He'd suspected she'd backpedal, but this was too much. Desperation—or possibly fear—was threaded beneath the surface of her throwaway tone. Even though he dearly wanted to keep her in his arms and make sweet love to her all through the night, it was obvious that sex wasn't what Lara needed. This time, he determined, they were going to face the emotional repercussions of their growing intimacy, not evade them with nonsense about sticking to the rules of her game.

Gently he pushed her away from him. "Lara, I'd like

you to come home with me tonight, but I don't want to make love."

Her eyes widened. She attempted a shaky smile. "'S'okay. I was planning something a little more nasty."

For an instant, he imagined again what nasty might entail. But the gust of involuntary heat was soon followed by a sorrow that she was still so mixed-up. Offering fantasy in place of a reality that could be so good if only she'd let it. He'd hoped that her phone call had been the breakthrough, but obviously this relationship wasn't going to be that clear-cut.

"Not this time," he said. "I'm not your sex toy." *And you're not mine.*

"Oh. I see." Lara's face registered a confused mix of emotions before she schooled them to cool disdain. Just like Tamar, he thought, afraid to show how much she cared. Little did she know that the paint on her face and the exposed cleavage and uncovered length of her legs made her seem more vulnerable than ever, like a little girl playing dress-up. Tears of a clown.

He moved toward her again, wanting to hold her and comfort her, but she backed away. A man came out of Viceroy's. Not the suit at the bar, but another patron with a beefy face and a paunch to match, trussed up like a rib roast in his tailored suit and tight white collar. He saw them and stopped short. "Trolling for action?" he said to Lara. Leering at her breasts, he gripped his groin in a crude gesture. "You look like a hot little piece. I got just what you want—"

In a haze of fury, Daniel reacted out of pure instinct. No time for thought. Just a whistle of air and then *thud,* the cretin was lying on the dirty cement, his bloated face smashed up against the rough edge of the curb. Lara had let out a small yelp of fear. Daniel went to her, shaking his hand. His knuckles felt broken, but that was a minor inconvenience. Protecting Lara was his prime concern.

She wasn't as grateful as she might have been. "*Are you crazy?*" she screeched. "You can't do that to a guy in a suit! You'll be sued." She grabbed the front of Daniel's jacket and hauled him toward the street, one arm waving to signal for a ride. A big checker cab was going to slide right by them, but she put her fingers in her mouth and whistled with such a piercing shrill the driver was persuaded to change his mind.

Before he climbed into the vehicle, Daniel looked back at the man he'd punched. The guy was starting to sit up, looking as logy as a felled heavyweight. Ash was smeared across his forehead. A slimy food wrapper was plastered to the side of his face. A few drops of bloods had splattered his sleeve from a split lip, but otherwise he seemed unharmed. Dazed, but unharmed.

As soon as the man shook his head and began to look around for his assailant, blubbering threats, Daniel pulled the door shut. Lara was giving his address to the driver, but he corrected it as the cab pulled away. Despite his earlier invitation, he'd rather send her back to her friend, Bianca's. Even though his intentions were admirable, his control was clearly not up to snuff. He didn't normally go around beating on men any more than he treated the woman he loved like a hooker. It was smarter not to have her in his house, especially dressed as she was. Get her going on one of her outrageous fantasies and she was too tempting to resist.

And this time, he must resist. The direction of their relationship depended on it.

Lara, though confused, seemed willing to let him have his way. "Ooh, your hand," she said, cooing with the proper amount of feminine solace. She took it carefully between both of hers and kissed the reddened, stinging knuckles. "Does it hurt?"

"Not anymore." He slung his left arm across the back of the seat with his fingers clenched, trying to ignore the urge to pull her in close to his chest.

She patted the top of his hand. "That was incredible. Neanderthal dumb, but incredible. And very brave." Her eyes turned up toward his, swimming with concern, green as a warm tropical sea. *Aw, hell,* he thought, and put his arm around her. He touched a kiss to her lips. Just one.

"Sure you don't want to take me back to your place, you big, brave hero?" Her voice was husky—very dangerous to his resolve. And then she made it worse for him, cuddling against him, her slender body feeling distractingly soft and pliable.

"You're going home," he said through clenched teeth. "To your friend's house, that is."

"That's home," she said simply. No explanation, though he hardly needed one by now.

She began playing with his hand, cupping her palm around it, lightly tracing her fingertips over his sore knuckles. When she murmured softly, he had to bend his head toward hers to catch her words. "I'm sorry if I went too far tonight. I thought it would be..." She breathed deeply and exhaled with a regretful sigh. "Wicked good fun."

He closed his eyes for a moment, struggling within. "It might have been. Another time. This once, I was planning on something a little more conventional. Given the evolution of our relationship."

She shot him a wary look. "That's kinda what I was afraid of. Do we have to get all formal and serious now, just because of...uh, you know?"

"Because you said—"

She interrupted. "Words are just words. They're not concrete. Not chains."

"Then why are you so scared of them?"

"I don't know. Words should be—" She stopped. Stuck out her chin. Her eyes searched his, charged with a combatant fervor. "Let's call a spade a spade. We're not talking about words. We're talking about...love. And I believe that *love* should be fluid and changeable. But it's not—not in most definitions."

"Can't we make up our own definition as we go along?" He grazed his palm across the unnatural barrier of the brunette wig, longing to see her gold-brown hair tumbled across her shoulders. He remembered wondering how it would look spread across a pillow. The answer was very good. Unfortunately, he'd had rare occasions to see it that way. She seemed to prefer anything but the conventional intimacy of a bed.

"Ideally we would." Lara pulled on her bottom lip.

"That's like saying, 'In a perfect world...'"

"Right. My point precisely."

The cab jounced in a pothole, going south down Broadway.

"Then what's the solution?" Daniel asked, though he could see no answer. Despite any reassurances he might offer, Lara had to make up her own mind. There were no guarantees. She had to discard her cynicism and become optimistic enough to believe in their chances of making it. "How can I convince you that love and marriage aren't to be dreaded?"

She'd dropped his hand and was withdrawing again, her face becoming a mask, beyond the garish makeup. Frustration tore through him. "God, Lara, sometimes you remind me so much of Tamar!"

"Tamar Brand? The perfect executive assistant, wife

and mind reader all rolled into one? Miss Johnny-on-the-spot?''

"That's your definition of a wife. Not mine.'' He had to look away from her. They were now caught in a snarl of traffic in the East Village, where a three-car fender-bender was clogging the street.

Lara aimed her gaze at the back of the cabbie's head. Her mouth was set. "I am not Tamar.''

"Aside from sex, you're just as closed off.'' When she didn't respond, Daniel stared out the window at the accident drama being played out for a gathering of voluble onlookers—New York street theater. After a while he said, "I had lunch with Tamar today, thinking it was time—past time—we became better friends. But she's not willing. She'd rather stay aloof. It's...sad.'' He turned back to Lara. "Do you want to live your life that way?''

"I am not Tamar,'' she repeated. She dropped her head into her hands as the cab began moving again, then suddenly raised it, her expression brightened. "Look at my aunt. Teal never married. She's strong, independent, productive and happy. She has family and friends. She's lived a good life, on her own terms.''

Damn that Teal, Daniel thought grumpily. "Then that's what you want? To live out your life all alone on Coppercrown Lake?''

Lara offered him a wan smile. "I thought you could keep visiting on the weekends.''

He shook his head. "That's not enough for me.''

"But I told you that I love you! Isn't that *enough?*''

He couldn't answer. His head was filled with thoughts of Tamar's detachment—which mirrored his own as well as Lara's—his parents' unhealthy mutual dependence, his own focused climb out of the lower class and how he'd overlooked so much along the way. Things like taking time for friends and family, the simple enjoyment of everyday life and the possibility that tomorrow would be even better than today. Everything he wanted to share with Lara and wasn't going to be able to. Unless…unless…

A wrenching pain gnawed at him from the inside out. He thought it might be his newly awakened heart breaking in two.

The taxicab had pulled up near Bianca Spinelli's graffiti-ridden storefront. Lara stopped him with a hand on his arm when he started to climb out to escort her to the door. "Don't," she said, her voice as dry as dust. "I don't need—" She gave a small cry, a gasp that caught in her throat. "I don't need your—your concern and devotion and, and—"

She couldn't finish.

He hadn't the heart to do it for her.

"When you do need it," he said quietly, "you know where to reach me. Even if you can't believe in…*its* power, I have *enough* for both of us."

Lara fled.

12

"A RECONCILIATION DINNER with the Gladstones." Lara plunked ceramic plates one by one onto the festively dressed dining table. "This is not a good idea."

"Meet the Gladstones," Bianca sang in tune to a familiar cartoon jingle. "Meet the Gladstones. Have a yabba-dabba-doo time—"

"Abba-doo-dime," Rosa chimed, toddling across the tile floor.

Bianca swooped in, taking her daughter's face in her hands and smacking kisses all over her round cheeks. "Very good. May you grow up to be an opera singer, *mia cara bambina.*"

"This is *not* a good idea," Lara repeated.

"Too late to back out," Bianca said.

"He won't come." Ian Gladstone didn't waste time on inconsequential details and unimportant social engagements. He had his wife for that.

"Quit worrying, kiddo." Bianca had telephoned the invitations. "Daniel will be here with bells on."

"Daniel! You invited him? I meant my father!" Lara clutched the back of a chair. "Oh, no. Daniel's coming? With my family? Oh, no, no, no." She cringed inside. She'd been feeling horribly embarrassed about the past night's incident—What was *wrong* with her, dressing up as a *hooker?*—and was not looking forward to seeing

Daniel again. Especially so soon. Seeing as she'd thrown herself at him. And he'd flung her back.

True, his rejection had come in the name of love...but still. She was stung to the quick.

"It's a reconciliation dinner for all those we love. Of course I invited Daniel, you goof."

For a change, Lara decided to stop thinking about her own love life and focus on Bianca's. "What about Eddie?"

Bianca frowned. "Eddie?"

"The father of your child. The love of your life. The only man in the world who can keep step with the Queen of the Discotheque." Lara reached for the wall phone, smiling pointedly. "Eddie should know as soon as possible that you have become reconciled with the idea of marriage."

Bianca's lips thinned in a matching smile. "You're so right. Make the call."

Lara dialed the shoe shop, somewhat peeved that Bianca had called her bluff. The dinner, which was to include both Shelly and her estranged husband as well as the elder Gladstones, was a disaster in the making. She didn't know how she'd been talked into allowing it, though her muzzy head—*This is your brain without sleep*—may have played a part.

Eddie was agreeable. He even offered to bring flowers, wine, dessert, arsenic—anything they needed. "That's done," Lara said, hanging up.

"One of us will be engaged before the night is through," Bianca predicted.

"Marriage, schmarriage," Lara muttered, feeling stupid and bumbling and childish about the whole thing. What would Teal do? she wondered. *Deep-six the lot of them. Dig in at the lake and refuse to budge.*

Not an option. Already she missed Daniel too much.

"What makes you think we won't have a disaster on our hands? You've met my family." Lara paced the tiled floor. Rosa chased her, her short legs churning. If ever there was a man who could take Ian Gladstone in stride, it was Daniel. Was that what worried her? That he would handle her family as easily as he handled her?

Leaving her with no defenses and no excuses.

Daniel had a way of putting things. She'd thought about their conversation all night, with a straighter head than she usually managed. Her ego-born battles with her father, her pity for her mother, her discomfort with their unequal marriage—they'd all been colored by the usual family complications and the limitations of her own thick head. Daniel had made her see that she needed to reach past those bonds. To embrace the possibility of…of…

That's all you get. All he can promise.

A possibility.

It didn't feel like enough to her.

Bianca hummed to herself, swaying her hips as she gave the penne pasta a stir. Rosa switched directions and went to cling on her mother's skirt, waggling her own diapered bottom in imitation.

"Stop being so cheerful," Lara said. "I'm having a crisis here."

"Ah, Lara." Bianca looked at her fondly. "That's no crisis. You're maturing before my very eyes."

Lara sat at the breakfast bar, hooking her legs around the stool. "Remember how we used to find a pair of pretty boys with earrings and attitudes and party all night, then at five in the morning go up on the roof to eat chorizo and chile peppers and recite e.e. cummings or Wallace Stevens to the dawn? We swore we'd never become dull married folk."

Bianca laughed as she swayed. "These days I'm more a Pablo Neruda girl." Her long patterned rayon skirt swished around her ankles. She was in sandals, a gold ring on one toe. Rosa, who'd plopped down to remove her shoes and socks, was equally colorful—her tiny finger and toenails were painted neon green.

"I for one have no intention of becoming dull." Bianca dropped a wedge of dripping Roma tomato into her mouth and chewed. "Mmph. Eddie told me the other day that our cells are continually renewing themselves. Every seven years or so, we become a whole new person."

Lara shook her head. "People don't change."

"Maybe not. It might mean that our tastes and experiences never grow old. Every seven years, it's like starting over. Life begins anew with a wealth of possibility."

There was a dramatic pause before Lara said in the flattest tone possible, "What a load of blarney."

Bianca caught her eye and snorted. "I know." They looked at each other and burst into laughter. They laughed until they were giddy, mostly because it felt so much better than angst. Rosa joined in, her big eyes sparkling, taking in the noisy joy as though it were nourishment. Which was what Lara had done, all those years ago, when she had found this place and the life teeming within it.

With Daniel, she'd renewed her zest. She may have cloaked that discovery in the guise of a sexual adventure, but they'd always been about more than mere fun and games. She couldn't fool herself any longer on that point.

This time, she wondered, holding her ribs as she sobered, would she retreat to her solitude or would she advance into the future, whatever it held?

Goodbye, giggles. Hello, anguish.

"I'm going to be a total girl and go take a bath," she told Bianca, checking the black-and-white checkerboard clock. "I have forty minutes before our first victims arrive." Her lips twisted into a self-mocking smile. "Hey, just enough time to go soak my head."

MICHAEL ROBINSON, Shelly's husband, was the first arrival, looking both eager and tense, but mystified by his summons to a dingy little art-glass studio in the East Village. He was a clean-cut M.B.A. who'd gotten into a dot-com business that had made a splashy debut but was now teetering on the edge of bankruptcy, not that you could tell it by looking at him. Except for a few faint lines on his forehead, he hadn't changed from the privileged college prepster who'd won Shelly's eighteen-year-old heart. The only rash thing either of them had ever done was to get married so young. They'd seemed happiest during the first days of their marriage, before work, parenthood and rampant consumerism had distracted them from each other.

Exclaiming over such generosity, Lara took the flowers Mike had brought—an aster bouquet for the house and a bundle of red roses for Shelly. She led him on the two-bit tour, pointing out some of Bianca's glasswork, then bringing him around to the back where the woman herself was offering wine and munchies. The gregarious Italian could set anyone at ease.

Eddie Frutt came in next, loud and boisterous, with a fresh shave and haircut, his arms laden with gifts: fruit, wine, flowers and a bakery box of puff pastry. "Ach! What happened to your lovely red curls?" Bianca shrieked. "Now you have no more hair on your head than my puny Uncle Alfredo, the one who looks like a chihuahua!"

Unconcerned, Eddie piled his offerings into Lara's arms and hoisted the laughing Rosa onto his shoulder. "Less for the little one to grab at,'' he said, and Bianca went over and took him by the ears to give him a big kiss.

Lara introduced the men and soon they were talking about how Eddie should make up a faux outdoor-adventurer name that would work better than Frutt's Footgear, set up a Web site with Himalayan wallpaper, quadruple the prices on his top line of hiking boots, and sit back to rake in the cash.

''Money, the common denominator,'' Lara whispered to Bianca, who, truth be told, was looking rather nervous beneath her cheer. Lara gave her a quick hug and a whispered reassurance that she didn't believe—for herself. If the evening was a success for anyone, it would be Bianca and Eddie.

Someone banged on the studio door.

''That would be for me.'' The blood drained from Lara's face. ''It's either the lady or the tiger.''

Daniel stood on the other side of the steel-reinforced security door. She'd intended to let him know right off that the reconciliation dinner wasn't her idea, but somehow the words wouldn't come. He was too darned good-looking. Not even spiffed up—he wore faded jeans and a gray sweater with a bright blue collar showing—but devastating all the same. When she looked into his eyes, longing swelled inside her and she lost all contact with solid ground. The man could lift her off her feet without a single touch.

So don't look into his eyes, you goof. Her gaze dropped to his midsection. *''Oh,''* she breathed. ''Wow.'' He'd brought flowers *and* wine *and* dessert—gorgeous freesia and yellow roses, a bottle of red and a bottle of white, plus another pink box from the bakery. Tied with a string and dangling from his finger. Not unlike her. She was a balloon on a string—all knotted up and hovering in midair, waiting for the pinprick.

"Daniel Savage!" Bianca pushed open the swinging doors. "*Pronto!* I've heard so much about you, you're already counted as a friend. Come in, come in. We are eating prosciutto and plotting a capitalist takeover of Avenue B." She flung up her hands, bracelets jingling, and said "*Pazzo!*"—Men!—before disappearing behind the doors again.

"That was Bianca," Lara said.

"I guessed," Daniel replied. "She's kind of unmistakable."

Lara felt awkward. You'd think they'd never been intimate, she thought. *Snap to. This man has been inside your body. Deeper than you ought to have allowed.*

"Do you want to come in?" she asked, then blushed furiously.

"All the way in," he said, his gaze direct. She couldn't be one-hundred percent sure he'd meant that the way it sounded. Was she mistaken, or were his eyes hot as molten pewter?

No mistake, she thought, meeting his gaze in midair. They were.

"You never miss a trick." She floated to one side to let him enter. "Except last night." She claimed the cake box, then the flowers, murmuring thanks.

"I like you better this way," he said, taking in her simple blouse, long red skirt and embroidered Chinese flats borrowed from Bianca.

She touched her cheek. Warm. "Mortified, you mean?"

"Don't be, Lara, my love." While his voice might have seemed soft and soothing, it remained as arousing to her senses as the stroke of his tongue against her skin. "Any other time," he continued, dropping an octave, "I'd have been all over you in the back seat of that taxi."

She peered at him through her lashes. He had the audacity to wink.

"Promises, promises," she said, as the doorbell rang shrilly several times in quick succession.

Not her father. He was the impatient type, but lazily so. He sat back and *expected* to be served. She threw the dead bolt and Shelly fairly leaped into the room, one hand clenched to the sleeve of her companion. "This neighborhood! My goodness. I thought we were going to get mugged on the doorstep."

Lara goggled at Kensington Webb. "We?" she repeated. "Uh, Shelly. You brought a guest?"

"Why, yes, of course I did." The young woman unbuttoned her coat. "I wasn't going to be the fifth wheel."

"Didn't Bianca explain...?"

Shelly cocked her head. The tendrils of her French twist becomingly framed her rosy cheeks and slender neck. Dressed in pink with pearls, she looked about twenty and completely naive. "Explain what?"

Kensington seemed unconcerned. He'd pulled out a handkerchief and was dusting off the front of his Abercrombie & Fitch topcoat.

Lara felt the heat of Daniel's body behind her. Oh, good, she thought. If she fainted, he'd be there to catch her. "It seems there's been a mix-up." She juggled the cake box and flowers, freeing up an arm to take the new guests' coats. "Um. I guess you'd better follow me." There didn't seem to be any way out of it, other than a convenient firebomb. "This way."

She led them through the swinging doors and into the living area of Bianca's eccentric lair. "This is my sister, Shelly Robinson," she told the assembled group. She nodded her chin in the direction of the men. "And Daniel Savage and Kensington Webb." Lumping them together might throw Shelly's husband off the scent. "Talk amongst yourselves. I have cakes to cut and flowers to arrange."

Bianca followed her into the kitchen and gathered up the coats Lara had dropped half on a chair, half on the floor. "Your face looks like cottage cheese. What did Daniel say?"

"Nothing. I mean, he was an imperfect gentleman. Just the way I like him." With shaking hands, Lara tore off the wrappings and jammed the bouquet into an art vase that looked like it had melted in the kiln.

"Then why do you look curdled?"

"Well, geesh. Let's see. Our dinner guests include an estranged couple and the man who'd screw them over for an opportunity to shake my father's hand. Plus a lover who insists on being in love—"

"The gall," Bianca inserted.

Lara grimaced. "And. And, and, *and* there's the late, great artist, himself, who probably wouldn't show up at all except that my mother will drag him here." She glanced around the kitchen. "Where did Daniel put those bottles? We're going to need lots of alcohol. Lots and lots and lots."

"Are you okay, Lara? You're echoing." Bianca thumped her on the back as if she had hiccups. "It won't be so bad. By the evening's end, you'll see. It's much better to get everything out in the open. In fact, I'm looking forward to it."

"I always suspected you had a sadomasochistic streak."

Bianca gestured. "Look at them, it's fine."

Lara put her fingers over her eyes. "It's going to be tragic. High drama always is."

"I'll serve the stuffed jalapeños before then. That way *everyone* will be red and teary eyed."

Lara stole a quick glance at the dining area. With Eddie paving the way, Kensington was being killingly kind, Shelly—surrounded by gorgeous men—jittery with excitement, Mike strained but trying to understand. And Daniel?

At the moment, he was ignoring the other guests.

He was watching *her*. With such a tenderness, so much caring and love—*and desire*—that Lara welled up. She swallowed, and swallowed again, but it didn't help. She began to know what Mount Vesuvius must have felt.

Blindly she extended her palm to Bianca. "Give me one of those peppers. *Now*."

LARA LOOKED like she had a fever. So did her sister. It might have been the dinner—there were enough spices, chilies and pesto in the ethnic meal to qualify their tonsils for emergency Red Cross relief, but Daniel sort of doubted that. They'd made it through the preliminaries okay, but now that the second round of wine had been poured and the main course served, the underlying tension had upped its heat from a simmer to a boil. Small bubbles of contention kept rising to the surface.

The doorbell gave one long imperious ring.

"My father," Lara said, and dropped a slice of bruschetta in her lap.

Daniel rescued it and set it on her bread plate. "He's late."

Kensington Webb, who'd lapsed into a bored silence, lifted his head like a bird dog sniffing the air for a buckshot partridge. He dabbed his mouth with a corner of the flea market fifties-style tea towels that served as napkins.

"He's really late," said Bianca. "What nerve. We've eaten all the jalapeños."

Shelly blinked, her face blank. "Dad doesn't eat peppers. Not around Mom, anyway. It's bad for his indigestion."

"Is someone going to answer the door?" Mike Robinson asked, keeping his eyes on his wife as he had for the past thirty minutes. Daniel couldn't tell if he'd figured out that she was with Kensington or if he was smitten all over again. Maybe both. There was an attraction between the estranged couple that was palpable.

"I'll do it," Eddie and Daniel said together.

Lara shoved back her chair. "Sit down. I will." She exhaled. "Do the honors."

"Presto." Bianca waved her napkin; crumbs flew. "Time to meet the parents."

For once, complete silence descended upon the dinner table. They all listened as Lara opened the door and exchanged greetings with the late-arriving guests. Mrs. Gladstone sounded worried, her soft voice trilling apologies. Mr. Gladstone said only a few gruff words, not sorry in the least. "I haven't been to Alphabet City since 1956," he was heard to observe.

Bianca snickered. "Neither have the beatniks. Or the mayor, for that matter."

"Or the waste commissioner," Eddie added.

They clasped hands and said in unison, "We're so blessed."

She kissed his knuckles. "We are."

"You mean that?"

Bianca was suddenly misty-eyed. "Yes, darling. I do."

"Dawling doo," chimed Rosa in her high chair.

Lara cleared her throat. She'd stopped just inside the doorway, holding another bakery box. The Gladstones stood beside her. "I hate to interrupt a tender moment, but here we are." Everyone stood, with much scraping of chairs and clearing of throats. She drew her mother forward, made introductions all around. "Everyone—Delphine Gladstone, my mom. She brought amaretti cookies and hazelnut biscotti."

Delphine was a tall, slender woman with a beautiful, fragile face and dark hair streaked with gray. She looked at the colorful, slapdash, all-in-one great room, then at the table, in a state of semi-wreckage. "We're terribly late. I'm so sorry, Bianca. We couldn't get a taxi, and then the traffic..." She seemed ready to crumple in humility. "I do apologize."

"My fault," said Ian Gladstone. "My daughters will tell you I'm never on time. Lara says it's because I expect the world to spin at my pace, not the other way around." He fingered his bushy white beard. "She could be right."

Lara gestured and said, "And here's the man who needs no introduction." She stopped there.

Kensington glided forward, practically genuflecting. "It's an honor, sir. A genuine honor."

Gladstone vigorously pumped the art dealer's hand. Kensington's eyes nearly crossed. "Webb, eh? Do I know you?"

Lara gave an audible sigh. "Kensington Webb from Kensington Webb Galleries, Dad. He represents me. I've mentioned it."

"We met once at Sotheby's, sir. They were auctioning your painting *Sediment, 1972.*"

Gladstone squinted. "You buy it?"

Kensington's obsequious smile faded. "The Tate did. For one million pounds. You don't recall, sir?"

"Bah! I pay people like you to remember that crap." By his expression, Kensington couldn't decide whether to be insulted or hopeful. It didn't matter. Gladstone had already moved away, his eye on Bianca. He took her hand and kissed it. *"Buona sera, bellissima,"* he said, taking measure of her hourglass figure.

Bianca thought that was amusing. Gladstone skipped Rosa, nodded at Eddie, looked Daniel in the eye. "Sir," he said, and they shook. Gladstone had a grip that could crush marble into dust. Daniel tried not to wince as the man squeezed his scraped knuckles, thinking that next time he'd go ahead and challenge the old guy to an arm-wrestling match so they could skip the bone crushing. Lara hovered, nervously reciting Daniel's professional qualifications, but Gladstone merely said, "Grmph," and released him to enfold Shelly in a bear hug.

"That was fun," Daniel muttered. He shook his hand until the blood came back to it.

"You got off light," Lara said out of the side of her mouth as the assemblage reseated themselves.

"What are we having?" Gladstone said greedily, tucking a cherry-printed napkin into his collar. His thick white hair was leonine, his broad face as rough and brown as if it had been hatcheted out of a slab of hardwood. The term *larger than life* sprang to Daniel's mind. No wonder Lara found it hard to compete. It was a wonder that she tried.

"The main course," Bianca said, ladling out the sausage penne and mushroom salad without apology. "We've eaten the appetizers." When the others had wanted to wait for the late arrivals, she'd insisted they begin. Her pasta waited for no man, not even a famous one.

"It's all right, Mom," Lara whispered when Delphine started in with the excuses again. "Bianca's dinner parties go with the flow. Have some of the bruschetta. There's goat cheese."

Shelly beamed. "This is fun. I never get to this side of town. Your house is something, Bianca. It's so eccentric."

"Quite colorful," Kensington said, looking like he meant *terribly gaudy*.

Delphine smiled bravely. "Now I understand why Lara came here so often. In my day, we called ourselves Bohemians."

"Were you both Bohemians?" Eddie asked the Gladstones.

"About four decades ago," Lara said. "Before Sotheby's and the like."

"Nothing wrong with success," Ian Gladstone said, tucking in with gusto. "Got to keep the little woman in dresses, shoes and handbags."

"Sure. Before you, Mom was wandering around Paris in sackcloth and bare feet." Lara tore off a chunk of bread and chewed voraciously.

Delphine frowned. "I've always had plenty of shoes...." Her voice trailed off to a strained silence.

"I like going barefoot," Bianca said to break it. "It's so tactile."

Shelly's mouth puckered. "But dirty."

"Now, now," Eddie said, mopping his plate with a crust. "My parents always said, 'No dirty feet at the dinner table.'"

Daniel grinned. "Mine didn't."

Kensington sniffed with distaste. "The very definition of class, were they?"

Gladstone glanced at the art dealer beneath bristly white brows, dismissed him and shoveled in a heaping forkful. "Good chow."

"Very tasty," Delphine said in quick agreement.

Gladstone mopped his mouth with the napkin. "I'll take another helping." His wife reached for the serving spoon.

Mike Robinson had been sitting in silence, now and then taking a bite of the food when he tore his gaze away from Shelly. Suddenly he dropped his utensils, picked up his wine, set it down, lifted it to his mouth a second time, then blurted, "When are you going to come home?" before gulping down all of it at once.

"You should have brought a case," Lara said to Daniel.

"What?" Shelly squawked. "Home?"

"Are you waiting for me to beg?" Mike threw aside his napkin and got down on one knee. "Okay. I'm begging. I want you back. Are you satisfied?"

Shelly covered her mouth. "O-o-oh," she warbled.

"Big mistake," Gladstone said, sucking his teeth as he stared at his son-in-law with disdain. "Now she's got you by the short hairs."

"Ian," censured Delphine.

He burped. "Just telling it like it is."

"Shelly?" said Mike from the floor.

She threw a distracted glance at Kensington, who'd pulled back his head like a turtle retreating into its shell.

"Don't look at him," Mike said. "Look at me, dammit." He did a double take. "Why *are* you looking at him?"

"I'm not looking at Ken, sweetie. Ken doesn't mean a thing to me."

Mike surged to his feet. "Ken?" he repeated. "You call him Ken? Is *this* the man you drove into the city with?"

Shelly paled visibly. "How did you...?"

"The boys told me. They e-mailed me."

"Oh, well, of course. It's not like they'd actually get to talk to you in person."

"Don't change the subject. I want to know what's going on between you and that oil-slick kiss-ass." He clenched his fists, glowering at the art dealer.

"Don't worry," Lara said. "Kensington doesn't want to sleep with Shelly. He wants to sleep with our father." All faces turned to her. She waved a hand. "In a manner of speaking."

"I really don't care for that manner of speaking," Delphine protested, but no one seemed to notice.

Kensington's features were pinched. "I am insulted."

Gladstone guffawed. "How do you think I feel?"

"Maybe 'get in bed with' is the more apt phrase," Lara said.

Shelly's voice rose above the ensuing murmurs. "I haven't been in bed with anyone!"

"Do you swear?" Mike said, putting his hand on her elbow and urging her up beside him. He stared into her eyes. It was a stirring Ken-and-Barbie moment. "Because I haven't been either."

"Of course not." Even though Shelly tried to pout, she looked thrilled. "You eat, sleep and breathe your business."

"We've turned the corner at last. The business is going to survive." Mike coaxed her away from the table. "I'll have more time for you and the boys..." he was saying as they walked toward the seating area, murmuring fervently out of earshot of the dinner party guests.

"You see?" Bianca smiled at Lara. "Love has unique properties. It's like a law of nature." She held up two fingers, ten inches apart. "Magnet. Steel. All we had to do was put them in proximity and—" Her fingertips touched.

Eddie pulled his napkin out of his lap, untucking his shirt as he did. He went down on one knee. "If that's so, we should have been living together two years ago. Bianca..." He took her hand. "You are my magnet. Let's make it official."

Gladstone peered across the table. He harrumphed. "What kind of proposal was that?"

"Not a proper one," Kensington immediately agreed.

Gladstone looked at him. "You still here? Make yourself useful, hey? I need more wine."

Delphine started to rise. Lara held her back. After a lengthy pause, Kensington skulked into the kitchen.

By then, Bianca was sitting on Eddie's knee, kissing his face all over. "You have a spot of pesto sauce on your tie," she said between kisses, "but that's okay because it's the ugliest tie I've ever seen." Eddie looked down and she kissed his bald spot. "Your shirt is untucked." She flung her arms around him. "And I don't care. Because I love you. I love you, Eddie Frutt!"

Daniel wanted to applaud, but instead he slid his arm around Lara's waist and gave her a kiss. He bent his knees, as though ready to go down. "Give you any ideas?"

She was startled. Not in a good way. "Don't you dare, Daniel Savage."

His heart dropped. "I wasn't going to." *At least not here.*

Lara watched him suspiciously. He couldn't tell whether or not she was secretly disappointed that he continued to stand erect.

"My goodness," said Delphine, blinking at the embracing couple. She looked at her husband. "Perhaps we ought to leave?"

Gladstone appeared to be enjoying himself, but he

stood, picked a sliver of blackened portobello mushroom off his beard, and said, "I need a cigar anyway."

"But we have all these cookies and cakes," Lara said, putting up a token protest. She seemed relieved as she followed them through the studio. Mike and Shelly joined the group, wanting to split a cab. They departed in a flurry of apologies, goodbyes and kisses. Lara stayed at the door until they were safely in a cab and then she turned to look at Daniel, her shoulders rigid.

"That wasn't so bad," he said, wanting to gather her up even though she was giving off as many don't-touch-me signals as a porcupine.

"Could have been worse," she admitted.

"Your father was fine."

"He's a boor."

"He's blunt. I liked him."

"Men usually do." She sighed. "He's a man's man. All that raging I-don't-give-a-damn-if-I-trample-on-the-little-woman's-feelings testosterone. For him, women are either maids or—or—"

"Hookers?" Daniel said, feeling one of his brows doing a Tamar arch.

Lara flushed bright pink.

"Did everyone leave?" Bianca came into the studio. Eddie followed, his face marked red with lipstick. He was holding hands with Rosa, who was beating on his thigh with her baby spoon. All three fairly glowed with happiness, unless that was the smeared lipstick.

"We didn't do dessert," Bianca complained. "And I was going to give everyone a mini art show afterward. Show off a little for the great artist."

"Don't worry about it," Lara said. "You were otherwise occupied." Her gaze traveled around the room, a large industrial space with exposed electrical conduits and raw cement-block walls, fitted out with worktables and slotted cabinets and drawers that held sheets of glass. Stained-glass artwork hung suspended from the rafters and in the barred window. "My father wouldn't have been interested anyway."

Daniel couldn't say that she was wrong.

Kensington pushed through the swinging doors, a bottle held out before him, his upper lip curled in a sneer as he peered into its neck. "The cork broke. Cheap wine." He felt them staring and looked up. Dismay crossed his face, then suspicion. "What did you do with Ian?"

"Sorry," Daniel said. "He heard there was cork in the wine, so he escaped."

"But this was my best chance to—" Kensington stopped himself. He looked at Lara speculatively, gradually transforming his demeanor from art shark to ardent suitor.

"Watch out," Daniel whispered to her. "Here comes the old drop-down and suck-up maneuver."

Her chin jutted. "Don't even think about it, Kensington. By God, I'll kneecap you if I have to!"

13

"TWO OUT OF THREE isn't bad," Lara said. They'd eaten dessert, Daniel had gone and Rosa was put to sleep. She swung her lower leg back and forth. "Not that I'd count on Shelly and Michael lasting without a number of dust-ups along the way."

"Every married couple has those," Eddie said, his hand on Bianca's knee.

"Are you two actually going through with it?" As thrilled as Lara was for them, she couldn't help feeling rather like an unappetizing party leftover. Left out. Or that burst balloon. In pieces. What happened to strong and independent, she wondered, turning in the rump-sprung armchair and curling her legs beneath her.

"We'll live together first." Bianca was snuggled beneath Eddie's arm on the chaise, her sandal-clad feet propped on the low, rolled arm. "Maybe we'll get around to the marriage thing before too long."

Eddie made a face that Bianca couldn't see. "We will."

"Will what?" she said, tilting her head back.

"Get around to the marriage thing," he said. "And soon."

"Ooh. So commanding."

"Patience did me no good."

Bianca wrapped his arms around her shoulders, resting her head in the crook of his elbow. Lara thought they looked the picture of domestic bliss, until Bianca said, connivingly, "There's a lesson for Daniel. You might clue him in, Eddie."

"Sheesh." Lara stuck out her legs and stretched like a cat, pulling her hair back from her face. "Leave us alone. We've been together for only a month or so. You two took five years!" She remembered when Eddie had moved back to New York from a stint in the Peace Corps and taken over his father's shoe store. She and Bianca had taken one look and declared him a middle-aged frump. Over several years of gradual acquaintance, they'd learned to love him for his genial, generous nature and respect for humankind. One of them more than the other.

Bianca patted Eddie's furry, freckled arm. "Only three years since we started sleeping together."

He heaved a sigh. "It took me a long time to persuade her to surrender."

"Surrender? Never!" She kicked a foot in the air for emphasis. "I haven't surrendered, you dope. I've triumphed."

Surrender? That was rich. Tugging on her hair, Lara watched the couple owlishly. *Surrender* was exactly how she thought of marriage, even love. That she was twisted enough to want to play out the same game in her sexual fantasies was something she'd come to accept. But just because she wanted to be conquered in bed didn't mean she wanted it in real life.

"Can't we both be the victors?" Eddie said. "I'm planning to go up to the roof and pound my chest like Tarzan, you know. I want everyone to hear about our big news."

Bianca chuckled. "Fair enough."

Lara twisted around again, trying out the lotus position. *So easy for them,* she thought, momentarily forgetting the past few years. *Why do I have to make it so difficult?*

Bianca was watching her with a brooding expression.

''You've either got fleas or you've got an itch. I vote for the second. Why didn't you go with Daniel and work it out of your system?''

''He doesn't want me.''

''Don't get all Sylvia Plath on us. Of course he wants you. A blind person could see how much he wants you.''

Lara scowled. ''Right. But it turns out he's an all-or-nothing sort of guy.''

Bianca shook her head. ''Sounds familiar, no?''

''No. I'm not...like that.''

''The hell you're not,'' Eddie said.

''Two out of three isn't bad,'' Lara insisted. ''Let's leave it at that.'' She put her feet on the floor. ''I should go to bed.'' It had been an eventful evening and there was a daybed in Rosa's room with her name on it. She could get psychoanalyzed tomorrow.

''Two out of four,'' Bianca said, stopping her.

''How do you figure?''

''Me and Eddie, Shelly and Mike. That's two.'' Bianca sat up, pulling her patterned skirt over her legs. ''You and Daniel—three. I'm putting a hold on that result. The fourth reconciliation was *supposed* to have been between you and your father.''

''We're not fighting,'' Lara said. She stooped to pick up her Chinese shoes. They had paper-thin soles; she folded them between her hands like tortilla rounds. All right, yes, she was antsy.

''You've been battling with him all your life.''

She shrugged. ''That's just family. The usual struggle.''

''Maybe so. Still, isn't it time you made peace? He's not gonna change. But you can.''

''Sure. I can accept his selfishness and his arrogance and his—his—disrespect. The way my mother has.'' Lara walked toward the bedroom, then turned back. ''Look.

Thanks for trying, Bianca. I just..." She was out of words.

"I know he doesn't value your work as much as you'd like, but he recommended you for the Viceroy's job, right? That was something. You've got to give him a chance. Be the bigger artist, if not the better one."

"It's possible he wants to try, too," Eddie put in, "but can't put it into words. Lots of guys have that problem, which is why they belch and grunt so much."

Lara laughed tiredly. So they were back to possibilities. Chances. She knew her friends were probably right. But she didn't know if she was ready to risk it all, not after guarding her feelings and nursing her broken confidence for so long.

"I'm done for," she said to Eddie and Bianca. "See you in the morning, okay? Don't stay up too late."

"Just long enough to keep my date with the roof," said Eddie. "I've got an announcement to make to all of the Lower East Side."

Bianca gave him an affectionate shove. "You mean a jungle call, you big ape."

Eddie beat his chest with one fist. "I am king of the jungle!"

Bianca laughed. "Or at least Avenue B."

AN HOUR OR SO LATER, Lara felt around in the dark for a pair of jeans, slipped them on over her pajamas and crept out of the bedroom with her jacket in one hand and the flimsy Chinese shoes in the other. Rosa stirred, then quieted with a soft sigh, her face angelic in the dim glow of the night-light.

In the dark, Lara made her way to the long farmhouse table. The door keys hung on a hook in the kitchen. She knew the code for the security alarm. She could sneak out easy-squeezy, no one the wiser. Except maybe her.

She pocketed the keys. Stopped for a moment when she heard a soft moan. Bianca, definitely, she thought with a smile, tiptoeing toward the couch.

A shaft of light from the street reached across the studio and under the swinging doors. Right before she sat, Lara realized she wasn't alone.

"Hey," a man said beneath her, squirming at her weight.

Lara leaped up, turned and threw her shoes—all in one motion. *Thwap, thwap.* "Aaaargh!" she yelled, whipping her jacket overhead, ready to defend the Spinelli household to the death.

"Yeowch," said Bianca, freezing Lara's upraised arm. The jacket dropped limply on her head. She pushed it away in time to see the shadowy bulk on the couch divide into two. "Lara? Umph. Hey, that's my rump, not the couch."

Lara gaped. "Bianca? Eddie?"

"None other." Bianca gave a strangled laugh. "Where's my bra?"

Eddie shifted. "Around your neck."

Lara took a deep breath. "Um, excuse me. Didn't mean to interrupt. I'll be going now." She closed her eyes and sidled toward the doors, one hand out to feel the way. "I'm not looking."

"You'll need your shoes," Eddie said.

"Hold on." Bianca flicked on a floor lamp. The rainbow colors of the stained-glass shade glowed to life.

Lara risked a glance. Bianca's skirt was bunched at her waist, but her bra was on, if unhooked. Her hair hung in her face. Thank heavens, Eddie was still in his T-shirt and boxer shorts. He held one of her shoes and was rooting among the pillows for the other.

"I thought you two were going up to the roof."

"We did. You couldn't hear Eddie shouting?"

"Not well enough to distinguish him from the usual night crawlers. The guy who lives in the alley screams warnings whenever a UFO lands." She hesitated. "Is this part of the marital blahs?"

Bianca shrugged. "We've turned over a new leaf, now that we're getting married. Risky sex is in. We thought the roof, but it was too cold. Eddie couldn't tell my nipples from my goose bumps."

Lara compressed her lips so she wouldn't laugh. "Can I have my shoes so you two can get back to it?"

Bianca grabbed the one Eddie was looking for. "Not so quick. Where are you going?"

Lara turned, trying to look blameless. "Nowhere special."

"As if." Bianca shoved her hair away with the back of her wrist. "You're going to see Daniel."

"Maybe. What of it?"

Bianca smiled. "Nothing. I'm just happy for you."

"Don't be. This is only one night. I'm not making any promises."

"Not exactly the right attitude, but it's a start." Bianca stood and gave Lara the shoe. "You'll never get a cab this time of night."

"I'll walk," Lara said. "It's not far."

"Not on your life. Eddie?"

He was already zipping up his pants. "I'll go with her."

Bianca's eyes narrowed. "But that leaves you to walk back alone. Too dangerous. I'm going with you."

"What about Rosa?"

"Genevieve's a night person. She'll come downstairs to sit with Rosa. Or there's Mrs. Occhipinto. She's usually up all night with chronic indigestion."

"Lou C. Bawl," Eddie said.

Bianca said no. "He's doing drag at The Pink Banana."

"Hey, really, that's okay," Lara said. "I don't want to disrupt the entire building." Which was what would happen if Bianca went upstairs knocking on doors for a babysitter. "I'll get a cab. It's not that late."

Eddie stepped into his loafers. Bianca got the key that opened the door to the upper apartments' stairwell. "Really," Lara said. They ignored her.

Five minutes later, she was on the sidewalk out front. Genevieve had come downstairs in a vintage peignoir and mules. Mrs. Occhipinto and the busybody crank who lived below her were both hanging out their windows to watch the goings-on. Bianca was explaining what they were doing—for the second time—in a very loud voice. "No, no, he's a *nice* man, Mrs. Occhipinto. It's Lara who's cracked."

"Who's using drugs?" said the busybody. "This ain't a crack house."

Lara stalked off.

"Remember to practice safe sex," Mrs. Occhipinto called.

Eddie and Bianca stayed on her heels all the way past Tompkins Square Park, even though there was plenty of traffic and activity and she wasn't bothered in the least, except for the usual lewd gestures and suggestive catcalls. When she turned onto E. 10th, Lara stopped and waved. "Okay, I'm fine. You can go home now."

Eddie, who was puffing, shook his head.

They followed her right to Daniel's front stoop.

"Okay, we're here," she said patiently. "Thanks."

"Are you sure he's home?" asked Bianca.

"There's a light on in his apartment. It's the first floor."

Eddie looked over the building. "He owns this? Sweet."

"A good catch," Bianca said, nodding.

"Now you're sounding like Mrs. Occhipinto," Lara said. "Okay." She took a deep breath, flexing her hands like a boxer, realizing that all the drama had distracted her from potential misgivings. "I'm going in."

"Atta girl," Bianca said. Eddie waved. They waited while she went up the steps, rang the doorbell and waited several excruciating minutes for an answer. When Daniel cracked the door, her friends departed, almost discreetly, walking with their arms wrapped around each other and Bianca's head on Eddie's shoulder.

Daniel craned his neck after them.

"My watchdogs," Lara said. "Never mind. I come in peace."

"You said I give you shattering orgasms." Daniel blinked sleepily. "Or was that just pillow talk?"

Her brows drew together. "Huh?"

"You usually come in pieces."

She smacked her head. "Oh. I get it. Are your wits never dull? Do you sharpen them at midnight so they're ready to go in the morning? What else should I know about you?" She took a breath. "I'm babbling, aren't I?"

"I'm listening."

She closed her eyes. Opened them. He was still arresting—broad, bare chest, drooping sweatpants, hair rumpled, eyes alight. "Okay. I'm calm. Sorry for getting you out of bed. Didn't you know that you were supposed to be awake all night, tossing and turning, thinking of me?"

His smile was lopsided. ‘‘I tried, but I fell asleep.’’

Could he be any cuter? She laughed as he locked the door behind them and then took her hand and led her through the crowded foyer. ‘‘I’m going to fix that,’’ she said, looking at the crack that ran through the antique stained-glass window.

‘‘Later,’’ Daniel said. ‘‘Right now, come to bed.’’

She closed his apartment door. ‘‘I didn’t come here for that.’’ She took off her jacket and hung it on a coatrack. ‘‘Well, not *only* for that.’’

He looked over his shoulder. ‘‘I was thinking of sleeping.’’

‘‘Gee. How flattering. You’re taking all of this in stride.’’

‘‘What is *this?*’’ he said, turning and studying her with a bit more attention.

‘‘It’s…’’ She wavered on her feet, feeling as lightheaded as she had on the first night they met. She wasn’t certain of what she meant in coming here. All she knew was that she’d had to.

‘‘It’s…’’ she repeated, her mouth dry as chalk. ‘‘I guess it’s enough.’’

He took one large step closer so that he was standing in front of her, filling her vision. He caught her face in his hands, smoothed his fingertips over her cheeks, warming skin cooled by the chilly walk. ‘‘For always?’’

‘‘It’s enough for now,’’ she whispered. ‘‘I don’t know about tomorrow.’’

‘‘Mmm-hmm.’’ He nodded, releasing her without kissing her. ‘‘That’s what I thought. So we might as well go to bed.’’ He started for the bedroom.

‘‘No.’’

He turned back to her one more time, his expression quizzical. ‘‘You have something else to say?’’

Lara licked her lips. Her head was filled with conflicting desires, but ultimately they all meant the same thing. She had to be with Daniel. If that meant sacrificing her independence and making it permanent, she'd do it. She'd be scared witless, and half-sure it wouldn't work, but she'd try.

"No, I don't have anything else to say." She took his hand, squeezed it, hoped that he would figure out how she felt without her having to explain. She was such a guy that way. "Let's go to bed."

14

In the darkened bedroom, Daniel watched her hold on to the end of the brass bed and stand one-legged to pull off her shoes and socks. His heart was beating hard against his chest, like a prisoner banging on the bars, begging for release. Lara had the key. It was hokey, he knew, but that's how he felt.

She was afraid. And cynical. But she was here.

He had hope.

For the past twenty-four hours, he'd been thinking of ways to make her see the truth and rightness of their relationship. His conclusion was that they'd best communicated through sex. Which also happened to be Lara's favorite way of distracting him from getting too close, from breaking down her barriers.

Why not make sex his method of extraction? It was a dirty trick, but she'd forgive him afterward, once she realized she really had wanted to go all the way... emotionally.

While she was busy with her socks, he surreptitiously opened the top drawer of his dresser, removed an item and slipped it into the pocket of his sweats. "Let me do that," he said when she unsnapped her jeans. He clicked on a bedside mica lamp, giving the room a golden cast.

He heard her zipper. "I can handle it, thanks." Her head was bent. She watched him from beneath hanks of loose, mussed hair that shone like honey in the lamplight.

She was that kind of woman—rich and sweet as wild honey, hard to capture but worth the trouble and sting.

"My pleasure." He put his hands on her hips and drew the jeans down. She wore pajamas underneath—black-and-white gingham checks. "Lift your leg," he said, crouching to run his hands along the length of it. She did one and then the other with her hand on his shoulder for balance. He pulled the jeans off and then tossed them aside.

The room was very quiet for a long moment until the blare of a siren from the street invaded their silence. Lara flinched. Laughed nervously. "I'm used to the woods."

"A bed is softer."

She inhaled, glancing at the rumpled quilt. "I didn't mean—"

He smiled. "I know." Still kneeling before her, he reached inside the cuff of the loose pajama bottoms and ran the back of his hand up her shin. Prickly. She hadn't shaved her legs for a while. It suited her, just as the no-makeup, uncombed-hair look did. He liked having her free and natural, without pretense.

Her fingers pressed into his shoulder as he caressed her legs with both hands, making long, luxurious strokes up and down her calves as he looked up into her face. "'My very dearest,'" he said, "'down on both knees before your beautiful body which I embrace.'"

Her eyes grew round, questioning him.

"Auguste Rodin, in a letter to Camille Claudel." He rose onto his knees to lip soft kisses between the gaps of the buttons of her pajama top. He nudged the waistband lower, revealing the smooth oval of skin indented by the tight rosebud of her navel. His tongue touched her there, dipping and licking until she shivered.

She held his head away, her fingers gentle as thistledown on his beard-roughened cheeks. "You did research." A soft chuckle. "I should have known. You're such a thorough man."

"And tonight I'm going to look and touch and taste every inch of you."

"You've already done that."

"Not as slowly or as thoroughly as I prefer." His hand dipped inside her pajamas. "I want to memorize you, inside—" his questing fingers plunged deeper "—and out."

"Hmm." Despite her moan, she kept her thighs pressed together. He inserted the flat of his hand between them and slid one finger up into her. She was warm and damp, slippery-smooth as satin. He swore he could feel the beat of her pulse, as if her entire body had become an exposed nerve.

She was breathing hard, a hand clenched on the knob of the brass footboard. "There's more than one way to get inside a person."

"You've always preferred this method." He pressed deeper, stroking her from the inside out, the knuckle of his thumb rubbing against her most sensitive spot. He whispered erotic words of praise against the soft curve of her belly, like a man at a shrine.

Her hips rotated. "Mmm. So...have...you...." He'd never heard anything sexier than the rich, lazy sound of her voice, brimming with the ultimate intimacy—desire born of love. Even though she thought they'd already made love, he was certain all they'd done before was a mere appetizer to the erotic banquet that would sustain their life together.

His hand stilled. "We can change that anytime you want, my love."

"Now?" Her features puckered. "How?"

He withdrew at a tantalizing pace. She caught at her

lower lip, her nose wrinkled with adorable dismay. He smiled, the wicked lift of his brows promising that her pleasure had just begun. Holding her gaze, he brought his hand up beneath his nose, dragging one glistening finger over his lips with a provocative deliberation. The fragrance of her arousal was outdone only by the taste.

Lara was transfixed. Her lips parted in sync with his; her tongue peeped between them, flickering there for a moment before she stopped and swallowed, her eyes closing. "What are you doing to me?" she whispered.

"Seducing you."

"But you've already done that."

"That was your body. This time I'm seducing your soul." He kept a hand wrapped around her knee; she wasn't allowed to withdraw. "You've opened your legs for me, Lara. Now you're going to open your heart."

She blinked. Frowned, remembering when he'd first asked. Despite everything that had happened, she felt no more ready. "You first."

He clamped an iron hand on one of her bare ankles and reached up to grip the stretchy waistband of her pajama bottoms. "Well, then. The first thing I need to tell you is..." He hesitated. *Don't hurt her.*

She sensed the change in mood. "Tell me what?"

"How bad you made me feel."

"I did?" Her stomach tensed against his knuckles, contracting as she sucked in a shocked breath. He slowly drew the pajamas down, past her hipbones, until he saw the curly wisps of her gold-brown triangle. She quivered but stayed motionless. Panting lightly. He slid the bottoms all the way past her hips, let them drop down her legs. The moment was charged both emotionally and erotically, as though a thousand silvery particles of electricity crackled between them. The heated scent of her acted like a drug on him, making his blood pound and his body swell. Confessing his feelings was just as affecting, in another way.

"You did. When you said you couldn't love me." He brushed outspread fingers over her thighs, savoring the feel of her silken skin. "It made me remember. My parents. They didn't love me—not the way parents are supposed to. I thought I'd moved beyond all that years ago, and then your rejection brought it all back up again. But do you know what I realized?"

Her loving hands smoothed over his hair, cradling his skull. "What?"

He looked up into her face. Her eyes were huge, shining with tears. "Don't cry," he said. "I'm not unhappy."

She nodded, her throat working.

He stood and kissed her, being as gentle as he could. He touched her eyelids with tingling fingertips. Her lashes were wet. "I realized—I remembered—that I could accept my parents for what they are. And what they are not. Because I'm not perfect, either."

She put a finger beneath her nose and sniffled. "Why is everyone trying so hard to teach me that?"

"Because it's something you need to learn really, really badly?"

"Okay." She squeezed her eyes shut for a moment, then blinked them several times. Holding in the tears. He shouldn't have told her not to cry. "I'll try," she whispered. "But that doesn't automatically make marriage any more palatable."

Lighten it up. "Ah, but you haven't tasted Chef Savage's recipe yet." He kissed the tip of her nose.

"I am not going to marry you."

He licked her bottom lip. "Try a sample," he coaxed.

"It's a special concoction, a new taste sensation—you and me together."

She gave a laugh that was husky and sultry but edged in wariness. "Oh, I've sampled."

He reached one hand around to her bare bottom and gave her a little slap. "And came back for more despite your allergies."

"I've gotten shots."

Chuckling in his throat, he pressed small openmouthed kisses along her neck, across her cheeks, even into her wild, ruffled hair. "I think we've wrung every possible pun out of this analogy."

"Not yet." With a deep sigh of pleasure, she wrapped her arms around him and closed the small gap between them. Their bodies melted together, pulsing with warmth and need. "I'm empty. I'm hungry. Fill me up, Daniel. Please. Fill me."

He ached. "You're not empty, Lara. Not even close to it."

"Part of me is. Not my body, but inside me. My heart, I guess, the vulnerable part of me that needs you...so much...and loves you...." She kissed him, her need so raw and her belly pressed so tight and hot against his erection he felt as though he were already inside her. "So much."

He'd thought he'd have to pry each one of those words out of her with a crowbar. Maybe she wasn't as dead-set certain as she claimed. With a little more coaxing...

"I'm very sorry I hurt you," she whispered.

"I'll think of a way for you to make it up to me." He smiled, showing her just a hint of his cockiness. "A kiss to start."

With his fingers tangled in her hair, he held her head still and brought his mouth down upon hers. She murmured sensuously, closing her eyes while he stroked her lips with his tongue until they'd grown damp and full. The murmur became a moan and he licked the pleasured sound of it off her tongue, deepening the kiss by degrees until their mouths were fitted together like the yin and yang.

"Not a bad way to begin," he said, keeping a tight hold on her, plying her with soft, biting kisses until she was shuddering against him.

By then, hot primal urges had nearly consumed him. He wanted to take her swiftly, have her squirming beneath him, soft, warm and willing—*or maybe not*—while he thrust deep and fast and then deeper and faster inside her. But doing it that way wouldn't last. Before he was through tonight, she'd have accepted more than his body into the very heart of her. He would fill her as she had filled him—with wonder and love and an unshakable faith in their future.

And he would have to make it irrevocable.

SHE'D FORGOTTEN that he was a predator.

Dumb, Lara. Very dumb.

The last thing she remembered with any clarity was him reaching into the pocket of his sweatpants. She'd been lax against him, made dopey and unaware by the magic of his kisses. There'd been a split-second warning—a wicked glint in his eyes as they darkened to slate—and then she'd found herself thrown flat on the bed with his big, hard body on top of her, holding her down. Although she'd struggled and bucked beneath him—out of sheer contrariness—he'd had her pinned but good, her arms flung overhead. He'd grasped both her wrists in one hand and wound something soft and silky around them, then threaded it through a curved brass bar in the headboard.

With a twist and a tug, he'd secured her arms in place and sat back, straddling her body, breathing heavily through his nose as he looked down at her with a smug, victorious, utterly *masculine* expression.

It had happened too fast, all in a blur, but she knew one thing for certain.

She was captured.

Lara exhaled through her teeth. Her body prickled with an awareness so sharp it hurt.

Twisting her head, she was able to glimpse her bound wrists. Gold silk. Was that...?

It was. Her panties—the ones she'd tucked into his suit pocket the night they'd met.

Daniel had withdrawn to the end of the bed, stretched out in a lazy sprawl. He was up on his elbows, his dark head resting against the brass footboard while he watched her work out the details of her predicament. His face was shadowed, his jaw and chin darkened with beard bristle. A small, sexy smile and the simmering calculation in his eyes completed the picture.

He looked utterly dangerous. She was thoroughly aroused.

"Very cute," she said, her stomach hollow and nervous. "Hoist on my own petard."

"There's a certain delicious inevitability about it," he agreed. He bared his teeth. Laughed with a grand sense of male satisfaction, making her feel like a sacrificial offering to the gods. One sex god in particular.

She curled her legs in closer, clamping them tightly in defense even though her arousal was dampening her there to such a degree her thighs slid against each other. All right, so she was turned-on. No wonder. The situation was incredibly provocative, as if Daniel had mind-read her most intimate fantasy.

And now here she was, laid out before him in only a half-buttoned pajama top. Like it or not, she was at his mercy.

Like it.

Nonetheless, she tugged at the silken bonds. Snug. But not so snug she couldn't eventually work her way free, given the time. And the desire. She wasn't yet at that point. All her desire was focused on Daniel.

"What happens next?" she asked warily.

"Guess."

"You, um, have your wicked way with me?"

He snagged one of her feet. "One might say that."

She arched her back, pulling against him as he tugged at her leg. For a moment she was afraid he was going to tie her foot to the bed, but apparently he only wanted to spread her thighs, because he was fitting himself between them, brushing against her in a very intimate way. Exquisite sensations shot through her. The mattress shifted beneath his weight, and so did she, her hips rocking against his, searching for the fulfillment promised by his virile body and the erection that was barely constrained—and not at all concealed—beneath his clinging sweatpants.

"What are you doing?" she whispered hoarsely, only half-aware that she was making soft moaning sounds in her throat that begged him to continue.

"Showing you," he said as he slowly unbuttoned the pajama top.

"Showing me what?" Her wanting him, begging for him, was nothing new.

"How far you'll go." He parted her shirt, making her naked for him. Naked for his pleasure. The positioning of her arms had pulled her breasts together and lifted them high on her chest, thrusting them forward, the nipples so prominent his gaze went straight to them. He licked his lips.

Her mind spun like a pinwheel. *Stripped bare.*

Hold on, she counseled herself. Her fingers wrapped around the cool curved brass. *Stay in control. He can't make you lose control.*

Ha!

Several seconds passed while he gazed at her bare body in its sacrificial display and she made a valiant attempt to pull her head together enough to answer. "How far will I go?" She paused, arching her back to taunt him. "Far enough, I'm pretty sure." She made a chuckling sound, but it was a fake. Suddenly she knew what he meant. This wasn't about sex. It was about love. It was about him making her surrender her heart.

I won't do it, she instantly told herself, even as she acknowledged that she already had. In every way but one. The one he was going to force out of her.

The ultimate female resolution. The sweetest, most cruel, most deceptive surrender of them all.

"Don't," she blurted. "Please."

He stopped with a fingertip poised above the puckered tip of one of her breasts. So close it was excruciating.

She shuddered. Every nerve ending in her body was screaming for his touch. "Oh, damn," she said, relenting, flexing her shoulder blades so her breast was pushed even higher—against his open palm. Pleasure hissed out from between her teeth as his fingers closed around her aching flesh. He put his mouth there, flicking her nipple with his tongue before sucking it deep, and that was so good she threw back her head, working her wrists frantically, wanting to feel him. Needing her hands on him.

The knotted panties held. She groaned, wrung with too

many conflicting emotions to keep track of which she was guarding. "This isn't fair."

Daniel looked up. "I can stop."

"You can untie me."

"Say the magic words."

Her eyes narrowed. "You're a bastard."

He wagged his head. "Nope, that's not what I want to hear." A sigh. "I suppose I'll have to torture it out of you." He stroked a fingertip around the circumference of her breast, making circles toward the areola, sending small tremors racing across the surface of her skin. The circles got smaller. She drew in a ragged breath.

His hand stilled. Her frustration was acute. "Did you want to say something?"

She bit her bottom lip. It was so tender and swollen even the smallest nip stung. "I've already said it." She looked into his eyes. "I love you."

He dropped a hand between her legs, covering her but not touching her the way she wanted to be touched. His eyes remained locked with hers. "And...?"

Suddenly she twisted sideways, somehow managing to get out from beneath him even though he grabbed at her hips. She gave a sharp kick, connecting with his shin. He laughed and reached for her again. She got her knees up beneath her, but the position was awkward with her torso extended toward the headboard where her wrists still held fast, even though they'd turned against the silk.

"Mmm, this is nice," Daniel said, reclining to run his palm along her ribs to her breasts. They hung free beneath her, and she cried out when he batted them, making them sway like fruit on the vine. He plucked at the sensitive tips, teasing them mercilessly. She wanted his mouth on her again, sucking until the ache inside her was eased. She pressed her face against her outstretched arms, fighting herself. It would be so easy to give in. So damned easy.

"No-o-o," she breathed, grabbing the headboard and shaking it in frustration.

"Do that again" Daniel said, clearly enjoying the view from his position beneath her swinging breasts. She snapped at him, which only brought her close enough for him to latch onto one of her breasts with his lips open. His tongue fluted around her nipple, laving it, and then she felt his teeth, tugging with erotic precision. Her eyes rolled back into her head. She sagged against her bound wrists, slumping toward his mouth, feeding more of her breast into it until the stream of sensation was running through her body from her toes to the tips of her breasts and straight into him. Into him. She was all the way into him.

"Untie me," she murmured against the top of his head. She shimmied coaxingly. "I want to touch you."

He moved to the other breast.

"Untie me, Daniel. I'll take you in my mouth. In my throat. I'll swallow."

His busy tongue quieted, but then he said, "Mmm, you already did," and went back to feasting on her.

She stifled a hysterical laugh. *That'll teach you to hold something back for negotiation!*

If their legs hadn't been intertwined, she would have kicked at him again. Instead she scooted out her rear end and tried to bring up a sharp knee, not to seriously hurt him but to get his attention.

He wasn't as absorbed in playing with her breasts as she thought. With a muttered oath, he caught her leg and levered it outward, using his weight to flip her onto her back again. Holding her down, he reached over the side of the bed and came up with a tie, which he quickly looped around her left ankle. She struggled, kicking her free leg in earnest now, but he dodged the blows by sliding off the bed out of range.

"Wildcats must be restrained," he said, tying her down so that her left leg was stretched flat, held securely in place by the tie. She'd closed her lids, her teeth gritted, but when she peeked he was staring between her legs with eyes as hot as molten silver and she couldn't stand it—she had to close her thighs even though she knew…oh, yes, she *knew* what he'd do….

He picked a sock off the floor, then discarded it as useless. She watched through her lashes as he untied his sweats and began to pull the drawstring from the waistband. Her breath came shorter and shorter. Her chest heaved; cool air washed over her dampened breasts. Every other part of her body burned with anticipation.

The cord came free. He leaned over the bed, the sweatpants drooping down to give her a glimpse of his taut backside, distracting her enough that he was able to catch hold of her ankle without trouble. She tried to wrench it away from him but he was too strong, and with a few quick lashings she was staked out upon the bed, her legs stretched wide. Totally open to his scrutiny. His lust.

His love.

Thrilling sensations boiled through her body, shocking her with the depth of their scouring heat. She felt as though she might crack open under his gaze, all of her hidden desires pouring out. It was too much. She had to move, to fool herself into thinking she hadn't already succumbed. There was a small amount of give in her position and she worked against it as well as she could, bending her knees, twisting her hips upon the mattress, not even caring that from Daniel's point of view, writhing was probably more enticing than surrender.

They'd been together enough times that her physical nakedness wasn't completely excruciating. What was worse—blistering, really—was the emotional exposure that came with it. The feeling of being without defense. She'd thought she'd been vulnerable before, but that had been nothing compared to this...this *submission.*

Perversely, she flowed with desire as never before. Daniel didn't have to touch her to know. He could see. He *was* seeing. Everything. The proof was there, she could feel it in exquisite detail—the swollen lips of her sex, the lubrication so copious it trickled into the creases of her legs with each buck and roll of her hips.

She turned her gaze aside, afraid to look at Daniel when she knew her darkest desires were written in her eyes.

A soulful moan came from deep in his chest. He shook his head, as if waking from a trance. Moving quickly, he dropped his loosened sweats without care and grabbed a condom from the nightstand before joining her on the bed. He knelt between her open legs. She trembled, eyes closed tight. But she had to look. She had to. Not facing him—and herself—would be the ultimate cowardice.

She saw his eyes first, blazing on hers. Windows to his soul—a fierce, passionate, zealous soul, the kind of man who would make a promise and stick to it, who would love her with all his heart until the end of time. She nearly smiled at that, even given her position, but then her gaze dropped lower. Past his muscle-banded chest and rock-hard abdomen...

She swallowed. He wasn't just aroused. He was *inflamed.* Ramrod stiff, pulsing with lust. And obviously holding himself severely in check.

Her nervous tongue stroked the roof of her mouth. Her body undulated before his. It seemed impossible for her desire to escalate, but it did, rushing through her in a series of surface frissons and bone-deep tremors. She wanted desperately for him to take her. To feel him inside her, pounding as hot and hard as her blood.

As if to soothe her visible reaction, he placed his palm between her legs. A whisper of a touch, but as devastating as a blatant thrust.

"Don't tease me," she pleaded, every cell in her body yearning for a deeper invasion. "I can't take it."

"You can." A fingertip parted her, most delicately. "You will." He leaned over her, his broad chest layering her with heat even though he didn't touch her anywhere but between her thighs, where she needed him the most. She could barely restrain the urge to spear herself on his probing fingers. "Tell me what you want."

She moaned. "You know."

"Say it out loud."

Hadn't she already given in enough? Embattled, she wrested at the bonds one more time. Her struggles had only made the knots pull tighter. *No reprieve, no escape. No excuse.* The truth was brutal and she had no choice but to face it.

Despite her hard-learned doubts, she wanted him in her life forever.

Forever.

There it was.

His fingertips stroked her sensitive flesh so lightly it was worse than not being caressed at all. She whimpered with frustration.

"Say it." His voice was rough velvet. "Say it..."

Her heart felt as if it might burst. "I love you," she said, "and I want to marry you." Although she'd thought it would be excruciating to admit, the words soared out of her, so huge and meaningful she was humbled by their importance. She gave a shaky laugh. "Damn, it's true. *I want to marry you.*"

Daniel kissed her then, deeply, with the strange combination of ravishment and unconditional acceptance she'd come to expect from him. Wonder, tinged with a certain amount of grateful relief, filled her up like never before.

So this was what it meant to surrender to love, she thought. This unalloyed joy.

When they broke apart, he reached up and untied her wrists, his jaw clenching with frustration at the momentary delay as she moved her body sensuously against his, goading him toward their inevitable joining. He undid her ankles. "There," he said, when she was set free. "Now say it again."

Her turn to be cruel. She wrapped her legs around his hips, inciting him so the penetration she craved would come quickly now. "I will. When you're inside me." *Not so very cruel.*

He smiled. And lifted off her a few inches so he could reach between their clinging bodies to plunge an inquisitive finger past her swollen entrance to test the hot liquid center of her. As if he needed to when they both knew she was as ripe to bursting as he. She propped her thighs higher, wider, absolutely wanton in her desire. Drawing back, he raised her hips in his hands, positioned himself precisely at her center, and filled her in one stroke. One devastating stroke.

That was all it took.

"I'm going to marry you," she said, not caring that she'd shouted the words as he drove inside her. It was too good. She came almost at once, lost in an erotic rush of sensation so pure it burned in her veins. Daniel groaned as she clenched tightly around his shaft, and after only a few deep penetrating thrusts he reached his own overpowering climax, spilling his essence deep inside her with his hands on her breasts and his mouth nuzzling at her arched throat. Lara's vision blurred. With passion. With tears. All the same—she was out of control, but it didn't matter because she was safe in love. And sure of one thing. She hadn't given in—she'd won. She was triumphant.

Yes—*triumphant!*

DAWN WAS EDGING past the row house roofs, bathing the walled garden in a rosy light, and they were still awake. Eating cold pizza in the kitchen. Licking tomato sauce off each other's fingers. Lara sat on the counter with her legs wrapped around Daniel's hips. They talked. They laughed. Frequently they lapsed into long silences. Silences filled with eloquence.

"So you really did mean it?" he asked, for the fourth or fifth time.

She put down the last gnawed crust, still ravenous. If this kept up, she was going to be one fat, happy housewife—the kind who got as she good as she gave. "I meant it. We're partners now, equal partners, and don't even think of trying it any other way. It turns out that I'm an all-or-nothing kind of girl." She cocked her head at him, pulling him closer by linking her ankles and tightening her grip. "Think you can handle me?"

He put his hands under her bottom, lifted her off the counter and carried her toward the bedroom. "I think that I can handle you just fine. Because what's right for you is more than good enough for me."

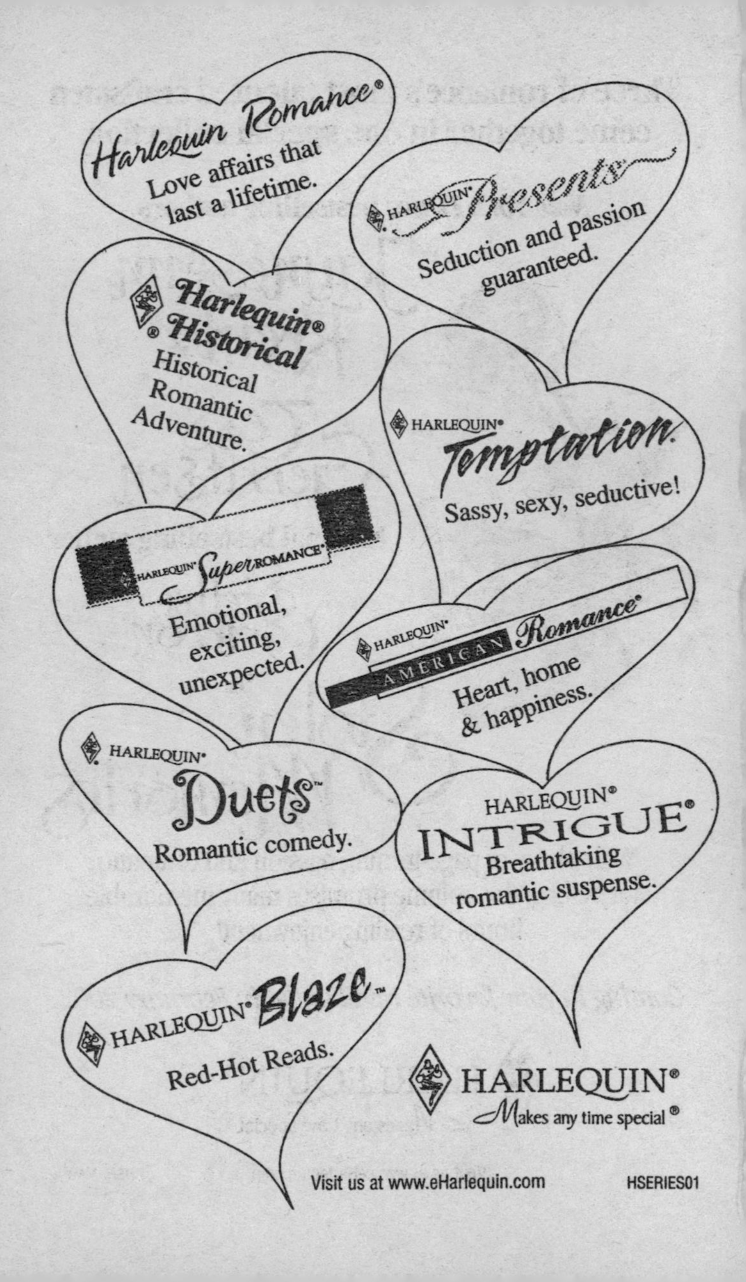

Harlequin Romance®
Love affairs that last a lifetime.
HARLEQUIN® Presents
Seduction and passion guaranteed.
Harlequin® Historical
Historical Romantic Adventure.
HARLEQUIN® Temptation.
Sassy, sexy, seductive!
HARLEQUIN® SuperROMANCE®
Emotional, exciting, unexpected.
HARLEQUIN® AMERICAN Romance®
Heart, home & happiness.
HARLEQUIN® Duets™
Romantic comedy.
HARLEQUIN® INTRIGUE®
Breathtaking romantic suspense.
HARLEQUIN® Blaze™
Red-Hot Reads.
HARLEQUIN®
Makes any time special®
Visit us at www.eHarlequin.com
HSERIES01